The
Paris
Mistress

The
Paris
Mistress

A Revolutionary War Mystery

Mally Becker

Author Photo Credit: Sharon Dobin

First edition

ISBN: 978-1-68512-430-4

Cover art by Level Best Designs

This book was professionally typeset on Reedsy.
Find out more at reedsy.com

To Ellin and Jeff

Praise for The Paris Mistress

"Someone is trying to kill American ambassador Benjamin Franklin in this wonderfully engaging mystery set in pre-Revolutionary Paris. Becca Parcell and Daniel Alloway are planning a wedding when a man is found dead, tied to a lightning rod. Their search for his killer will take them to Notre-Dame, the chic perfumeries of Paris, and a ball at Versailles, presided over by the doomed Marie-Antoinette. A sly and witty Franklin makes a delightful addition to this sparkling, clever series."—Mariah Fredericks, author of *The Lindbergh Nanny*

"Exploring a little-known aspect of the Revolutionary War, this intriguing mystery demands that Becca and Daniel uncover the spy in Benjamin Franklin's Paris home. Becca is shrewd and passionate, equally adept at speaking French and solving mental puzzles, and a heroine to root for. With scenes set all around Paris, from the seediest alleys to the palace at Versailles, and with fresh, engaging prose, this is Becker's best yet."—Karen Odden, *USA Today* bestselling author of *Under A Veiled Moon*, nominated for the Agatha, Lefty, and Anthony Awards (2023)

"A trifecta of delights for fans of historical mysteries. First, there's the Benjamin Franklin we never knew from school. Second, our couple, Becca and Daniel, find their romance tested when a murder disrupts their wedding plans in Paris, and they are asked to become spies to solve the crime. Third, readers will meet a slick, charming, and treacherous villain that is a delight. *The Paris Mistress* is steeped in vivid but unique period details. The pace is unrelenting, and this is riveting history with stakes and teeth."—Gabriel Valjan is an Agatha, Anthony, Derringer, and Shamus nominated author. He writes the Shane Mystery series, set in seventies Boston

"A delightful combination of brilliant plot, well-researched history, and a little snuggly romance."—C.L. Tolbert, author of the Thornton Mystery Series

"A wedding in Paris! That's what Rebecca Parcell dreamed of when she set sail to marry Daniel Alloway. Instead the couple finds themselves embroiled in a traitorous plot to stop the French King from continuing to support the American Revolution, with Dr. Benjamin Franklin right in the middle of it all. Deftly plotted and rich in historic details, Mally Becker's *The Paris Mistress* will leave you wanting more."— Cathi Stoler, award-winning author of The Murder On The Rocks Mysteries and The Nick Donahue Adventures

"An exciting adventure story set in turbulent times, featuring the legendary Benjamin Franklin and the notorious court of Marie Antoinette. With powdered wigs and perfumes, satin dresses and taffeta birthmarks, the era comes alive, transporting the reader at a white-knuckled gallop to its surprising conclusion."—Nina Wachsman, author of *The Gallery of Beauties*, nominated for both the Agatha and Silver Falchion Awards and for the newly released *The Courtesan's Secret*

Cast of Characters

- Rebecca Parcell–A young widow who has twice served as a spy for liberty. She arrives in Paris to marry Daniel Alloway, her partner on those two missions. Becca believes that her days serving General Washington are over.
- Daniel Alloway–A former British prisoner of war and former printer. Daniel arrives in Paris six months prior to Becca's arrival to begin a new life as the European agent for a wealthy Philadelphia merchant.
- Lady Augusta–Becca's mother-in-law and mother to Becca's deceased first husband. She accompanies Becca to witness her wedding in Paris.
- Edward Bancroft–Secretary to the American Peace Commission in Paris. Mr. Bancroft lives with Benjamin Franklin at his home outside of Paris.
- Captain Charron–Captain in the Paris Prefecture of Police.
- Gabriel d'Aumont–An assistant finance minister at Versailles who supports American independence and befriends Benjamin Franklin, Becca, and Daniel.
- Jude Fenimore–An American merchant who resides in Paris. Jude Fenimore shares the trans-Atlantic voyage from America to France with Becca, Hannah, and Lady Augusta.
- Monsieur and Madame Fargeon–Owners of a perfume shop on the rue du Roule beloved by French nobility.
- Benjamin Franklin–Writer, scientist, and Founding Father. Benjamin Franklin was America's first diplomat, serving as American Minister (Ambassador) to France from 1776-1785. He resides in a mansion located outside of Paris, the Hôtel de Valentinois in the village of Passy.

Franklin and Daniel form a bond over stories of their early days as printers. Daniel, Becca, Hannah, and Lady Augusta become Franklin's guests for the summer.

- Mrs. Hannah–Becca's mother and a healer. Having fled from France with her family as a child, Hannah reluctantly returns to Paris to witness Becca's wedding.
- Queen Marie-Antoinette–Requires no introduction. Queen of France.
- Michael–A talented baker who is inspired by the American fight for independence to seek a more just French society.
- Renée–A saleswoman at the perfume shop on the rue du Roule. Jude Fenimore's lover.
- Patience Wright–One of the most famous American sculptors of her day. Dr. Franklin gives Patience a home in Passy for the summer.

Prologue

Passy, France

His name would be synonymous with cowardice. He'd be remembered for abandoning his country when it needed him most. At best, he would be an entry in a jestbook, a drawing of a stout man holding a kite.

"Don't scowl, Benny. I'm trying to sculpt your mouth." With feather-light movement, Patience Wright peeled away a sliver of cream-colored wax. It curled and fell, lodging between two blades of lush grass.

Benjamin Franklin's eyebrows rose in honest shock. "I am reduced to a *Benny?*" Only his closest friends were permitted that informality.

He sat on a mahogany chair the servants had placed on the lawn with his back to the pale, elegant Hôtel de Valentinois, his borrowed home outside of Paris these past five years. He wore his plum-colored "ditto suit," as he called it, with vest, coat, and breeches cut from the same cloth. One of his feet rested on a red and blue needlepoint footstool, the other, on a Turkish rug that protected his boots from the wet grass.

"If I can call the King of England by his first name, I can certainly call you Benny." Patience pointed at Franklin with the thin blade she held between thumb and index finger, then turned back to the lump of wax on the table set before her.

"Isn't that why their Majesties forced you out of England? They didn't appreciate you calling the king Georgie, did they? Franklin was sharper than he intended. He was accustomed to flattery, flummery and false praise

v

from men and women alike after decades of fame. He was not accustomed, he admitted to himself, to American women who treated him as if his good will was of no significance.

If Congress accepted his resignation, that is exactly who he'd be, a man of no significance. He pushed away the thought.

"I left England because the lords and ladies of the realm would not see the good sense of acknowledging America's independence," Patience sniffed.

"Of course. My apologies," Franklin murmured, hardly paying attention. He imagined how Congress would be nattering on about the letter of resignation he'd sent off by ship in March. The jackals who whispered that he was too old, too lazy, and too ineffective to continue as ambassador to France would be toasting their luck at the City Tavern in Philadelphia.

By his estimates, it would take them another month or so to conclude that he was irreplaceable. Who else could negotiate a peace with the English? Not that sanctimonious popinjay, John Adams. The French court hated him. Franklin had meant his resignation letter to quiet his critics. *You overestimate your own value.* Franklin shoved that thought away, too.

"The frown, Benny. Don't scowl," Patience repeated.

Franklin forced his lips into a small, pleasant smile, the one he wore when posing for posterity.

Patience stepped past the wax bust and strode toward Franklin. He wasn't entirely certain she would stop in time to avoid toppling him from his chair.

Franklin forced himself to remain still as she lowered her face to his. The morning sun highlighted the gray at her temple, the web of lacy wrinkles extending from her eyes. She was a tall, awkward woman whose rough hands shaped the most elegant sculptures in Europe.

"You might have been permitted to stay in London if you'd kept your opinions to yourself," Franklin added in a gentler tone.

"And do *you* ever keep *your* opinions to yourself? Stop speaking, Benny." She backed away, seemingly satisfied by whatever she saw in his expression.

This time, he laughed at her blunt speech but obeyed.

The musical crunch of carriage wheels on nearby roads and the sun's warmth on his neck finally soothed his thoughts and set his mind adrift.

The screams jolted him.

One woman's voice, then another, rose and fell as if the world were ending.

His bad foot, the one he kept on the footstool, hit the ground. The pain in his toe exploded and the new pain in his hip left him breathless. Franklin stood, leaning on the cane left by his chair.

Two servant girls in matching white aprons and clogs gripped each other for comfort. *Mon Dieu*, one trilled, her voice as high and wild as a bird's song. The other shook her head, as her screams turned to tears. *Au secours.* She called for help.

A gardener in clothes brown as the soil came running. All three stared up, speaking in French that was too quick and too distant for Franklin to understand.

Patience turned in the same direction as the servants, lifting her gaze to the roof of the grand house behind them. She dropped her blade and gasped.

More slowly, Franklin followed her lead, straining his neck, looking higher. A rag, he thought. A tan and white rag had wrapped itself round the lightning rod. *His* lightning rod. He'd had it installed on the roof to great fanfare. It was the first lightning conductor in the entire country of France, he'd been assured.

Franklin's body seemed to grow heavy as if it accepted the truth of what he saw before his mind translated the image. Not a rag. His heartbeat galloped. His hand rose shaking to his chest.

A body was tied to the lightning rod, a man in tan breeches and matching tan vest. His head lolled on his chest, his black tricorner hat miraculously still affixed to his head. The figure leaned forward as if ready to dive from the roof.

Calm. He ordered himself to remain calm. At seventy-five years of age, it should take more than a body tied to a lightning rod–*his* lightning rod–to spark panic.

Franklin heard his own voice as if it belonged to someone else. The voice that was his and not his said, "Mrs. Wright, would you run to the house and instruct the butler to take at least two goodly-built men to the roof. Ask him to bring the healer woman with them."

Mrs. Parcell's mother, Hannah, had kept to herself since her arrival. But a woman trained as a healer couldn't possibly turn down a request for help.

Franklin took a deep breath and waited for his heart to slow. He focused again on the man tied to the roof, ignoring the aching heat in his foot and the lightheadedness that accompanied his shock.

Franklin told himself to observe carefully and not engage in idle speculation. He was a scientist, after all, and a renowned scientist at that. But when a crow landed on the man's head, dislodging the hat and sending the bird into the air again with protesting *caw-caws*, Franklin swallowed the acid bile that rose in his throat and turned away.

Chapter One

Six Weeks Earlier

Whrite, billowy sails luffed before collapsing into lifeless piles on the deck. Beige-colored side ropes snapped in the stiff breeze. The brigantine's hull shuddered as it came about.

Standing on the quarterdeck of the *Windborne*, Rebecca Parcell clamped one hand to her straw hat as the ocean wind tugged at its brim. A month into their voyage from the new world to the old, she no longer noticed how her legs and hips shifted for balance aboard the privateer's ship.

"A single reef, gentlemen," Captain Roberts bellowed.

A battalion of men, none of them gentlemen, clambered up the rigging. Canvas sails tightened beneath the clear blue sky, and the vessel leaped forward into the wind.

Becca's spirit rose. The captain had said they might make landfall in France within days if the wind held. The wind was holding.

How soon would she see Daniel again? They'd been separated for more than ten months.

She followed the progress of one young crewman in particular. He shimmied up the ropes—the rigging, they called it—beyond the gaf sail on the main mast. She swallowed past the lump in her throat and forced herself to keep an eye on him.

"I am not enamored of heights, either. 'Tis a job I would pay to avoid."

Becca winced. She knew that voice.

1

Jude Fenimore stood behind her on the quarterdeck, his pale blond hair gleaming white in the sun. His blue eyes were wide-set, his nose thin and straight. Only sun-blistered red skin along his nose and the top rim of his forehead marred the perfection of his appearance.

Mr. Fenimore had been kindness itself from the moment they met at the Capes of Delaware, two strangers waiting to board the ship. She had detested him from that first meeting.

Guilt stabbed her. It wasn't his fault that he resembled her deceased husband. Her philandering, disloyal, traitorous British spy of a husband, Philip. *God rest his soul*, she almost forgot to add.

She and Philip had only been married for three years, and he had been gone for more than two. There were days now when she strained to recall his precise features, his voice. Mr. Fenimore brought her dead husband back to life.

He turned from Becca to the two women she loved most in the world. Becca's former mother-in-law, Lady Augusta Georgiana Stokes Parcell, and her mother, Hannah. They'd insisted on undertaking the difficult journey to France with her. Neither could imagine missing Becca's wedding, they'd said.

"We hear that France is the civilest society on Earth." Lady Augusta said to Becca. "We have asked Mr. Fenimore to school us on Parisian courtesies." Her face shone each time she looked at him.

So Lady Augusta saw the resemblance to Philip, too, Becca thought with dismay. Becca didn't have the heart to discourage this shipboard friendship with the man. She hoped her mother-in-law wouldn't suffer when he left them at the end of their journey.

"I was telling your lovely companions that in France, you must say exactly what you mean but appear not to mean it at all." Mr. Fenimore aimed his smile at Becca. "Or say the opposite and make it appear that you thoroughly believe it."

"What on earth for?" Becca tucked a lock of wavy black hair back into the straw hat. She knew she was being rude. She didn't care.

"Rebecca." Lady Augusta's tone was censure enough.

"What on earth for? For amusement, Mrs. Parcell." Jude laughed. "The French crave amusement, because, beneath their frothy surface, when given a choice of believing the best or the worst of the world, they always believe the worst. Flirtation and style, *toujours* the style, make life bearable, you see."

"I do not see. And how is it you are an expert on the French temperament?" Dear god, couldn't he leave her alone? He brought out the worst in her.

His smile faltered for a moment, then returned. "I do business in Paris. I moved there from London when the war began." Mr. Fenimore extended one silk stocking-clad leg, swept an arm forward, and bowed as if to lighten his own mood. "Back to the subject of French manners. Now, you must flirt with me." The lace at his wrist rippled in the breeze.

And how did he manage to keep his linen shirts white after twenty-nine days aboard the ship when her blue muslin gown was stiff with salt and layers of dirt that she was better off not contemplating? The ship's quarters were too tight to allow for servants.

Facing her silence, he prodded, "Madam, as you are fair and lovely, be generous and merciful to one who is your slave."

"You are making fun of me." Becca's cheeks burned.

"Indeed, I am not. The practice of flirtation will serve you well, especially at Versailles, will it not, madam?" He turned to Lady Augusta for confirmation. His pale skin glistened, as if the spring air suddenly blazed with summer heat.

Lady Augusta's expression softened, as it always did when she was in Mr. Fenimore's presence.

Becca's behavior toward Mr. Fenimore was indefensible. She struggled to think more kindly of him and of her poor, dead husband. Without Philip's treason, Becca never would have come to serve General Washington as a spy. She never would have met Daniel Alloway. Without Philip, she wouldn't be here, caught between the new world and the old, on her way to wed the only man she could imagine marrying. She felt her lips curve into a smile at the thought of Daniel.

"There. Memorize the expression that graces your face at this very moment, Mrs. Parcell," Mr. Fenimore crowed. "You will conquer all of

Paris with that countenance." His forearm pressed against his side as if pained by a sudden cramp.

Becca felt her eyes narrow. He was schooling her on how to lie.

"My daughter is practicing to be a wife, not a *coquette*." Hannah sounded uncharacteristically stern.

"I mean no disrespect, madam. *Désolé.*" He lifted his hand to his heart and bowed so deeply, appearing so mortified, that Hannah and Lady Augusta laughed.

Désolé, Becca repeated to herself. I am sorry. Becca appreciated the way that Mr. Fenimore wove together English and French, as if to acquaint them with the language they'd need to conquer.

Her gaze veered to Hannah. She was shorter and slighter than Becca, but they shared the same dark blue eyes, wide cheekbones, and black hair. And the two of them already spoke fluent French.

"Don't let anyone know I was born in France. Promise," Hannah had whispered as they were rowed out to the *Windborne*.

"But why not?" Becca had protested.

"The Catholics made life difficult for us, my parents said." The lines on Hannah's face seemed to deepen at the memory. "We left, and I had nightmares for years." She had been born in France but left as a young child. "I...I am nervous returning."

"You are American now. It will be fine." Becca had clasped her mother's hands between her own, studying Hannah's face. She watched her mother's moods for signs of the blue devil. That was what Hannah called her dark days. There'd been fewer of them since she'd come to live with Becca and Augusta in Morristown.

The blue devil had claws. They had grabbed Hannah after Becca's birth and not let go. When Becca was three, Hannah fled, convinced Becca and her father would be better off without her.

Becca's throat tightened at the sudden memory, the shock of discovering her mother alive last year. They had found each other in Philadelphia, where Becca and Daniel were searching for traitors. All Becca's life, she'd been told that her mother was dead. How angry she'd been to discover the lie.

4

Becca forced her attention back to the present, to the sound of water rippling over the hull and metal rings clinking on stays. "You've made this voyage before, Mr. Fenimore. It can't be too much longer, can it?"

"We might make land as soon as tomorrow. That's what Captain Roberts tells me." Fenimore's skin seemed even paler than usual.

Becca nodded. Paris was a landlocked city, and they would dock in Nantes. She patted the pocket she wore beneath her gown to feel the reassuring whisper of crinkling paper. Daniel's latest letter was safe there.

He would arrange to pay for the carriage to take them to Paris. He would leave more instructions for them at the port. He described where they would live until the wedding with such detail that she could almost taste the sweet, tart oranges that grew there.

In his letters, Daniel spoke little of his new job as Mr. Barnes's business agent. Daniel had been gone for 302 days. Becca kept count.

"You've been such pleasant company," Mr. Fenimore began.

Was that sarcasm in his voice?

"If I wanted to assure myself that you were well taken care of, where might I find you three ladies after we make landfall?"

Becca let the early evening breeze cool her cheeks as she turned to face east, away from Mr. Fenimore and toward Daniel, toward Paris and the future. She wasn't about to encourage a friendship with their fellow passenger in France.

"We'll be staying outside of Paris. A place called Passy," Augusta volunteered. "Do you know it?"

"With Dr. Benjamin Franklin," Hannah added. "Mr. Fenimore?"

Something in her mother's voice, some emotion trapped between fear and surprise, made Becca spin round just as Jude Fenimore's face went slack.

His chest rose and fell as if starved for air. He fell to his knees, one hand holding the side of his rib cage, then collapsed with a hollow thump on the deck.

Chapter Two

D aniel Alloway inhaled the acrid scent of printers' ink and wished himself anywhere but here. Standing next to Dr. Franklin's printing press catapulted him into the past—into grief—and that wasn't a place he willingly chose to go.

Newly printed pages hung overhead, drying on ropes that crisscrossed the ceiling. Muffled voices rose from riverboats passing nearby. The building was near the edge of their host's property with a view of the Seine River.

"Tis a fine typeface, is it not?" Franklin squinted at the tiny metal squares held fast in a narrow tray. The letters glinted silver in the morning light streaming through the windows.

"Fine, indeed." Daniel pretended to study the composing stick and its parade of letters. His fingertips recalled the feel of setting type, his hands, the act of locking type into place in the frame. He'd thought that all of life could be condensed into the words and sentences he created one letter at a time.

And now? He'd never again feel the magic of transforming a writer's thoughts into print. The work required strength. It required two hands. His right hand was still scarred from the injury he incurred when he escaped from a British prison ship in New York Harbor. His palm was still frozen as if it were forever scooping water from a lake.

"But I warrant you didn't bring me here to discuss type." Daniel swept his good hand round the one-room building where Franklin had installed his press.

Franklin's gaze dropped momentarily to Daniel's hand, then rose again.

"I didn't mean to cause distress, Mr. Alloway. I was merely searching for a private place to speak." His expression softened. "That's partly why I wanted a printing press again. I missed the work, too."

Daniel brushed off the sympathy. "The setting makes me blunter than I might otherwise be, Dr. Franklin. You needed a private place for what purpose? I'll admit to feeling penned in here."

Franklin laughed, and relief washed over Daniel. His bluntness was forgiven.

"Shouldn't your Mrs. Parcell be arriving any day?"

Becca's arrival had nothing to do with this meeting. But Franklin's question was polite, and so Daniel answered. "Yes, her ship should arrive soon, though it's deucedly difficult to tell how long any voyage takes. I've paid at the post-house in Nantes to send a messenger ride here as soon as they arrive. I'll leave to meet them on the road and bring them back myself."

"Good. When she arrives, I shall require your services and hers," Franklin continued.

"Her services? I can't imagine what you mean." Daniel tilted his head, studying the older man until he realized that Franklin studied him in the same manner. No more than a handful of people were privy to their missions for General Washington in New York and Philadelphia.

Franklin swept up a soft cloth from a nearby hook with one hand and a small metal letter from a wood case with the other. He polished the *S*, returned it to its small bin, then picked up a *P*. "Clean. Good. Good." A pause. "General Washington sings your praises, as do Alexander Hamilton and your employer, Mr. Barnes."

"I know, Dr. Franklin. I read the letters of introduction they wrote before presenting them to you last fall. They were too kind."

"I didn't mean the letters of introduction." Franklin half turned to Daniel, his cheeks crisscrossed with fine wrinkles. Part of his face remained in shadow. "I know about Mrs. Parcell's husband. I know about the plot you discovered in New York City and about the counterfeiters in Philadelphia." His watery blue eyes grew sad. "I know a bit of your history, too."

Something heavy settled in Daniel's chest. "I don't know what you think you know, but...."

"Please stop. Lying doesn't suit you. I have my own sources of information."

Daniel didn't answer. Grief over the death of his wife Amelia and infant son Silas had driven him to America before the War for Independence began. Becca had brought him back to life. None of that was Franklin's business.

"And I require your services, as well." The jocular, distracted elder statesman was gone. In his place was a Benjamin Franklin Daniel hadn't seen before.

"I have a job, Dr. Franklin, a fine one working here for the richest man in North America. I won't put that at risk."

And then Daniel understood. "I thought we were merely agreeable guests you wished to add to your menagerie. I was so grateful for your invitation that I didn't let myself ask why you invited us to live here." He swept his arm out as if to take in all of the Hôtel de Valentinois, its stone walls, manicured gardens, endless silent servants, and view of Paris in the distance.

There were two other Americans staying at the chateau, a sculptress and Dr. Franklin's personal secretary.

"America has been generous to me, Dr. Franklin. But I've paid my debt to her. So has Becca. The war will have to continue without us. And I won't put Becca in danger, not even to keep your fine roof over her head."

Franklin had charmed Daniel at their first meeting. He'd hoped the famous American could use his influence at court to help untangle a shipping problem for Mr. Barnes. Within an hour, the two former printers were comparing favorite inks and papers, sharing childhood stories. Was Franklin wooing him even then?

Daniel had leaped at the invitation to stay here until he and Becca wed, and, more importantly, he was grateful for the chance to leave Paris. The pickpockets. The sound of fights at two in the morning. The smell of decay everywhere. It was a city of mud and danger. He couldn't leave Becca, Augusta, and Hannah in such a setting.

Daniel was angriest at himself. He was a gifted liar and even more talented at catching others in lies. Franklin had fooled him.

8

"We are friends, Mr. Alloway. Do not doubt that." Franklin opened his own arms as if to embrace Daniel. "I wouldn't have extended an invitation to live here otherwise. 'Tis a small favor I'm asking, an important favor but one that doesn't put you or Mrs. Parcell in any danger."

"What is it you want, Dr. Franklin? As briefly and clearly as possible," Daniel said.

"I do apologize. I have become too accustomed to the French court." Franklin blew out a long breath through pursed lips. "An ocean of words accompanies even the simplest request. And this is a simple request."

Daniel raised one eyebrow. "Nothing about you is simple."

"You may be right." Franklin sighed. "I shall begin again. The chateau's owner, Monsieur Chaumont, offered me the use of his property to keep me and the American delegation away from spies and gossips. It hasn't worked. Whitehall and the King of England know my business almost as soon as I know it. So do the French, for that matter. There is a traitor in my household. Briefly and clearly, I am spied upon."

Franklin stepped to the only chair in the roughly built space, an unfinished pine seat. "I must sit. Excuse my rudeness in not offering you a chair."

"Not at all." Daniel's shoulders tightened. Was Franklin in pain or merely seeking a more sympathetic hearing? In either case, his curiosity was aroused. "I won't ask how you've learned they know your secrets. I'll assume you're correct."

"You'll *assume* that I'm correct?" Franklin slapped one knee with his hand. His voice rose.

"Does the great Dr. Franklin never make a mistake?" Daniel couldn't help himself.

"This is why we are friends, Mr. Alloway. You speak to me as if I am a fourteen-year-old printer's apprentice. Sometimes, I need reminding that I am not yet just a statue on a pedestal." Franklin's laugh was a goose's honk.

Daniel went back to Dr. Franklin's puzzle. "Many hands touch correspondence. How do you know the leak originates here? Pouches of letters are stolen from ships. Becca—Mrs. Parcell—only receives two in three letters I send."

"I tested my hypothesis." Franklin's face lit with pleasure. He suddenly looked years younger. "I made some ridiculous claim about General Washington's next moves at the dining table. And I heard those claims repeated in newspapers out of London two weeks later."

"So one of your guests is betraying you." Daniel leaned back against a wall and crossed his arms.

"A friend or a servant. There are too many to keep track of."

"It would help if you were more careful with your papers. I've seen correspondence from the French government lying scattered in the sitting room and the library."

"I am not a private secretary, Mr. Alloway." Franklin's face darkened. Do not tell me how to represent my country."

Franklin was open to limited criticism, it seemed, and Daniel had gone too far. But he wouldn't apologize for telling the truth. He scanned the workshop. There were two windows, and the single door to his left was closed. It didn't mean no one was listening to them. Would he look like a fool if he whipped open the door and window to check?

"What do you want from us?" Daniel asked reluctantly.

"You live with us now. I want you and Mrs. Parcell to listen to all the residents here. Only to listen. Your history with traitors may make you hear and see with a certain sensitivity."

"Sensitivity?" It was Daniel's turn to laugh.

Franklin nodded.

"And only listen?"

Another nod.

"Listen to whom?"

Franklin's lips curled into a satisfied smile as if Daniel had already agreed. He began to recite the names of his guests.

"I don't understand why you trust us," Daniel said. "General Washington and the others could be mistaken about me. Perhaps I fooled them all. I may be a British spy, too."

"Yet another spy at Passy. I swear the place is filled with them," Franklin said with good cheer. "You are filled with 'maybe's' and 'perhaps's.' Perhaps

I have someone watching you."

Daniel wondered if he and Dr. Franklin wore the same look of speculation as they stared at one another now. They burst into laughter at the same time.

"Will you help me?"

"I will help you. But Mrs. Parcell will make up her own mind. I don't speak for her."

"Indeed? And she will be your wife?" Franklin's pale white eyebrows rose.

"As quickly as I can arrange our wedding."

"And you do not speak for her?"

"She speaks for herself," Daniel repeated. "Always."

"How...interesting."

Daniel grinned. "She is interesting and more. You will like her."

Chapter Three

"I am fully recovered. A touch of *mal de mer*. A wicked case of seasickness." Jude Fenimore leaned against the ship's rail overlooking the Port of Nantes. He peered past Becca to speak to Hannah and Augusta.

"I have a delicate constitution, you see."

Hannah's dark eyebrows, so like Becca's, dropped into a straight disbelieving line. "Seasickness? You should have allowed me to examine you."

"There was no need. Your tea has refreshed me entirely."

Jude had woken from his faint quickly but pushed Hannah's hand away when she sought to examine him. He drank the relaxation tea she prepared from poppies and recovered enough to stagger to his narrow room within the hour.

"Lady Augusta and Hannah suffered terribly with the boat's motion," Becca said. "But seasickness comes at the beginning of a voyage, not the end."

"I doubt seasickness keeps track of time." He shrugged.

Becca squeezed her eyes shut. They were scratchy with lack of sleep. She opened them to find Jude studying her.

"I regret that you lost a night's sleep on my account." His lips curved into a half smile. "Though I am surprised you bothered to watch over me, given your distaste for me."

He'd slept on the floor below deck near the boat's stern, where the captain and senior crew ate. The crew had made Jude a nest of blankets. Becca had watched him until sunrise by the flickering light of a single candle.

There was no point in denying the truth. "You remind me of someone who caused me distress. I treated you badly. I kept vigil to apologize." She didn't mean to sound surly. Becca could speak of numbers and mathematics without end. Speaking of her own emotions left her awkward and tongue-tied.

Jude had grimaced and winced in pain as he slept but never roused. Once, he moaned, "No, René," so loudly that she reached out her hand to shake him awake and end the nightmare. She would have called Hannah if he'd gotten worse.

By dawn, she no longer saw a pale ghost of her dead husband when she looked at him. She saw only Jude, and her irritation with him vanished. It was difficult to dislike anyone when you'd seen them asleep and vulnerable. He'd seemed years older at rest than awake.

"Ahh. You were making penance." His smile was gentle. "Apology accepted." He shook his head. "But I didn't expect the kindness."

"Who is René?" she blurted out.

He went still, then smiled again. "I don't know. You tell me."

"You said his name in your sleep. You said, 'No, René.'"

"A dream, I suppose. I don't recall." Jude shrugged.

"Tighten the sails," a voice overhead rang out.

The bow swept left, and Becca staggered, clutching the rail to stay upright.

The jib sail came down first, then the main. "Ready to anchor," another voice called. Minutes later, the wooden masts were stripped naked, the crew folding sails. Without its forward motion, the ship pitched and rolled, subject to the wild, living sea.

"The anchor, boys," Captain Roberts shouted with his Scottish burr.

Chain slid through metal with a *rat-a-tat-tat*, and the anchor plummeted to the harbor floor.

* * *

The *Windborne* anchored in the bay until the harbormaster gave permission to tie off at one of the docks. As the sky lightened from apricot to a watery blue, Becca scanned the busy port crowded with ships.

Women in colorful aprons displayed vegetables, bread, and meat for sale. Crews hoisted barrels filled with fresh water or goods for sale onto boats. In the distance, Becca spied a long line of Black men in chains wearing little more than loincloths.

She averted her eyes, sending up a quick prayer that Missy and her son were well and still free. Captain Roberts had told them of the slave ships in Nantes. "From West Africa, they come. Then the French slaver traders go on their merry way to the Caribbean or America."

"Merry way?" Lady Augusta had said.

Roberts grimaced. "Not merry at all, trading in human life."

Behind them soared a fairy tale castle with white towers, jutting turrets, and dark-gabled spires. The house of the Dukes of Brittany, Captain Roberts said. It seemed light enough to float in the air, with only the heavy yellow bricks at its base tethering the castle to earth.

But Becca's mind drifted back to Daniel. Three hundred and three days had passed since she'd seen him. She patted the pocket tucked within her skirt again to feel the reassuring outlines of the letter she kept there. His letter.

"I have become familiar with an entirely new typeface, thanks to Dr. Franklin," Daniel wrote. "I dream of schooling you in this French alphabet. It shall require many lessons."

Becca's cheeks heated. She imagined the warmth of his skin as she drew letters on his palm, along his arms, then in the hollow of his throat, and along his chest beneath a summer moon in a Philadelphia garden last summer. It was their private game of touch and tease. Daniel had unknowingly started it when he drew an *A* on the palm of her hand to show her how printers invented different alphabets.

They would travel in a large coach, he had written. He would come as quickly as he could to meet them on the road.

The breeze was buttery soft and the weather warmer than it would have been at home. The modest homes here, with their tile roofs and wooden shutters, were different, too.

"Are you ready now?" Becca called to Hannah and Lady Augusta. She stepped onto the gangplank and waited for the vibrations underfoot to signal that the two women were following. But she waited alone on the narrow plank of wood over the Loire River. Becca whirled back, calling again. "Shall we go?"

Hannah and Augusta stood arm and arm, appearing as anxious as if they were about to dive into the harbor fully clothed. Their voices were low but not low enough.

"What will you do?" Augusta asked.

"It won't happen." Hannah paused. "Was it foolish of me to come?"

"Then we are both foolish. I swore I would never return," Augusta said.

"It was dreadful here," Hannah said.

"Entirely dreadful," Augusta echoed.

"For her, we did it." Hannah swept her unruly dark hair off her forehead.

"For Becca," Augusta sighed. Her silver hair was held rigidly in place. Even with her impeccable posture, she stood at least five inches shorter than Hannah.

"You didn't want to come? Neither of you?" Becca took three quick steps back up the walkway. Her eyes stung. "Why didn't you say something? You didn't protest. Neither of you even complained when you were sick the first two weeks." None of the herbs Hannah carried with her had relieved their odorous, painful malady.

Hannah and Augusta exchanged glances. Neither spoke.

Below them, dock workers hurried by pushing wheelbarrows with yellow and orange fruit. Members of the crew rolled barrels from the cargo hold to the dock.

"How didn't I see? Of course, neither of you wanted to return to Europe. I've been blind."

Hannah patted Becca's arm, murmuring, "There, there."

"If we didn't want to come, we would have stayed home. Has it crossed your mind that neither one of us would think of missing your wedding?" Augusta stood even taller, as petite as she was. She had fled from England and her husband's creditors.

"You could have said something when Daniel and I told you we would marry in Paris. You didn't even try to change our minds." The breeze whipped a strand of hair across her face.

"Mr. Barnes needed Daniel here. He left for France so quickly." Hannah's gaze slipped to Augusta. "Paris was the only choice."

"Of course it was." Augusta nodded to Hannah.

Becca's gaze slid from one woman to the other and back. "When did you two start to agree about anything?"

"We don't know what you mean." Augusta and Hannah raised their chins.

"You've disagreed on what to eat for supper, what herbs make the best tea, and how to clean curtains" And—it seemed to her—on which of the two Becca loved more. They had politely detested each other since the moment Hannah came to live with them in Morristown last year. "Seasickness brought you together," Becca said.

"Whatever can she mean?" Augusta said to Hannah, who shook her head.

"All it took for the two of you to become friends was a queasy stomach." The two women had shared a small room in the officers' quarters and nursed each other through the worst of the disorder. They'd emerged as friends.

"Don't fret, dear. It will be fine." Augusta patted Hannah's hand, then pulled her forward.

"Of course, it will be fine," Becca snapped. She hovered for one more moment.

"Go ahead, Becca." Augusta's voice was kind but distant. "We'll find our way down when we're ready."

Becca flew down the final few feet of the gangplank, eager for the feel of solid ground beneath her feet. Even more eager to reach Daniel.

She jumped to the dock. It buckled, rising and falling like ocean waves. She staggered in surprise. Captain Roberts's arm shot out and steadied her.

"Go slow, missus," he said. "People talk of getting their sea legs. S'harder to get your land legs back, me thinks. It'll take a day or so. Step careful til then."

Chapter Four

Becca pinched her cheeks again to create a natural flush.

"No need to punish your face that way. Your Mr. Alloway will find you lovely enough." Jude Fenimore's eyes were closed; at least, they seemed to be closed. His blond head rested against the cracked leather carriage bench he shared with Becca, Lady Augusta, and Hannah.

Becca's face flushed even more with embarrassment. It was too soon to expect Daniel to find them on the road. She knew that. And yet he could be here soon. He might be just miles away. And pinching her cheeks would bring color to them. Three days in this mildewed diligence coach had done little to improve her appearance or her temperament.

They would continue on to Passy, near Benjamin Franklin's home, unless Daniel met them sooner on the road. Jude would travel on to Paris.

Becca pinched her cheeks again.

Without opening his eyes, Jude added, "They'll expect you to paint your face white when you go to Versailles. And you'll want a wig for appearance at court. If your Mr. Alloway is to be successful, he'll need to know important people who can do him favors. That means he will go to court at Versailles and be charming."

Jude opened one eye and studied her. "He can be charming, can't he?"

Becca wasn't sure which of Jude's statements she should address first. "Yes, Mr. Alloway can be very charming," she said, copying Lady Augusta's most disapproving voice.

Daniel never powdered his hair, which he tied low at the back of his head. His collar and sleeves bore little lace, and he dressed in clothes that were less ostentatious than those most men wore in society. His simple style suited him. His appearance suited her. She felt a flutter low in her belly at the thought of Daniel.

She moved on to another question. "And how exactly do women here paint their faces?" A few women in New York City and Philadelphia powdered their faces white.

His smile grew broader. "They buy cosmetics made from lead. Their faces are pure white."

"You can't be serious." She shuddered at the thought of wearing a white mask.

Jude seemed to enjoy her reaction. "Going to Versailles bare-faced would be considered bad manners at best."

"And at worst?"

"It would be considered insulting." Another smile. "You wouldn't want to insult the king, would you?"

"I don't even want to see the king, not any king." Jude had just cracked open a door to the future, and Becca wasn't certain she liked what she saw. Would she need to accompany Daniel to balls at Louis XVI's court? She could hunt, track traitors, and decode ciphers, but she could not dance the minuet.

The traffic thickened as they approached the town of Le Mans.

The carriage horses neighed, protesting at the additional strain of pulling their weight up a rise. The woman next to Becca and other passengers sat forward as if that would help push the coach up the incline.

As the carriage slowed, Becca's breath grew shallow. The future had arrived while she'd been daydreaming like a young girl.

Where would they live? What would she do with herself when he worked? Would there be room for Hannah and Augusta? When could they all go home? *Would* they all go home? She hadn't spent a moment thinking beyond the first moment she'd see Daniel.

Becca asked a final question, more to distract herself from her sudden anxiety than out of any real interest. "How do you know so much about cosmetics in France?"

"I am a merchant. I am required to be charming, too." Jude smiled.

The dull thud of horseshoes on dirt was replaced by the crisper clip-clop of hoofs on cobblestones. The carriage driver called to his horses.

Becca began to protest that Jude hadn't answered her question when a gleaming black carriage pulled next to them. It stopped by a crumbling reddish-brown wall that spoke of times so ancient that she couldn't imagine them.

A tall man in a brown velvet coat with large gold trim and gold buttons, a white wig, and a black tricorn hat leaped from the carriage. In the noonday sun, his hat cast a shadow that hid his face. His long lace sleeves fluttered as he strode toward the diligence coach.

Becca had seen imaginary Daniels at every coach stop. All it had taken was the sight of a tall, thin man like this one. She was ready to turn away when the most current not-Daniel swept his hat from his head and waved.

He towered over the small knot of people waiting for the carriage.

"Daniel," she whispered.

Two passengers, a man and a woman, blocked the carriage door. The woman muttered and patted the side of her black gown as if checking her pocket to make sure she'd left nothing behind.

Becca thrummed with impatience until someone below helped the woman down.

She leaped into Daniel's arms.

* * *

Servants jostled Becca and Daniel out of the way as they carried trunks and bags from the coach to waiting passengers.

Daniel released Becca slowly, his fingertips lingering at her waist. "Will you marry me, Mrs. Parcell? Or have you changed your mind?" What he meant was, "I have waited too long for you."

She threw her head back and laughed. "We shall wed tomorrow unless you are free sooner?" Her eyes shown with joy.

"The English elope to Gretna Green. I don't know where overeager couples in Paris go. But if you decide on that course, m'dears, may we accompany you?" Augusta said.

"An elopement?" Becca sounded wistful.

"Would you prefer to elope? The sooner, the better." Daniel grinned.

"I have missed enough of Becca's life," Hannah interrupted. "I should like to see my daughter have a proper wedding." She swiped the back of her hand over her eyes. "I am sorry for all the years I've missed with you."

"No more apologies," Augusta cajoled. "You promised."

Promised? What else had the two women discussed on board the *Wind-borne*? "Of course you shall see me wed. Why else have we all come?"

Daniel nodded.

"Yes," Augusta said. "There is a wedding dress to be made, a party to be arranged, and a minister to be found." Her eyes narrowed. "But in the meantime, Mr. Alloway, why are you dressed like a Frenchman?" She pronounced 'Frenchman' as if it were a skin disorder.

Daniel squinted down at his breeches, his vest, his shoes. Nothing seemed amiss.

The three women stood in a semi-circle, heads tilted, arms crossed. Their gaze dipped to the crystal-studded buckles on his shoes, rose to the embroidered flowers on his green damask jacket, and ended at the lace collar of his shirt.

"Mr. Alloway looks…." Hannah's voice trailed off as if she couldn't think of a word to complete the sentence.

"Quite fancy," Becca offered, her head tilted to the same degree as her mother. "Quite fancy. I barely recognized you at first."

He widened his arms as if standing for inspection. "Don't I look like a member of the gentry? The sort of man you'd hand your good French *livres* to in exchange for Mr. Barnes's goods? Why, that's the point. I need to look the part." The lace at his wrists luffed like the sails on Captain Roberts's ship.

Daniel had hardly recognized himself when he donned these clothes. And now? The silks and linens were a costume, as much of a disguise as his false identity had been in Philadelphia.

20

"So your clothing is a disguise, just a disguise you use to do your job." Becca smiled in relief.

She understood. Daniel nodded. "I don't stand out at Versailles dressed like this. I quite disappear, in fact. You'll see."

Lady Augusta *hmphed* in disapproval. "You shouldn't dress as the French do. It doesn't suit."

Becca stared at the crystal-studded buckles on his shoes again and winced.

Daniel tried again. "But Paris is the whipped cream of Europe."

The three women exchanged glances that suggested he'd lost his mind.

"Whipped cream and men's clothing? I don't understand," Becca said.

"Yes, speak clearly, Mr. Alloway," Augusta demanded.

"It's Voltaire. I heard it at Versailles." Daniel was met with blank stares. He tried again. "It is different here. Style—the whipped cream—matters as much as substance. Sometimes more."

"Whipped cream has no substance. You do," Becca said.

"A fine compliment, Mrs. Parcell." He stared into her eyes until Augusta cleared her throat. "We should leave. It will still take a few days for the four of us to arrive at Dr. Franklin's." He turned to signal his carriage driver, who was feeding the horses.

"There will be five of us, not four." Augusta waved to a stranger standing by the diligence coach.

Jude reached them in two easy strides. Bowing, he extended a silk-stockinged foot that was only slightly grubby after the log trip from Nantes. He tipped his hat with one hand,. "Jude Fenimore. Your servant, sir."

"As I am yours," Daniel returned the gesture.

"Mr. Fenimore has kept us safe since we arrived in France. He'll continue on to Paris with us," Augusta said as if the matter were settled.

Augusta and Jude smiled at each other as if they were the best of friends. Becca hardly glanced at the man.

Daniel felt his shoulder muscles unlock. "If you've kept these women safe, sir, we'll find room for you. I owe you a debt of gratitude."

"And I am grateful to you, as well, for your hospitable offer." Jude grinned. "I'm happy to sit with the driver if you can accommodate me at least to

Passy."

"A capital idea." Daniel smiled, too. "I'm grateful to you, but my gratitude doesn't extend to giving up my seat."

"Passy? We are going to Passy?" Hannah's normally ruddy face turned pale.

"Yes. Didn't Becca tell you? We'll be staying with Dr. Franklin," Daniel said.

"She said he lived outside of Paris." Hannah kneaded one hand with the other.

"And so he does. In a village called Passy. Is that a problem?"

"Certainly not." Augusta stepped in front of Hannah, blocking his view of her.

Daniel turned to Becca, raising his eyebrows.

She shook her head and shrugged. "What is it?" Becca stepped toward her mother.

"Merely the ride." Hannah wrapped her arms around herself.

"A short walk in the fresh air, and she will be well." Augusta pulled at Hannah's arm. The two women stepped away, petite Lady Augusta in her bright yellow gown with hardly a wrinkle and Hannah with her wild hair and limp muslin gown. Their soft voices sounded to Daniel like doves cooing at sunset.

Chapter Five

Becca's hand rose to her neck as the carriage finally, blessedly, came to a stop. "Do lunatics live here?"

"Quite a few." Daniel sounded pleased.

Out the carriage window, an old man in a brown suit swung a long-handled mallet over his head. He whooped in delight.

"Don't tell me that's Benjamin Franklin," Becca said.

Daniel nodded. "He most certainly is."

Nearby, a tall woman leaned on the mallet she held as if it were a cane. "It's your turn, Gabe," she called to a young man in a light green silk suit.

Gabe pulled the mallet back.

Dr. Franklin whooped again just as Gabe tapped his mallet against a ball. With a crack, it rolled across the lawn, coming to rest just to the left of a white hoop.

The tall woman cheered as the shot missed its mark.

On the sidelines, a middle-aged man glowered, holding a ream of papers.

"Foul, sir." Gabe slapped his hand against his forehead. His suit shimmered in the afternoon sunlight. "The doctor ruined my shot on purpose." A smile removed the sting from his accusation.

He spoke English with a French accent and turned to the carriage as it came to a stop. His face lit with pleasure. "There you are, Mr. Alloway. You must convince Dr. Franklin to stop cheating. It is unbecoming."

The tall woman snorted. "You simply cannot stand losing to an American."

Daniel grinned at Becca. "They're playing ground billiards. A game. *Jeu de mail*, they call it. And Dr. Franklin does like to cheat. Come. Meet my

23

friends."

"I thought they were about to beat each other with those sticks," Becca murmured. She pressed her back against the leather seat, not quite ready to leave the safety of the carriage. "I thought they would kill each other."

Daniel leaped to the ground and clapped the Frenchman on the back, then returned to help each of the women from the coach. Jude climbed down from his seat next to the driver. He stood back, waiting near the carriage.

"But this is marvelous," Augusta said with surprise. "I expected some dark, ancient castle."

Becca's gaze traveled up the rise of the rich green lawn to the stone building that glowed pearl white in the afternoon sunlight. Its center courtyard connected two matching three-story houses that were capped by elegant black tile roofs. A line of lime trees bordered the walkway.

"The view from the back is even better," Daniel said. "That's where you'll find the orange trees. I'll take you to see the gardens and the path to the river. You'll see Paris from there, too. It's only three miles away."

Becca forced a smile. Did Daniel already love the French so much that he wanted to settle here forever? She tried to imagine herself still here in three years or five, and her mind went blank. "What can I or Morristown offer you after this rich life?"

He leaned in, whispering. "All that I need, Becca. That's what you offer me."

His warm breath on her neck raised goosebumps but didn't stop her worry.

"Introduce us to these three goddesses, Mr. Alloway," Dr. Franklin crowed, calling Becca's attention back. She had looked forward to meeting her friend Sally Franklin Bache's famous father. But she found herself tongue-tied now that she was face-to-face with one of the most famous men in all of Europe or America.

"You must be Juno, the Roman queen of goddesses." He bowed to Augusta.

"I've never been compared to a goddess, but I shan't complain." Augusta dipped a curtsy as gracefully as a woman half her age.

His eyes lit with interest as Lady Augusta rose. "Enchanted, madam. Dr. Franklin at your service."

Becca's spine stiffened. He did look enchanted by Augusta. Too enchanted.

"And you must be Minerva, the goddess of wisdom." Franklin bowed to Hannah, who nodded curtly.

"And I know you, Mrs. Parcell. You are Venus, the goddess of love, for you have stolen Mr. Alloway's heart."

Becca dipped an awkward curtsy, too tongue-tied to answer.

"French women would take the comparison to a goddess as a compliment. I hope you do, as well," the Frenchman said. "Gabriel d'Aumont. Your humble servant." His features were sharp, his heavy-lidded eyes kind.

"I barely know what to say." She felt her cheeks heat.

"You're embarrassing Mrs. Parcell, Gabe. You and Benny must both stop," the tall woman said. "I'm Patience Wright." She bobbed a curtsy. "Pleased to meet some American women. There aren't a lot of us in Paris."

"I have papers for Dr. Franklin to review, and they won't wait," the glowering man interrupted.

Franklin's face tightened with displeasure. "Edward Bancroft would introduce himself if he had any manners, but I shall do it for him. Mr. Bancroft is my good friend, and he serves as private secretary to me and the commissioners who will soon, God willing, begin negotiating a peace with England. I doubt I should get anything done without him."

Bancroft frowned even harder.

Couldn't Dr. Franklin see the hatred in Mr. Bancroft's expression? Had there been an argument, Becca wondered.

Franklin focused for the first time on Jude, but he addressed Daniel. "You bring me a surprise guest, Mr. Alloway?"

"No, sir." Jude stepped forward, away from the carriage. "Not a guest. A temporary visitor. Mr. Alloway and the ladies offered me a ride. I'll be continuing on to Paris."

All good humor fled Patience Wright's face.

"You have business in Paris? And you're an American, you say?" Franklin asked.

"I didn't say. But, yes, I am an American. I'd fallen on a bit of hard times, and I am back to make my fortune." Jude's tone was so lighthearted that

Becca couldn't tell if he was serious about hard times.

"Mr. Fenimore is trying to arrange credit to sell French fabrics to Americans," Daniel said.

Hannah and Augusta exchanged glances. Becca pinched her lips. As if American women had money for French fabrics in the midst of the War for Independence.

"You're invited to stay for our midday meal. Our new pastry chef is quite good." Franklin patted his round stomach as if its size proved his chef's excellence.

"The chef is gone for a week. Some emergency at home," Bancroft said.

"Have lunch with us in any case, Mr. Fenimore." Franklin ignored his secretary.

"A kind offer, but I best be off."

"I may be able to assist you, Mr. Fenimore," Gabriel d'Aumont said. "Do you have a calling card?"

"Give him one, Jude," Daniel urged. "Monsieur d'Aumont knows all the bankers and merchants in Paris. He is an assistant minister of finance."

"I do, and I am." d'Aumont bowed with an ironic flourish.

Jude's face lit with hope. He pulled an embroidered silk wallet from his pocket and extracted a slim card that he handed to Gabriel. "You can find me here for now."

"We shall see you again? You will visit?" Lady Augusta asked.

Becca felt an itch between her shoulder blades as if some invisible predator stalked her. But this wasn't the forest where she'd hunted as a child. She studied Dr. Franklin and his guests more closely.

Patience stared at Jude with hatred.

Augusta watched him with longing.

Monsieur d'Aumont assessed him with a cool, analytic look as if the visitor was a row of numbers that didn't add up.

Jude scanned the house and grounds, avoiding their scrutiny.

Franklin beamed at everyone but saved his biggest smile for Lady Augusta.

And Edward Bancroft glared at Becca as if she'd stood up and giggled in church in the midst of the sermon.

Who was the hunter, and who was being hunted? It was a fanciful notion. She was tired from the ride, Becca told herself. That was all. Nothing was wrong.

Gabriel d'Aumont broke the tension. "I have never heard you all so silent. Did you mention pastry, Dr. Franklin? Am I also invited for supper?"

"You are always welcome." Franklin clapped his hands.

"Welcome to a free meal here four times a week," Bancroft muttered.

d'Aumont ignored him. "Farewell, Mr. Fenimore. T'was a pleasure meeting you."

Moments later, the wheels of the coach turned, spitting gravel across the drive.

Patience Wright dropped her mallet and strode toward the house. Edward Bancroft handed Franklin one paper, then another.

Gabriel d'Aumont leaned on his mallet and seemed to contemplate the afternoon sky.

"Come, ladies. I'll see you settled in your rooms," Daniel said, seemingly eager to remove them all from the scene.

* * *

"That wasn't the 'jolly company' I promised you," Daniel said an hour later.

He and Becca stood alone on the third-floor landing of the Hôtel de Valentinois. Candles flickered in bright gold sconces, casting shadows and scenting the space with beeswax. Hannah and Augusta were still unpacking in their rooms.

"They were gripped by bad humors. That's what my mother would call it." Becca tilted her head. "Don't they want us here? You sensed something, too. I could tell."

Daniel's shoulders unknotted. For the first time since Becca had jumped from the diligence coach into his arms, the awkwardness that beset them on the journey was gone.

"It was odd," he said. "*They* were odd. But I don't think you had anything to do with their 'humours.' Patience Wright hated Jude Fenimore on sight. I could see that much."

"It wasn't my imagination, then." Becca's blue eyes widened. They were almost purple in the shadowy hallway. "And Gabriel d'Aumont seemed to study your every reaction. How does a French minister have time to 'stop in' in case you happen to be available?"

"An assistant minister." Daniel grinned. "Gabe notices everything about everyone. 'Tis the only way to survive the backstabbing at court, he says. Dr. Franklin's secretary was watching your every step. I find myself with a sudden, intense dislike of Edward Bancroft."

Becca rewarded him with a smile. "And the more strained all his guests appeared, the happier your Dr. Franklin became." She paused. "What is going on here, Daniel?"

All Daniel wanted to do was gather her into his arms, to feel her warmth against his after their long separation. It felt miraculous to have her here. Instead, he scanned the stairway and the hall. They were still alone. Daniel gripped her arm gently and pulled her further into the shadows, away from the stairs.

"Someone in the house is sharing American secrets with the English. That is what Dr. Franklin believes." He relayed the rest of his conversation with Franklin in the print shop. "A spy in our midst, Benjamin Franklin said, and now I am imagining spies everywhere."

"But we are done with spying." Becca fisted her hands on her hips.

"That is what I told Dr. Franklin." Daniel took a deep breath. "I said I would help him. The Congress hasn't accepted his resignation letter, and he is still our best hope for peace with England. How could I refuse? As for whether you choose to help..." He trailed a finger from her wrist to her elbow. "...I told him that you make your own decisions."

Her dark eyebrows rose in surprise. "You said that?"

He nodded.

"Ask me to marry you," she said.

"But you have already agreed to marry me."

"Ask me again."

Would he ever understand her entirely? He doubted it. "All right. Will you marry me?"

She lifted herself on her toes and kissed him lightly. "How can I refuse a man who allows me to make my own decisions?"

He swept his arm around her waist and kissed her again. This. He craved this.

At some point, she raised her face to his and exhaled, "The carriage ride was torture."

"It was long."

"I don't mean the length of the trip." Becca's eyes were luminous and slightly unfocused. "I meant our audience. Hannah, Augusta, and Jude didn't stop watching us for a moment."

He kissed the skin along the side of her throat, inhaling the scent of lavender, cedar, and something that was purely Becca.

She shuddered, then scraped his earlobe with her teeth.

His thoughts sputtered to a stop.

"And each night, I joined Lady Augusta and Hannah in one room." Becca's hands slipped beneath his linen shirt.

"While I joined Mr. Fenimore in another." The heat built in his chest.

A door slammed below. Footsteps crossed the hall and ascended one flight, then a second.

"*Stront.*" Daniel breathed an old Dutch curse, just one of the cornucopia of French, German, Portuguese, and Dutch curse words he'd picked up in the disreputable waterfront taverns of Elizabethtown. He smoothed his vest.

Becca straightened her gown and tucked a strand of dark hair behind her ear.

"My apologies," Mr. Bancroft called up to them, not sounding apologetic. "You have business with that French chap. Dr. Franklin asked me to fetch you."

Daniel stepped in front of Becca as if she needed protection.

"Go. I shall be fine." Becca poked him in the back.

More footsteps, light and quick. A moon-faced girl holding her charcoal gray gown to her shins clambered up the stairs, stopping a few steps below them. Her eyes were wide and curious. She curtsied, pointed up and to the right, then curtsied again, all while smiling at Becca.

"She wants you to follow her to your room. She'll unpack and help you change for supper." Daniel lowered his voice to little more than a whisper. "And what do you make of Dr. Franklin's request? Will you help him?"

Her broad forehead furrowed. "I should like to. But won't I be too busy with our wedding plans?"

"Are you coming, Mr. Alloway?" Bancroft barked, then swiveled and ambled down the staircase, mumbling under his breath.

Daniel stopped himself from uttering yet another curse and followed Bancroft down the stairs.

Chapter Six

Nude women frolicked with pink-cheeked Cupids across the walls and sky-blue painted ceiling. Becca shifted her gaze to the front of the room. A half-sized onyx statue of a man stared back at her, wearing only a cloak that displayed more than it hid.

A week since their arrival, Becca still hadn't grown accustomed to the mansion's exuberant decoration.

"This room is ruining my digestion," she muttered to Daniel. There was no place to rest her gaze without staring at lusciously painted naked flesh.

Dinner conversation fell away. Benjamin Franklin coughed into a napkin to hide his amusement. Patience Wright hiccupped a laugh and took another sip of wine.

They were dining *en famille*, as Franklin called it. Lady Augusta and Hannah sat on either side of him at the foot of a table that seated twenty-four. Becca had counted the chairs. She and Daniel sat across from Patience and Gabriel d'Aumont, who seemed to be a regular guest.

"It does take some getting used to." Hannah giggled.

Becca's embarrassment evaporated at the sound. Hannah's fear of living here in Passy—whatever its source—was lifting. She'd been so worried that letting her mother come to France had been a mistake.

"The French have strict rules when it comes to deportment and fashion. But they are less strict with regard to other matters." Franklin pointed to the ceiling, with its painted figures and gold, carved moldings.

"The French are not the only ones less strict when it comes to 'other matters.'" Patience smiled at Becca. Her eyes gleamed with malice above the almost-empty glass of burgundy she held to her lips. It wasn't her first glass of wine this afternoon.

The insult landed squarely. Each night, Daniel slipped into Becca's room after the house grew silent. He left before first light. They were to be married, after all, and it was no one's business but their own.

Hannah's spoon clattered to her plate.

Becca studied the artist. What accounted for this attack? Patience had seemed unconventional when they first met on the front lawn. Her hatred for Jude was clear, but she'd welcomed Becca. Something must account for this sudden, irrational change.

Daniel's chair scraped the parquet floor as he pushed back. Becca wondered if anyone else heard the growl in the back of his throat.

Beneath the white linen tablecloth, she placed her hand on his thigh. "Please," she whispered.

He stayed seated, but she felt the tension in his muscles.

"Did you mean anyone in particular, Mrs. Wright?" Becca widened her eyes, mirroring the sculptress's expression. If Mrs. Wright wanted to push her, she would push right back.

Patience's smile grew wider. "Why, I meant no offense. Polite conversation in France is so broad. It covers many more topics than are permissible in America." She raised her wine glass in a toast. It was empty. A servant moved to refill it. "Isn't that true, Monsieur d'Aumont?"

"*C'est vrai.* That's true." Gabriel lounged back against the carved mahogany chair. "But at home with our loved ones, we value kindness above all else." Gabriel's rebuke was diplomatic but direct.

Becca was grateful. She would thank him later.

"Actually, I expected I would have you running from the table in tears," Patience interrupted. She slurred her words.

Franklin frowned as she half-emptied her glass again.

"Why, you're almost strong enough to face the ladies at Versailles." Patience sipped, then thumped the goblet on the table. It wobbled, spit droplets of dark red wine onto the white tablecloth, and settled upright.

"You are testing me?" Becca's chest tightened with anger.

"One is tested repeatedly at Versailles. You will become accustomed to their insults." The artist's small mouth pursed. Her acorn-brown gown bore dabs of paint and stains from the wax she used in her sculptures.

"Then I shan't go to Versailles," Becca said.

"If you're asked, you'll go." Patience scanned the table and sighed as if disappointed by her reduced circumstances.

In London, Mrs. Wright had been fêted by royalty. In France, she was just another artist clamoring for commissions. Becca felt an unexpected jolt of compassion.

Into the awkward silence, Augusta asked, "Have any of you heard from Jude Fenimore? He said he would visit again soon. I hope he has not forgotten us."

Becca relaxed as much as her stays permitted. The men sat back in their chairs. It was as if the room exhaled with relief at Augusta's change of topic.

Four servants whisked away the consommé bowls and silently replaced them with gold-rimmed plates of chicken that scented the air with butter and white wine. Another servant refilled Patience's cup.

"Are you certain you've never met Mr. Fenimore before?" Augusta asked Dr. Franklin. "I had the impression you knew all the American merchants."

"I only know the Americans here who want to complain or ask me for a favor. Your Mr. Fenimore must never have had a problem that required a favor."

"If that's the case, I must learn his secret," Daniel sniped. "I don't know of a single voyage that's gone smoothly, not with the war."

Gabriel d'Aumont voiced an opinion about how much longer the War for Independence could last. Dr. Franklin told a story and soon, the servants were replacing empty plates with smaller ones for dessert.

Becca eyed the pastry before her. She lifted her fork, inhaling the scent of tart lemon and sugar, and took a bite. The lemon layer cake was laced with flecks of poppy seeds and filled with thick layers of lemon curd. Buttercream, lemon zest, and vanilla danced on her tongue. "Oh my." She looked up in astonishment.

The laughter round the table was good-natured.

"Our new dessert chef has returned," Dr. Franklin said. "This confection proves it. With pastry such as this, I may never leave France."

The dining room door at the far end of the room slammed open. Becca jumped at the sudden sound.

Edward Bancroft burst into the dining room with a heavy canvas bag over his shoulder. The heels of his black leather shoes were caked in dirt. He dropped the bag and fell into the empty chair next to Gabriel.

"At least you are in time for dessert," Franklin said as a servant slipped a dessert plate in front of Bancroft. "I hope it's not something as frivolous as work that's kept you from the midday meal."

"Just your work, sir." Bancroft produced a thin smile before his lips fell into their habitual expression of discontent.

"You didn't mention any new matters earlier." Franklin's frown matched Bancroft's.

"Nonsense, is what it is." Bancroft sounded angry. "Now strangers are throwing correspondence to you over the fence."

"You pique my curiosity. Were you scouring the grounds, waiting for such an offense?" Franklin asked.

Becca felt the tension between them. Dr. Franklin didn't sound like someone who had resigned his post, and the two didn't sound like old friends.

Bancroft hesitated. "One of the gardeners found the letter and fetched me."

"And it took you the entire length of our meal to retrieve it?"

Bancroft's back stiffened. "I took the time to read the correspondence. I am, after all, your private secretary."

Franklin extended his hand, palm up.

Bancroft retrieved the tote bag, sighing loudly. He ignored the waiting hand and set several sheets of parchment on the table next to Franklin.

"We shall take coffee in the sitting room," Hannah said.

Becca half rose. Her mother was right. The two men needed privacy to discuss their business.

"No need," Franklin answered absently. He slipped a pair of wire-rimmed glasses from his vest pocket and set them on his nose. The paper glowed ivory in the afternoon light as Franklin read. Becca thought his hand trembled for a moment.

"Thank you, Mr. Bancroft," Franklin said. "As you say, 'tis nonsense."

Bancroft reached for the papers.

Franklin slid the parchment out of his reach. "Chef has outdone himself with this dessert." He turned to the butler, who stood by the door. "Perfection should be recognized when it is achieved. Can you ask the chef to come?"

Becca's gaze slid to Daniel. His eyebrows rose. He, too, seemed to notice the clumsy way Franklin cut off discussion with Edward Bancroft.

Moments later, a tall man wearing a chef's round white cloth cap, long, loose pants, and wooden clogs ambled through the door. Short tendrils of black hair streaked with gray escaped the edges of the cap. His expression was wary. He was almost as thin as Daniel had been just months off the British prison ship when Becca first met him. The chef's features–deep brown eyes, down-curved nose, and wide mouth–all seemed slightly too large for his thin face.

"I have never eaten such pastry, and my guests agree. Well done," Franklin called in French.

The chef bowed with the dignity of a prince. He rose, surveying the empty dessert plates with satisfaction, then lifted his eyes to the guests. He turned from Franklin to Augusta and Daniel, then to Becca.

He blinked twice and frowned. His gaze turned to Hannah. His dark eyebrows rose. The pastry chef looked away, then back at the two women as if puzzled by them.

"Is the lemon cake your own invention?" Gabriel asked.

"Of course." The chef frowned.

"But the filling. I have never tasted the like," the Frenchman said.

"Lemon curd, it is called." The chef grudgingly smiled, which saved his face from ugliness. "My mother's recipe."

"And the seeds?" Gabriel asked.

"They are poppy seeds," Hannah said.

The chef studied Hannah, who bit her bottom lip in response to the examination. "May I return to the kitchen now?" he asked.

Franklin nodded, and the man bowed twice as he retreated from the room

"I suppose he is unaccustomed to being congratulated on his skill," Dr. Franklin said with amusement.

"Or he is shy around beautiful women." Gabriel swept his hand round the table to include all four women at the table.

"What a delightful meal." Augusta stood, staring at Patience for one beat too long, as if to imply that the meal was anything but delightful, thanks to the sculptress's outbursts. "I shall retire to rest. But don't forget, Becca. The dressmaker will be back in an hour."

Hannah rose, too.

"Must we see the dressmaker every day?" Becca's curiosity about the dessert chef receded. "I can barely move when she is working." The tiny, sharp stab of pins at her wrists, her waist, her ribs, her back made Becca feel like a caged animal.

"You will need more than one gown, especially if you are to accompany Daniel to Versailles," Hannah said.

Patience rose and staggered as she turned to the door.

Gabriel shot up and took her arm in time to stop her from falling. "Tell me how your work goes?"

"Quite well, of course. Quite well." She leaned on him as they exited.

Becca had felt like a compass pointing east toward Daniel for so long. How ridiculous that she'd given so little thought to what it would be like to live in the shadow of Versailles. Perhaps it was Patience Wright's snide question or the threat of having to visit Versailles. It might have been the thought of the dressmaker's pins. All she wanted was to escape the mansion. "Do you have time for a walk, Mr. Alloway?"

He rose and offered her his arm.

* * *

The scent of manure rose from the vegetable gardens. Two servants stooped over lush green lettuces with ruffled edges. Their soft voices carried like music on the light breeze.

Becca stepped into a row of green vines that climbed seven feet tall. The curtain of pea plants provided some privacy.

"Did you hear Mrs. Wright?" Becca hissed. "Did you see her face and Gabriel's? Do they all think I am your Paris mistress?"

She paced. "I don't want to care about them. I didn't come to France to care about them." She turned, stabbing Daniel in the chest with her finger. "I came to marry you.

"I don't care what color my wedding dress is or what they're wearing at Versailles or whether the neckline needs more or less lace or if the napkins and tablecloths will match." She took a breath. "I would marry you wearing a burlap sack. I don't care if we serve oatmeal at the wedding. Have the chef decide on the desserts. He seems quite competent."

"I will go to sleep happy tonight thinking of you wearing a burlap sack." Daniel teased.

Becca scowled. "Let Augusta and Hannah spend all day asking *your* opinion of what punch, what cake, what petticoat to wear, and see how patient you are then. I am quite miserable."

"Is it the gown that makes you angry?" Daniel studied her. "Or is it me?"

"I don't see you, Daniel."

"I am right here." He shook his head.

"That's not what I mean." What *did* she mean?

He stepped even closer. "I come to you every night." He stroked her forearm, from elbow to wrist, and lifted her palm to his mouth.

At the touch of his lips, Becca's breathing slowed. "I am not complaining of that." In the dark, especially in the dark, everything between them was honest and true.

"Then what?"

"You have something to do, something that keeps you occupied. You are with Mr. Barnes's customers or ship captains, or you are off to Versailles to consult with Gabriel."

"I am building a life for us. A future. The war can't last forever."

"And I am planning for a wedding, a single day, not even an entire day, as if it were everything." Why did she sound bitter?

Daniel's head snapped back as if she'd slapped him.

"I am saying this all wrong." Becca rested a hand on his vest, feeling his heart beat beneath her palm. "This is what I want. To be married to you. But what shall I do with myself?" She hadn't known that was the problem until the words tumbled out.

He raised his head. Footsteps. Becca heard them, too.

"I don't care, Daniel. I don't care if anyone hears us. I love you, and I will marry you. But your day is filled with challenges and tasks, and new people. How shall I fill my day? With ground billiards? With needlepoint? After what we've done for General Washington and Mr. Hamilton, how am I to spend my days thinking about lace fichus and the fashionable size of hip pads?"

"We will find our way. That is not the type of wife I want. I want you, *ow melder*." My love. He whispered the endearment in Cornish, the language of his childhood.

Becca swallowed past the lump in her throat. "I want to be a good wife, truly. Only, I don't know...."

"There you are." Benjamin Franklin's voice boomed. He stepped through the curtain of green tendrils at the end of the garden row.

"Mr. Alloway, shall we show Mrs. Parcell where you and I spend our time? I think she would quite enjoy seeing my print shop, don't you?"

Becca curtseyed, feeling her cheeks heat. How much had Dr. Franklin heard? "I would indeed enjoy that, Dr. Franklin. But Lady Augusta and Hannah will be expecting me. The dressmaker is coming."

"I've arranged to pay the dressmaker for the extra time she will spend here," Franklin said. He lifted his black-lacquered cane, pointing it toward the river. "Now, come."

Chapter Seven

Daniel focused on the raft of folded papers that Benjamin Franklin held as they wound their way down the brick walkway toward the edge of the property closest to the river. He managed to hold his tongue until they reached the printing shed. "It's not the press you're wanting us to see. It's the letter Mr. Bancroft handed you."

"Am I that obvious?" Franklin's pale eyebrows rose.

"Yes, you are," Becca laughed as Daniel said, "Certainly not."

Franklin glanced up the slope to the house as if to make certain no one had followed. "I've always enjoyed a good view of a river. Shall we?" He extended the point of his cane, now coated in rich soil, and pointed to three large tree stumps that rested nearby.

Becca spread her wide pink and white gown and sat on one log. Franklin settled on another.

Daniel took the third. He watched overhead as a large white Osprey made lazy circles in the sky. It landed out of sight, somewhere on the river.

He lifted his face to the sun for one last moment of peace. Daniel had the feeling that he wasn't going to like whatever Dr. Franklin was about to say. "All right. What was in the letter that so rattled you?"

"You noticed that, too?" He extended the papers to Daniel. "It might take a while to read it aloud. But I want Mrs. Parcell to hear it."

Daniel didn't reach for the parchment. "I agreed to listen for anything your guests said that suggested treason. I haven't heard anything that identifies your spy, if there is one. But you are going to ask for some new assistance now, and there will be more to it. We are getting married, Dr. Franklin. We don't have time to do more."

"Read the letter, Alloway. Do me the great favor of reading it."

Daniel lifted one eyebrow.

Franklin's hand was still extended.

He took the parchment, rubbing the paper between the fingers of his good hand to test its quality. It was an old printer's habit. "Heavy stock. A fine weave. Expensive paper."

"Indeed, it is. Read it aloud," Franklin repeated.

"Why don't we have paper of this quality in America?"

Franklin didn't answer.

Daniel sighed. There was no point putting off the inevitable. He opened the long letter, and reluctantly began.

Moments later, he raised his head. "This writer, this...." He found the name again. "This Charles de Weissenstein thinks you can stop the war?"

"Keep the sarcasm from your voice, Mr. Alloway. Continue." Franklin's expression was jovial, which alarmed Daniel. There must be worse to come.

There was. "We'll never be independent of England, and even if we were, we'd make a hash of it," Daniel said after reading the letter. "There's nothing surprising in that from an Englishman's point of view."

"And that is the point of the message?" Becca murmured.

Franklin poked himself in the chest. "Not quite the point. I am the point. He wants me to propose conditions of peace directly to King George that do not include independence."

Daniel read:

I do not at all guess what are America's views, nor what will please her; but if, in the present State of affairs, any reasonable proposals for accommodation come from you, the Crown must attend to them ... Why not offer some conditions directly to the King himself?

Daniel had the urge to drop the letter as if it were a scrambling rat he held by the tail.

"And if I follow through on his proposition," Franklin said, "I will be made a peer of the realm and granted an annual pension for life. All I must do...."

Daniel read the next paragraphs. "All you need to do is go to the Cathedral of Notre Dame and give the man with the red rose a note?" Daniel scoffed. "A note with terms for peace that leave us tied to England. You're not taking this seriously?"

The note read:

...specify your Preliminaries in writing; and carry them Yourself to the Cathedral Church of Notre Dame between the hours of twelve at noon and one; either on Monday the sixth of July instant, or on Thursday the ninth...you will find my emissary in the aisle of the right hand on going in, on the same side (if I mistake not) where the huge statue of St. Christopher is. I have asked him to stick a rose in his hat, which he will hold in his hand up to his face....

"Toss the letter. Drop it into the Seine," Daniel said.

"Really, Dr. Franklin, wouldn't it be best to ignore the letter?" Becca added. "And I don't see how we can help." She winced. "I apologize, sir, for offering advice to you of all people. I am sometimes too bold."

Franklin's face softened. "There's no need to apologize for honesty, m'dear. Truth is a guest that should always be welcomed."

Becca tilted her head. "Your daughter quotes your most famous sayings all the time, but I am unfamiliar with that one."

"I created it just for you." Franklin waggled his eyebrows, and Becca laughed again. He hesitated. "Does Sally quote me often?"

"Indeed, sir. She couldn't be prouder of you," Becca said. Sally Franklin Bache was Becca's closest friend in Philadelphia.

"She is a loyal girl, more loyal than I deserve." Franklin rose slowly. The bottom of his cane picked up mud as he paced. "I can't throw this letter in a fire, not yet."

"The river would do," Daniel said.

Franklin ignored him. "The letter may be exactly what it appears to be, an attempt to bribe me into helping England regain a stranglehold on America."

"How can they doubt your loyalty to independence?" Daniel asked. Then he understood. "It's your resignation, isn't it? Whoever wrote this thinks you have given up on America because you have resigned your post," Daniel said.

"Congress has not accepted my resignation. And they won't." Franklin glowered.

"You encourage honesty. You can't be angry when you don't like its sting," Daniel snapped. He turned to Becca. "Congress will see there's no one else but Dr. Franklin who can negotiate a peace with England, and they will insist he stay on. His enemies in Congress will have to hold their tongue. That was the whole point of resigning."

"But what if the letter has another goal?" Franklin asked. "What if it is intended to make America appear untrustworthy, unstable, just as peace negotiations are set to begin?"

"You mean, what if the goal is to make *you* appear untrustworthy." Daniel felt the pull of Franklin's curiosity and intelligence and cursed himself for responding. He didn't want to be drawn in. He didn't want Becca drawn in.

Franklin nodded. "I mean both."

"If the letter is made public, some will think you've accepted the bribe no matter how you deny it." Becca paced in one direction, crossing paths with Franklin pacing in the other. "Any peace terms you bring to Congress would be suspect."

"And some will wonder how many American politicians have received offers to sell their country for a pocketful of gold," Daniel added.

Becca's eyes were half-closed in thought. "Then you will need a witness at the Cathedral of Notre Dame."

"Do I?" Franklin's smile was dazzling.

"If the letter is a jest," Becca began, "then you need someone who can attest that the man with the red rose never came. If the letter is in earnest, then you require a witness who can swear you never met him."

"You have a wonderfully logical mind, m'dear," Franklin purred.

Daniel's chest tightened. They were all dancing to Franklin's tune. "Let the Paris police go. You have influence at court, and everyone in France is enamored of the great Dr. Franklin. Go to the police. They'll be your witness."

"I shall." Franklin's expression turned serious. "But that's not enough. I want to know who sent this letter. I want to know who the man with the red rose is, if he exists. And I want people I can trust..." He nodded to Becca, then Daniel, "...to watch the French police." Franklin stamped his cane into the mud and winced as he tugged it out.

"I would be happy to help," Becca said brightly.

"I thought with the wedding that there wasn't a moment of your day not filled," Franklin said.

"You were listening to us in the vegetable garden." Daniel's voice rose. Franklin was offering Becca exactly what she said she lacked: a purpose.

Franklin shrugged, but there was triumph in his expression.

"It will be a pleasure to assist you." Becca and the good doctor smiled at each other. They both turned to Daniel.

Daniel and Becca had separated in Philadelphia because of his urge to keep her away from even the slightest danger. If he could wrap her in cotton wool to keep her safe, he would. But then she wouldn't be Becca. Daniel struggled not to protest. "We will watch for the man with the red rose. Only watch."

"It is settled then." Franklin bowed.

Chapter Eight

Beneath the fragrance of incense and wax, Becca inhaled the scent of ancient wood and stone. The soft hairs on her arms lifted as if her skin felt the echo of five hundred years of prayer.

She took Daniel's arm, and they strolled through the Cathedral of Notre Dame on the day named in Dr. Franklin's letter, Wednesday, July 6.

They were surrounded by masses of flickering candles. Above them, the impossibly high ceiling arches strained toward heaven. The church hummed with the hushed voices of the faithful.

"Are you more comfortable now?" Daniel asked.

She nodded. "The cathedral welcomes everyone. I never knew a place so grand existed." Becca had never been to a Catholic church.

"Your nerves were understandable," Daniel said.

Around them, women in drab tea-colored gowns lit candles. Men dressed in silk suits and those garbed in rags prayed. One child pushed another to the ground, and a priest in a long black cassock stopped their howling fight. The parade of Paris passed before them. And there was light, candlelight, everywhere.

"I hope that Hannah and Augusta have a chance to see the cathedral before they leave for home," Becca said. The thought of their leave-taking was painful, and Becca changed the subject. "Have you found anyone who knows the letter writer?"

"The not-so-Honorable Charles de Weissenstein? No," Daniel said.

They began their third circle round the inside of the cathedral.

"None of my contacts here know a man by that name," Daniel said. "Gabriel will visit again in another day or so. He seems to know everyone. We shall ask him."

"What type of name is 'de Weissenstein'?" Becca asked.

"Flemish, I think. It's a Belgian name. I'm coming to believe that the real letter writer merely borrowed it to keep his own identity secret."

"The letter could be a jest."

"We'll know soon enough," Daniel answered mildly. "There's St. Christopher."

They walked toward the statue. No one could miss it, Becca thought. It rose twenty-eight feet high near the west entrance to the cathedral. St. Christopher bent forward as if launching into motion, balancing a young child on his back. His expression spoke of pain and patience.

They strolled across the nave, passing a cleric in long robes, two ladies, one in pink stripes, the other in yellow damask, then a man with one leg and a cane.

"But when will he come, this man with the red rose?" Becca asked.

"If such a man exists, you mean. I have my doubts."

"We have circled the church twice already."

"We could pass the time speaking of wedding stockings," Daniel teased.

"That is not amusing," Becca said. "Hannah and Lady Augusta are taking such pleasure in our wedding. I am trying not to complain about the details."

"We won't need to circle a third time." His arm tightened beneath her hand. "He's there. Don't turn."

Becca forced herself not to look at the base of the saint's statue, where she imagined the man with the red rose waited. *One black tile. Two. Three.* She counted them to control her impatience. They strolled slowly, looking left and right as if they were two tourists awed by the cathedral. Since awe was exactly what Becca felt, it took very little work on her part.

Her breathing quieted as if she were hunting in the woods where she'd spent her childhood. They circled behind a massive sculpture facing St. Christopher across the way.

They peered out from behind the statue. The man Daniel had spotted sauntered into view.

A bright rose was tucked into his tricorn hat. Its wide brim hid his face. Becca could only tell that his hair was powdered white and curled above his ears in the fashionable manner. He wore dove gray breeches and a matching coat with silver embroidery.

A wealthy man, Becca thought, if the silk taffeta suit was any indication.

When he reached St. Christopher, the stranger plucked the rose from the hat and twirled it between his thumb and index finger, holding his pose as if for a painting. Beneath the saintly sculpture, he appeared as small as a giant's toy.

"How could anyone think Dr. Franklin would betray his country?" Becca whispered. She leaned forward, mirroring St. Christopher's pose across the way.

"We are here to watch. Only to watch." Daniel gently laid his hand on her arm.

Heels clattered at the cathedral's entrance. Three men in matching navy coats with broad red cuffs and red vests marched through the west door.

"Soldiers?" Becca asked.

"The Paris police, just as Dr. Franklin promised," he said. "The *gendarmes*."

A few church visitors ducked into the shadows. Others stared at the unusual sight of police in the cathedral.

The man with the red rose lifted the flower above his head again, then swiveled toward the men in uniform, his hand still raised.

But no matter whether Becca stood on her toes to peer out or stooped, that hat still blocked his face.

"He doesn't seem worried at all," Daniel said with surprise.

"That is it exactly," Becca murmured. "He wants the attention. Why invite one of the most famous men in the world for a secret meeting in the most public place in Paris?"

"To make sure he is seen," Daniel whispered. He craned his neck toward the rows of seats that filled the center of Notre Dame Cathedral. "But are we his only audience, or is there someone else he knows is watching?"

Becca scanned the little of the church she could see from this vantage point.

She brought her attention back to the police. One spoke softly to the man with the rose. Another gripped his wrist and yanked him forward. The man with the red rose turned one last time back as if to memorize the lines of the church, its majestic power. A sweep of light poured through a high window, lighting his face.

"If I must be your guest, lead the way." Jude Fenimore bowed to one policeman and then the other. His expression held amusement.

Anger left Becca breathless. How could this spy, this American traitor to independence, be the same person who'd charmed Lady Augusta and Hannah?

"Fenimore isn't surprised to see the police," Daniel said slowly. "It's as if he knew they'd be here."

"How brazen he is. He must have laughed when we invited him back to Passy," she said.

"He must have meant to befriend you on board the ship. How did he know you'd be on that brigantine, or was it luck?" Daniel asked.

Becca didn't have an answer. "He is a cruel, traitorous dog. A man willing to betray his country, curse him. A man who toys with women." Her voice was raw. *Stop*, she told herself. *Jude is not Philip. You know he's not.*

"Did Mr. Fenimore toy with you?" Daniel swung around to face Becca.

Becca shook her head. "Jude Fenimore looks like Philip. The resemblance upsets me, especially now." She wiped her eyes with her sleeve, because Jude looked even more like her dead husband through the haze of her tears.

She'd forgiven Philip for his treason and his affairs, but she couldn't forgive Jude for his treason, at least not yet.

The police led the way to the cathedral's massive front door.

Becca shot out from the shadows. Not to speak. Not to interfere. She needed Jude to see her. Jude needed to see the accusation in her eyes. Her quick footsteps echoed on the black and white tiles.

Jude and his captors whirled in surprise.

His face filled with dismay. He reached out his arm as if to hand her the rose or ask for forgiveness. Becca couldn't tell. But a second later, he winced, slapping a hand over his ribs before standing tall again. The flower fell from his fingers, spilling blood-red petals on the marble tile.

She froze, confused by Jude's reaction.

One of the policemen pulled him back. Another went still, studying Becca.

"Look, m'dear." Daniel's voice boomed. She hadn't heard him follow her into the open. He pointed to the statue of St. Christopher and took her arm. "Have you ever seen anything so grand? Not where we are from."

The *gendarmes* watched Daniel with identical closed expressions as he gestured to the ceiling, to the columns, and to the explosion of colors in the stained glass rose window.

"Are there other churches we should see before we leave for Brussels?" Becca hoped Daniel saw the gratitude in her eyes. She hoped the police didn't hear the shiver in her voice.

"There's one more church we should visit, m'dear. Saint-Chapelle." Daniel used the English pronunciation of saint and chapel, instead of the musical French version, *sân sha-pell*.

The *gendarmes* turned from Becca and Daniel. One officer snorted his opinion of foreign tourists who couldn't bother to learn the language. The two others laughed in response.

Which was when Jude tensed. The rest seemed to happen slowly, though it must have taken mere seconds. Jude's dove gray jacket strained against his back.

The police didn't seem to notice.

He lowered one shoulder and swerved. His shoulder served as a battering ram, and he shoved the policeman holding his arm off balance. The second officer reached for him a moment too late. Jude lurched for the door.

"Pardon," he said as he backhanded a young man, who tripped and tumbled into the three officers.

Jude disappeared to the flapping sound of clamoring birds taking wing on the grand stone plaza outside the church.

Chapter Nine

Displaced by the police, the pigeons landed with a shake of their feathers and settled again in minutes.

"They've caught him by now, for all we know." Daniel winced in the bright sunshine as he scanned the open space for Jude and the police.

"Mr. Fenimore can hang." Becca hugged herself. "And I hope he does. Let us go back to Passy."

"We should follow the police." Daniel took her arm, and they crossed the crowded space, aiming for the carriage and driver Dr. Franklin had lent them.

"We told Dr. Franklin that we would watch for the man with the red rose. We have done enough." Becca's wide mouth was set in a grim line.

"If you want to see him hang, you have to catch him first." Daniel took a regretful look back at Notre Dame.

Had someone in particular been watching Fenimore to make sure he accomplished his task? Even if that were true, they'd be impossible to identify, whether or not they were still inside. Daniel had no reason to stay. But still. He would have liked to walk through the church one more time. Though he wasn't Catholic, the church had offered him a sense of peace he'd rarely felt elsewhere.

She held her arm out. "Look. I still shake, Daniel. I am that angry. I am done with Mr. Fenimore."

"Finding answers will make you less angry." He faced her. "You saw Fenimore. He was performing. And the only thing that upset him was seeing you."

The expression on Jude's face had looked to Daniel like fear and regret, and he didn't like that at all. "Does Mr. Fenimore regret losing your esteem?" Daniel asked. "Or is he sorry that you saw him because he has something worse planned for Dr. Franklin than a letter thrown over a fence?"

They walked further into the plaza. Daniel scoured the nearby street for any sign of Jude. He exhaled his frustration. The man had disappeared.

"It is a puzzle, isn't it?" Becca asked. "Did you see the expression on his face when the police arrived? As if he expected to be arrested."

Daniel's focus shifted as strolling Parisians turned at once in the same direction, like metal shavings drawn to a magnet. He angled in their direction, exhaling with satisfaction. The *gendarmes* had bolted across the nearby street, the rue Neuve Notre Dame. Their uniforms flashed blue and red in the warm summer sunshine. They disappeared at the first corner.

"I'm glad my boots are comfortable," Becca said grimly. She lifted the front of her gown and ran.

The Cathedral of Notre Dame sat on the Île de la Cité, a small island in the midst of the Seine River. With its warren of narrow, medieval streets, the island made up the oldest part of Paris. Becca and Daniel swerved past women in worn, colorful gowns holding straw market baskets. Children dancing in the still-muddy streets jumped out of the way as carts passed. A store owner stepped out of a doorway and threw a bucket of slops into the already foul-smelling street.

Becca leaped just in time to save herself from the worst of the offense.

The police were out of sight again, but Daniel couldn't make himself stop searching. Not yet. "Where would you run if you were Mr. Fenimore?"

She shook her head. "I don't know. But I'd feel trapped on an island like this."

"You're brilliant. He'll cross off the island." He flashed her a smile. "Here. Turn here." Daniel pointed. "There's a bridge further down. It crosses the river."

Human traffic flowed past Becca and Daniel as if all of Paris intended to cross the Pont de Notre Dame to or from the Right Bank. Tiny stone and brick stores with gabled roofs dotted the bridge. In between, Daniel caught narrow views of the river that flowed beneath them.

"There." Becca's hand rose to point as she caught her breath.

The *gendarmes* stood at the far end of the bridge. One of the three pushed another. They were arguing.

"We're not the only ones who have lost your Mr. Fenimore," Daniel said.

He and Becca stepped behind the shelter of a half-open shop door.

"He is not *my* Mr. Fenimore." She flung the words at him.

He offered her the truth as an apology. "I didn't know Fenimore existed during your voyage, and yet I found myself jealous of the month he spent with you on the ship while I waited here."

"I spent the month begging the wind to bring me to you more quickly." She inched closer to Daniel. His upper arm came to rest against hers as they watched the police argue.

A pink-and-white lacquered carriage passed to their right, its color so bright that it drew Daniel's attention. The coach drew away, leaving Daniel staring at a one-legged beggar leaning against a railing between two shops. He held out a worn felted cap for alms. His gaze rose high above Daniel's head, as if he were blind or embarrassed to be found begging. The beggar inched forward, straining to keep the police in his sights above the crowds.

One policeman slapped the other on the back. The third shrugged and spat as if that ended the discussion. Instead of crossing back to the island, they ambled away.

"They don't seem upset that Mr. Fenimore has escaped." The light wind whipped a single strand of Becca's dark hair across her forehead. She tucked it back beneath the feather-covered hat she wore.

"And they were awfully gentle with him in the cathedral," Daniel said. Memory pulled him back a year to Philadelphia. Arrests weren't gentle. He had escaped once from the sheriff there. The sheriff's men had made their displeasure clear after they caught him a second time. His ribs had been tender for weeks. There had been nothing gentle about his arrest.

They headed back toward the cathedral when Becca swiveled. "I hate that we've lost Mr. Fenimore." After a moment of silence, she tugged at Daniel's arm.

He turned. The one-legged beggar leaned over the waist-high stone wall that lined the bridge between storefronts. His thin back strained, and he hopped back a half step to rebalance. He lifted his crutch over the wall.

One hand appeared, clasping the crutch as the beggar pulled. The second hand followed, grabbing the wall. The rest of a disheveled Mr. Fenimore came into view, rolled over the wall and staggered to standing. He'd lost his broad hat in the escape, and his white-blond hair shone in the sun. His gray breeches were torn, exposing pink skin along one thigh.

Fenimore dug a hand into his pocket and pulled out a fistful of wet paper money, shoving it into the beggar's hand.

"Jude Fenimore," Becca called to him.

He took off without answering.

Becca and Daniel flew after him. They passed the muddy shore of the Seine, and Fenimore turned left, then right onto a broad street of three and four story shops and houses, all with balconies and gabled roofs.

Becca was fast, as fast as any woman could be weighed down by stays, a stomacher, petticoats, hip pads, and a gown. But not fast enough to keep Fenimore in sight, and Daniel wouldn't leave her unaccompanied.

They lost him on another block of small shops and apartments that smelled of flowers, lemons, and cedarwood.

A woman with a face painted white as a summer cloud with dots of red rouge on each cheek peered out the door. Behind her, Daniel caught a flash of shelves filled with small bottles that extended to the ceiling.

The woman looked left, then right. At the sight of Becca and Daniel, she disappeared. An invisible hand flipped the sign just inside the front display window from "*Ouvert*," open, to "*Fermé*," closed.

"Now, why would they close up shop like that in the middle of the day?" Daniel took two steps and rapped on the front door. No one answered. He rapped again.

The click of the lock was unmistakable. He and Becca were not welcome.

Daniel pounded until the side of his fist grew numb.

A window squeaked open above him.

"Daniel, move," Becca shouted.

Her warning saved him from the bucket of slop that rained down from above. He craned his neck to find a tired matron with frizzled gray hair holding the bucket. She blew him a kiss.

Daniel couldn't help himself. He laughed, extended one stockinged foot, and executed the most courtly bow he could manage.

The woman slammed the window shut with a final crack.

"My charms do not extend to French women, it seems."

"That is lucky for me," Becca said, then grew serious. "I think Hannah, Lady Augusta, and I shall decide that we require French perfume."

"Perfume?"

"Number eleven rue du Roule. The perfume shop." She pointed to the small brown and white sign set in the window. *Parfumerie*, it read in an elegant script. "I don't see how it can hurt to ask whether they saw Mr. Fenimore run past."

Chapter Ten

Daniel and Becca tumbled into the grand mansion in Passy. Becca lifted the muddy hem of her gown to avoid marring the gleaming white tile floor.

"Is Doctor Franklin available?" Daniel asked the dour butler, who spoke enough English to understand the question.

The servant had the face of a middle-aged cherub with a round chin, round cheeks, short, round nose, and receding hairline. His hands rose, palm out, as if to block their way. "The doctor, he is busy." The butler's eyebrows tented, rising on the diagonal high in the center of his forehead. His round brown eyes beseeched Daniel for help. "This afternoon, he is—he is—it is Tuesday, monsieur."

"Tuesday." Daniel exhaled hard. "Of all the bad luck. We will have to wait. There's no getting around it."

"You shall wait. Yes." The butler smiled with relief and bowed himself out of the entryway.

"Ridiculous." Becca started for the staircase with its gold banisters. "After all we have seen this afternoon."

"There is more to see in Dr. Franklin's rooms, but you will not want to see it." Daniel blocked her.

"What are you saying?" Becca tilted her head.

"You can't go up. Dr. Franklin is taking an air bath."

"What on earth is an air bath?" Becca raised her face to his.

"Dr. Franklin likes to spend time naked in sunlight. He thinks it improves his health. And don't look up at his terrace on a Tuesday afternoon. You

54

might find him there taking one of his air baths."

"But today is Tuesday." Becca's face went blank. Then she laughed, the sound echoing off the marble tile and stone columns of the front hall. Daniel couldn't help himself. He joined in, letting the cleansing, joyful sound wipe away his worries about Jude Fenimore, at least for a moment.

Wiping his eyes, he said, "I can talk to Dr. Franklin myself, unless you prefer I wait with you until he's finished."

She shook her head. "Go. The sooner Dr. Franklin hears about Mr. Fenimore, the better."

* * *

Daniel stepped onto the terrace outside Benjamin Franklin's bedroom to find him sitting on a straight-backed wooden chair without clothes. An inkpot and quill pen rested on a small, round table nearby. He squinted up at pages of accounts he held in one hand, pages of bills in the other.

Franklin twisted, "Every American in Europe seems convinced that our government should repay them for each dollar they spend here. I will not regret giving up this part of the job." He scooped up a thin white blanket that lay puddled on the floor and casually placed it over his lap.

His skin was freckled and lax, which shouldn't have surprised Daniel but did. Franklin had a young man's curiosity and enthusiasm that usually made Daniel forget his age.

"Tell me." Franklin pointed to a nearby chair upholstered in fuchsia silk. "What did you see at Notre Dame?"

Daniel sank into the chair. He recounted all that had happened from the moment they arrived at the cathedral until his narrow escape from the bucket of slop at the perfume shop.

Franklin stared out over the lawn with its lengthening shadows. "The letter was a juvenile trick. That is all, though it makes me angrier than I can say." He stood, wrapping the blanket around himself like the image of an ancient Roman statue Daniel had printed in a book once.

Franklin drifted into his bedroom and stepped behind a green screen painted with a landscape of flying white cranes and craggy mountains.

Daniel waited, leaning against the bedroom's yellow silk-covered walls.

"I may be indiscreet in many ways. But as I am one of the most remarkable figures in Paris…" He paused. "That is merely the truth, Mr. Alloway." He shimmied his lifted arm into a white linen shirt sleeve. "Even my appearance at Notre Dame, where I cannot have any conceivable business, would naturally cause speculation."

"Naturally," Daniel agreed.

Franklin's voice grew muffled as if the linen shirt now covered his head. "And if I were seen to deliver any letter to anyone at the church, as the letter instructed, there might be very mischievous consequences."

"Mischievous consequences. 'Tis an understatement. All would guess that you had betrayed your country. So you agree with me?" Daniel asked.

"Didn't I just say I agreed?" Franklin's tone was razor sharp. He stepped around the screen, fully dressed in his characteristic brown breeches and matching vest. "Yes, that letter is an attempt to embarrass me and our government," Franklin said. "And yes, I agree that whoever is behind that nonsense bribery letter may be planning more. It is a crooked, dark path you describe."

"I don't understand why the police gave up so easily after Mr. Fenimore ran from them. This was more than a juvenile jest."

"Even in Paris, Mr. Alloway, it is not a crime to hold a red flower inside a church." Franklin peered at Daniel, forehead furrowed. "Undoubtedly, the police thought their search frivolous and knew that they would be unable to hold Fenimore on any sort of charge. It was enough to scare the traitor away, I hope, perhaps for good. This may be the end."

Franklin smoothed his vest and pulled at his cuffs to straighten the sleeves. "I will be visiting a neighbor, a most amusing woman. I am certain she would enjoy meeting you and Mrs. Parcell. Would you care to accompany me?" "She plays the pianoforte remarkably well, and the company will be amusing."

"I thought you were angry, as angry as could be. You're dismissing the matter now. Why don't you sound more vexed?" Daniel blinked at the change in conversational direction.

"I am an old man, Mr. Alloway. Anger is rarely productive, and it resolves almost nothing. In fact, the hotter emotions do little more than ruin one's health and digestion. You have done even more than I asked and returned with a well-observed report. You have your work for Mr. Barnes and a wedding to plan. The Paris police did enough to scare your Jude Fenimore away. They won't try something so nonsensical again."

"You are correct, sir. They won't try something so nonsensical again. They'll try something more effective, more destructive." Daniel studied Franklin. He was more worried than he let on.

"I would hate to take up more of your time," Franklin swiveled left, then right. "Now, where did I put those papers?"

"You left them on the terrace." He was being dismissed, Daniel realized with a start. He couldn't walk away without pushing one more time. "But this isn't the end; at least, it may not be the end," he argued. "Fenimore and his friends may plan more to hurt you, to hurt America. And I am worried for Mrs. Parcell. Fenimore saw her at the cathedral."

"I have forwarded the mysterious bribery letter to Versailles. I shall consult with Gabriel d'Aumont's superior if that puts you at ease. All will be well.

"I almost forgot, Franklin added, "There is correspondence for you." He pointed to the sloppy pile of papers near his chair. "I asked Mr. Bancroft to arrange everything. I think you will be pleased." At the scowl on Daniel's face," Franklin repeated, "all will be well," before he sailed into the hall.

Daniel stared at the empty doorway, exhaling a sound halfway between a growl and a moan. The old grief wrapped itself round his neck, choking him.

All will be well was a wish or a lie. The meaningless phrase haunted him and would until the day he died. "All will be well," Daniel had said to Amelia, his much-loved wife, even as she burned with childbed fever, even as she weakened on the last day of her life. A part of him had died with Amelia and Silas that day. He hadn't meant to risk love again, but Becca had brought him back to life. She challenged him, baffled him, and, finally, loved him.

He scooped up the message Franklin had mentioned, and, as he left to join

Becca, Daniel wondered whether Franklin was lying or wishing when he'd used that most detestable of phrases: all will be well.

Chapter Eleven

Becca paced the shadowy landing at the top of the staircase, waiting for Daniel. But the door to Benjamin Franklin's bedroom remained closed, and she drifted down the stairs without a plan. Her kitten heels echoed on the marble stairs.

Numbers were simple. They were straightforward. You added them correctly or incorrectly, and it was easy to tell the difference. Her own emotions were a mystery.

Becca tightened her hand on the banister and squeezed her eyes shut. Why had she stepped out to face Jude at the church? Because she'd wanted him to know there was a witness to his treason. But that was no reason to forsake common sense. And that was exactly what she had done.

If only Jude Fenimore didn't look so much like Philip.

She'd been so angry at the way he'd manipulated them all by ingratiating himself into their lives on the ship. She was furious at the way he'd wormed his way into Augusta's good graces. Becca had been impetuous. What if she had made things worse in ways she couldn't yet know?

I won't be careless in my speech, she promised herself. *I will consider before I act.*

She could hear Hannah and Augusta talking nearby. But there was a third voice she didn't recognize, a man's voice. Becca followed the sound to the half-closed door of the salon.

Her footsteps slowed with rare indecision. She meant to tell Augusta about finding Jude at the Cathedral of Notre Dame. But what good could come of bringing her mother-in-law sorrow? Perhaps that was as much a mistake as showing herself to Jude.

"What is he saying?" Augusta demanded. Her voice carried to the hallway outside the salon.

Hannah spoke in rapid French.

Becca's hand to flew to her mouth. Her mother hadn't spoken a word of French since their arrival. She hadn't wanted questions about her French roots.

The male voice responded in the same language.

"Hannah, for goodness sake. Tell me," Augusta repeated.

I will consider before I speak, Becca repeated silently. Hannah and Augusta had not invited her into the room. They need not know she'd heard them. She could leave this moment. But the conversation was clearly important to the two women she loved.

Becca stepped into the room. "Tell me, too, please."

Hannah and Augusta looked nothing alike, but their eyes widened in the same manner at Becca's entrance. Their mouths pinched into matching small circles. They sat together on a sofa, one woman tall and dark, the other petite and gray-haired. In front of them, a small black lacquer table displayed a silver tray holding jewel-like tartlets with glazes of rich reds, blues, and yellows.

Their gaze shifted at the same time to the dessert chef, who was almost hidden by the door.

He held his white chef's cap in his hand, pinching and turning it as if kneading dough for bread. He examined Becca as if he were memorizing her face. His left ear carried a small smudge of flour.

She allowed the scrutiny for one beat, then two. "What is it you want with my mother, monsieur," Becca asked in French.

"I wanted only to ask her a question." His deep brown eyes widened. "You speak French, too."

"What question?"

"I thought I knew your mother," he said. "I couldn't be certain, of course. Too much time has passed. I told myself that I was imagining the resemblance."

Hannah translated for Augusta.

"Too much time? A resemblance? I don't understand. You can't know her," Becca protested. "My mother's family moved to America when she was so young."

"I was a child then, too." The warm smile he shared with Hannah almost erased the bitterness in his voice. "We were not lucky, not like your mother. We did not leave then."

Becca turned to Hannah and, in English, asked, "What does he mean?"

"You should have told Rebecca sooner," Augusta said.

"Don't tell me how to talk to my daughter," Hannah snapped.

Their new friendship still had cracks, Becca noted. The tension between them crackled.

"You told me there would be no more secrets between us after Philadelphia," Becca said.

Hannah's face reddened. "This isn't a new secret. It is a very old one, and I didn't think it mattered." She straightened her shoulders. "Also, I didn't want to ruin your excitement coming to France."

"You are giving me a headache." Becca sank into a nearby chair. Honesty might cause problems, but secrets were worse. "Monsieur, how do you know Mrs. Hannah?"

The cook's austere expression softened. "My grandmother lived with us until the day she died. Her best friend lived next door with her family. A child almost my age lived in that house. A girl. I taught her to catch frogs."

"In the stream," Hannah said.

He smiled. "She followed me everywhere."

"You threw rocks at me once to make me go away." Her face glowed.

"Pebbles. Only pebbles," he said.

"I cried."

Becca shallowed her breathing. How could this be?

"And my grandmother sent me to apologize to you."

Hannah searched the chef's face. "I thought you disliked me."

"I did not care for girls at the time." The edges of his mouth tipped into a half smile.

"My mother left France when she was so young. How can you possibly remember each other?" Becca asked.

"I was five," she said.

"And I was seven. I remembered you because you were a good memory," he said to Hannah. "There are not many good memories from then. But without the picture, I would not have said anything."

"What picture?" Becca challenged.

"My grandmother kept a drawing of her closest friend with her always. It hung in her room, especially after we left the village. You and your mother both look so like the drawing," he said to Becca. "I saw you both at dinner. I remembered the little girl I knew, and I remembered my grandmother's drawing. So I come to ask your mother." His lips tightened as if he were unaccustomed to smiling.

"Can this be true?" Becca asked Hannah.

"Of course it is true." The chef's chin rose. "My name is Michael Corbin. Ask anyone. I am an honest man from the village of..."

"From the village of Batilolle." Hannah smiled.

"As you say." Michael nodded. "The village is gone now."

"Gone." Hannah sighed. "My memories are not all good, either, from that time," Hannah added in English. "My father was accused of stealing sheep."

Becca didn't interrupt. Her mother never spoke of her own parents nor of her days in France.

"My father paid a neighbor to hide us in a hay wagon before they came to take him to jail. Then we made our way west to America," Hannah said. "The stories he told me of France scared me."

"My father was the neighbor who saved your family. His kindness ruined ours." Michael's voice was distant, as if he were talking about the weather.

"You understand English?" Becca asked.

"Some English." He nodded to Becca.

"Ruined your family? How?" Hannah's hand rose to her neck.

"The police came looking for your father after you all were gone. They broke down our door. The sound of wood splintering that night. I hear it in my nightmares. My father wouldn't say where he took your family. The police beat him."

"To Passy," Hannah said softly. "Your father took us to this village."

Michael swallowed hard. "My father couldn't work. Not for a year. When we couldn't pay the taxes, the noble landowner pushed us out." He made 'noble' sound like a curse. "We were lucky a cousin up north took us in."

"And your father?" Hannah asked.

"He walked with a limp for the rest of his life. God rest his soul," Michael said.

"What of the other families in the village?" Hannah asked.

"There were more taxes, more tithes due every year. They couldn't pay, and the landowner threw them out. And we were all Protestant, not Catholic."

Augusta and Becca exchanged a look of confusion.

"There has been violence here against Protestants for hundreds of years," Michael said. "There was little sympathy in our village for those that were arrested or beaten in our village for what? For being poor. For being Protestant. For both. It took a while, but we all left."

"And now?" Michael's chest rose and fell with anger. "We are approaching a moment of crisis and a century of revolutions."

"Mind your tongue," Becca hissed. "You don't know who is listening. You speak without care." She might as well be chastising herself. It was the message she still needed to learn.

Michael spread his arms, palms up. "In France, even humble bakers argue philosophy. I am only quoting Voltaire. What harm can come of that?

"Yet your daughter is right." He bowed to Hannah. "I share my opinions too freely. You must excuse me. I feel as if I still know you. I grew up imagining that you were catching bears in the new world instead of frogs." Michael's face filled with wonder.

Hannah's expression mirrored the baker's. Becca felt the urge to interrupt their unexpected intimacy.

"Is this why you were scared to return?" Becca asked her. "It was so long ago."

"Long ago, but nothing has changed," Michael said in French.

"No one will remember one family from a village that no longer exists,"

Becca argued. "There's no reason for you to be nervous."

"There was one policeman my father thought would chase him to the ends of the earth. A black-haired devil." Hannah shook her head as if to shoo away the memory. "But you are telling me that I have been scared for no reason."

"I say the opposite." Michael stepped toward Hannah. "Dr. Franklin's reputation protects you here. Do not stray far. France seems peaceful, but something dangerous grows here. More and more people are as angry as I am with the nobles who live off our labor. Go home as soon as you can."

His expression softened. "My family will be happy to learn that you are well and that you have raised such a fine daughter." He did not turn to Becca. "I could not be more pleased."

Becca's eyes slid from the chef to her mother and back. If Becca flung the entire tray of tarts into the air right now, she didn't think either Hannah or Michael would notice.

Michael bowed and slipped from the room.

Minutes later, Daniel strode into the salon, holding a single page in his hand and wearing a wide grin.

"Your meeting with Dr. Franklin went well?" Becca stood.

"Not particularly," he said, smile still in place.

"Then what?"

With a flourish, Daniel handed her the parchment. "It's about our marriage license. Our presence at the town hall is requested two days from now."

Becca sprung from the chair to leap into his arms.

Chapter Twelve

S unlight streamed through the dining room windows the next morning, highlighting red strawberries, a gleaming oval chafing dish filled with oatmeal, soft-boiled eggs still in their shells, three types of cheeses, and a freshly baked loaf of bread. Daniel inhaled its yeasty scent as he reached for the silver pot of hot chocolate.

Thump, step, pause, thump step, pause. Benjamin Franklin's unmistakable footsteps echoed in the hallway. But there was a hesitation to the pattern this morning.

Daniel replaced the pitcher on the sideboard and met Franklin in the doorway. "Your gout is worse today." It wasn't a question. He took the older man's arm, surprised when the proud Dr. Franklin allowed the courtesy.

"The lightning spooked my horse last evening." Franklin grasped the arm of his dining room chair and lowered himself, wincing as he sat. "T'was the oddest thing. He is a steady creature even in bad weather."

"On your way back from the neighbor's house?"

Franklin nodded. "The horse reared, and the carriage tumbled. A wheel broke." His smile was grim. "I almost broke with it. My hip is much abused."

"Wasn't anyone with you?" Daniel hadn't heard Franklin return from the party next door. The late-night storm had woken Daniel and Becca. They had made love to a symphony of thunder and lightning.

Daniel grabbed the wooden bowl sitting next to the chafing dish, filling it with oatmeal. "Here." There was no need to ask Franklin what he wished to eat for his morning meal. It was the same every day, always served in a wooden bowl.

Franklin nodded his thanks. "The driver, of course. He ran back to the party in the rain for help."

"You waited alone in the carriage, then? Daniel examined Franklin more closely, taking account of the shadows beneath his eyes, the lines of exhaustion around his mouth.

"Mrs. Wright and Mr. Bancroft accompanied me to the party, but they decided to stay on. Yes, I was alone." Franklin's face tightened with irritation as if Daniel had said exactly what he was thinking, that a man of Franklin's years shouldn't be traveling by himself.

"Consult with Mrs. Hannah about your injury. She is a brilliant healer. Her medicine soothed my bruised ribs last year."

"Perhaps later. I am posing for Mrs. Wright this morning." Franklin lifted his face as if imitating a statue. "She believes that her services might be in greater demand here if she can exhibit a sculpture of me in Paris."

Patience sailed into the room wearing a blue canvas apron over her maroon floral gown. "Are you speaking of the most accomplished sculptress in Europe?"

Franklin laughed. "Indeed, I am."

She sat and lifted her hand, displaying a neat bandage around her palm. "A hazard of my craft. I slipped and cut myself with my favorite carving blade. I hardly feel it."

"When did you hurt yourself?" Daniel asked.

"This morning early. I was working on my bust of Dr. Franklin. I was careless." Patience was brusque. She rose to fill her plate, ending the conversation.

Edward Bancroft entered next. His face was paler than usual, and his eyes red-rimmed. He reached for the silver coffee pot and poured its contents into an ivory porcelain cup before sitting across from Daniel. His hands shook when he raised the cup to his lips.

"A late night, Edward?" Franklin winked. "I hope you enjoyed yourself."

"*Hmm*," Edward grunted without raising his head from his cup.

Hannah, Augusta, and Becca arrived soon after and took their seats. Becca sat next to Daniel.

Conversation ebbed and flowed as the residents of the Hôtel de Valentinois came fully awake over their morning meal. Three hard knocks brought Daniel's attention to the dining room's entrance.

"I hope it is not too early." Gabriel d'Aumont stepped into the room. He was dressed in dark green breeches decorated with embroidered vines in ivory silk. His white wig was perfectly curled and looked as if it could withstand a windstorm without a strand of hair coming loose.

Daniel wondered how early d'Aumont rose each day to achieve his fashionable appearance. He wondered what news couldn't wait.

"You could move in with us, Monsieur d'Aumont. It would save the wear on your carriage." Franklin gestured to the assistant finance minister to take a seat.

"I am honored to be the subject of your jest, Doctor Franklin." Gabriel smiled at each guest at the table in turn. "I do have business. No, not with you, Mister Alloway. Not directly with you. I am here to inform Dr. Franklin that the Paris police will arrive this afternoon."

Edward Bancroft's cup clattered as he lowered it into a saucer, spilling a pool of the dark liquid in the process.

Hannah gasped. Her hand rose to her neck.

Becca shifted as if ready to spring from her chair.

"Why in Hades are the police coming here?" Patience lowered her injured hand below the table.

"*Mon dieu.* I did not mean the upset." Gabriel's eyes widened. The assistant minister's command of the English language was normally perfect. This lapse was a sign of how much their reaction surprised him.

It surprised Daniel, too.

"The police are coming to report to Dr. Franklin on a small matter." Gabriel studied the group and seemed to decide that the less said, the better. "On a small matter that Dr. Franklin requested. That is all."

Daniel emptied his mind and allowed impressions of those at the table to wash over him.

Patience didn't return Gabriel's gaze. But Daniel saw her take a deep breath and relax.

Edward Bancroft appeared no more comfortable than he had the moment Gabriel mentioned the police.

Hannah leaned toward Augusta, who patted her hand.

Becca turned to Daniel with hollow eyes and mouthed the words, "I am sorry. I am so sorry."

He understood Hannah's fears of the police and Becca's regret about confronting Jude Fenimore at Notre Dame. The police would have questions about their presence at the Cathedral. But what secrets were Patience Wright and Edward Bancroft hiding that made them tense at the mention of the *gendarmes*?

"Will you have a few minutes for me after breakfast, Gabriel?" Daniel asked.

* * *

"The police will tell Dr. Franklin about the man with the red rose. Is that it?" Daniel asked as he shut the library door.

"Of course." Gabriel leaned, arms crossed against an octagonal table in the middle of the book-filled room.

"Mrs. Parcell and I saw him."

"At the cathedral?" Gabriel asked slowly. He pushed himself away from the table.

Daniel nodded.

"Why were you there?" Gabriel stepped across the red and blue rug to face Daniel.

"To watch for him. Only to watch." Daniel knew where this conversation would lead, and he didn't care for it at all.

"At Dr. Franklin's request, I assume. He wanted his own witnesses?"

Daniel didn't deny it. "The man with the rose escaped your police, but we recognized him. Jude Fenimore is his name."

"You say his name as if I should know him." Gabriel's dark eyes narrowed with suspicion.

"You met him the day I arrived with Mrs. Parcell. He was the blond merchant who continued on to Paris." Daniel prodded. It would have been so easy to withhold all this information. A lie by omission.

Gabriel shook his head. "I don't quite…Ah. We were playing a lawn game. Your Mr. Fenimore hardly said a word. Are you certain it was him?"

"We shared a carriage for several days. I am certain," Daniel said.

"My friend, you put me in an impossible position." Gabriel threw his arms into the air. "The letter Dr. Franklin showed us is ridiculous, almost silly. But the man with the rose ran from the police, and now you say you know him. You spend time with him in France. And worse, you live with Dr. Franklin. Do you know how that sounds?"

"I know exactly how that sounds. It sounds as if Mrs. Parcell and I are linked to Mr. Fenimore's plot. The police might even think we were partners." Daniel circled the room. He had paced a jail cell in Philadelphia last year in the same manner. He didn't relish a meeting with the French police.

"Daniel," Gabriel exhaled. "I am an official of the French government. I will attest to your good character, but I cannot keep this information from the police. Your Dr. Franklin is almost as precious to France as our king. Tell me, at least, that you will have nothing more to do with this matter."

"Dr. Franklin has told us to leave it alone now."

"Good. That is something," Gabriel said with satisfaction.

"But we can't." He held his hand up when Gabriel started to argue. "We can't stop until we know that whoever wrote this bribery letter has nothing else in store for Dr. Franklin."

Gabriel threw his head back. *"Oh la vache."*

"You are calling for a cow, or have I translated that incorrectly?" Daniel grinned.

So did Gabriel. "Yes, it means, 'oh, the cow,' and it is impossible to explain to a foreigner why it is the perfect expression for the present moment." He sighed. "Promise you will tell me everything you learn. I will try to help."

* * *

Sitting at the walnut desk in his bedroom later that afternoon, Daniel folded his letter to Mr. Barnes with satisfaction. A customer had tried to cancel a shipment of indigo that had already left Savannah on one of Mr. Barnes's ships. Daniel reported that he'd found another customer willing to pay a greater amount for the goods.

The *gendarmes* hadn't arrived yet, and work kept Daniel from thinking too much about the police interview to follow.

He stretched his cramped left hand. Before his accident, Daniel had written with a fine, elegant hand. A fine *right* hand. It still required extra effort to force his left-handed writing into legibility.

There was no point in regret. If he hadn't escaped the prison ship, he'd be dead. One numb, frozen hand was not a terrible price to pay for life. That was what Becca said. It had only taken him two years to adopt her eminently sensible, no-nonsense attitude.

He lifted his gaze to the bedroom window just beyond the desk. Benjamin Franklin sat posing for Patience Wright. The sculptress stared at a block of white wax, then walked to Franklin and returned to the wax block. Before them, the gardens, lawn, and cloudless sky promised a never-ending summer.

The sudden screams pulled his attention to the lawn below. Two servant girls stared up at something high above the third-floor bedroom. Daniel leaned forward and yanked open the window.

Franklin stood, then sat so quickly Daniel thought he'd collapsed. Last night's carriage accident had hurt the old man more than he admitted. Daniel would talk to Hannah about creating a poultice to soothe his pain. But not now, not with two servant girls frightened to death at something on the roof.

He spotted Patience Wright running toward the house. Daniel sprinted to meet her.

"Mrs. Hannah," Patience bellowed up the stairs, then turned to Daniel. "Where is she?" Her breath came in short puffs, reminding Daniel that she was at least as old as Hannah.

"What's happened?" he asked.

Patience ignored him, calling again for Hannah. Lifting her skirt to her shins, she started up the stairs.

Hannah ran from the back hall, followed by Michael, the baker. "What's happened?" she called to Patience, repeating Daniel's question.

"Follow me," Patience wheezed.

Hannah joined her; so did Michael.

Becca met them on the third floor landing. "Has something...."

Patience flew past her.

"We don't know," Daniel called as Becca joined them.

They turned left into the other wing of the house. Patience burst through a door at the end of the hall and disappeared up a set of stairs. Her footsteps thumped on the plain wood steps. She threw open the door to the roof and screamed.

Chapter Thirteen

The breeze was stronger here without the trees and bushes that blocked the wind below, and yet the dark roof captured more of the day's heat. A ribbon of perspiration trickled down Becca's back. "There," Patience sobbed, pointing left.

A man was tied with rope to Benjamin Franklin's lightning rod. His body was limp, his head bowed as if in prayer.

Patience hugged herself, bent over almost double. She shook. "Help him, someone."

"Come, Becca," Hannah said calmly.

At a distance of fifteen feet, Becca's throat went dry. Blond hair is not so uncommon, she assured herself.

At ten feet, she faltered. The chiseled jaw. The straight nose. "It is Jude, isn't it?" Her shoulders curved forward, and she looked away. She sensed Daniel behind her before he rested a hand on her shoulder.

Hannah reached Jude first. She lay her hand on his forehead. Her lips moved, though Becca couldn't hear what she said. A prayer, perhaps. Then Becca's mother held her palm under his nose. She was checking for life, for breath, Becca knew. Hannah turned to them all and shook her head. "He's gone. Help me lay him down."

"It's too late to help, based on what I can see," Daniel said.

"Can't you do anything for him?" Becca's eyes stung.

"We can pray for him," Hannah said. "No less nor more than that."

Jude was kind to her. Jude was a traitor to their country. Both were true. Becca had cursed him. Cursed him in a church, and then he was dead. As if her words had power. She knew that wasn't true. But the thought brushed against the edge of her mind, like a wolf circling its prey.

Becca saw Jude again in her mind's eye, recalling his look of surprise and horror at the sight of her at Notre Dame. She couldn't have known it was the last time she'd see him. He had reached his hand out to her, dropping the rose. She would never know what he meant by the gesture.

In silence, Becca and Hannah untied the knots that held Jude to the lightning rod. Her hands shook. Hannah's didn't. Michael and Daniel lowered him to the ground.

Daniel rose, widened his stance, and swayed.

Becca placed her hand on his lower back. She searched his expression. She knew how the ship's dead haunted him.

"The memories," he confirmed. Memories of the British prison ship is what he meant, Becca knew. Memories of the dead soldiers whose bodies he'd been forced to carry to the deck.

Michael and Hannah watched him with concern.

"Fine. I am fine," he said gruffly. He softened his voice. Managed a smile. "I am truly fine."

They stood in a circle round the body. All of them except Patience. Becca craned her neck, searching for the artist. She still stood by the stairs, hugging herself. She had stopped crying.

"He's almost smiling," Daniel said. Jude's expression was thoughtful, even quizzical. His eyes were closed, his mouth relaxed. "He seems more at peace now than he did when we knew him."

"There's nothing suggesting he feared for his life," Becca said. Who was to say whether Jude was more scared for himself or for her when she confronted him at that cathedral? She'd keep that thought to herself for now.

"He is soaked to the skin," Hannah whispered. "He was placed here during the rainstorm last night." She crouched over him. Her delicate fingers reached for Jude's wrist. She turned one of them, then changed position and reached for the other. "He did not pull against the rope. There are no bruises."

Michael said something in French. Hannah answered in English. "That's right. I don't see signs of violence, either. There is no blood. There are no cuts or bruises, though I shall look more closely."

Hannah's calm manner didn't surprise Becca. It matched her own slightly-distant approach to untangling mathematical puzzles.

Becca pointed to the soaked lace along Jude's right sleeve. "There is a stain here." A light brown stain about the size and shape of a thumb marred the cuff.

"It is hard to tell what that is after the rain. Dirt, perhaps?" Daniel suggested.

Hannah continued her examination, making note of the stain, but withholding judgment.

"I shall inform Dr. Franklin, and I will fetch a blanket to cover this man. Murdered or not, he deserves respect." Michael added in French. He backed away, trotting past Patience Wright on the way downstairs.

"I doubt Dr. Franklin will be able to climb those stairs," Daniel murmured.

A charcoal gray bird coasted past Becca, and she followed its progress until it dove below the roof line. She fought the urge to follow Michael back into the house. It was unnatural to feel closer to the sky than the earth, to stand as tall as birds soaring through the air.

"The rope reached round his shins." Hannah's voice was soft. She pointed to fine tears in Jude's white stockings. Hannah reached for one of them and rolled the wet silk down, folding it back as delicately as if Jude were a young child who required help undressing. She sighed. "A horrible thing. Look."

A red line, like a narrow trunk of a tree, started at Jude's ankle and rose, spreading like branches across his calf.

Hannah raised her eyes to Becca and Daniel. "Struck by lightning, he was. The blood will leave a mark beneath the skin like this sometimes. I have seen it."

"Who would tie a man to a lightning rod?" Daniel muttered a curse and stepped away.

"And with a storm coming in," Becca added.

Hannah gently rested a finger on Jude's leg with its odd red pattern of blood beneath the surface. "I wonder whether he was still alive when the lightning hit him."

The question made Becca queasy.

"His expression. He appears pleased, almost happy. I wouldn't expect that if he felt pain. And there are no signs he struggled." Hannah frowned at Becca and Daniel. "Do not look at me as if I am the monster who placed him here."

"He didn't tie himself to the lightning rod." Daniel's tone was dry.

"Who could be so cruel?" Becca asked.

"One of us," Daniel said. "A servant or one of Dr. Franklin's guests must have let Mr. Fenimore in."

"Then Dr. Franklin was right. There's a spy in his midst," Becca whispered to Daniel.

"Or just a murderer," Daniel answered.

"The poor man." Hannah smoothed his soaked vest and tugged at Jude's linen shirt. She lifted her palm, then placed it back on his vest. She tilted her head in puzzlement, then lifted the shirt. "The poor soul."

Jude's belly was distended as if he were several months pregnant.

"Did the lightning cause that, too?" Becca winced at the sight.

"Dr. Franklin might know more about what electricity can do, but I don't think so." She covered his chest again with the shirt. "But his stomach bothered him at sea."

"And then, at the cathedral, he winced and held his hand to his ribs. It hurt him there, too." Becca said.

"There's one last thing to do." Daniel sank to his knees. "Sorry, old man," he said to Jude. "You won't mind if I relieve you of a few knick-knacks." He slipped his hand into one of Jude's pockets. It was sodden but empty. The other pocket held a dull coin and a small, wet handkerchief. Daniel pulled out both objects.

Daniel opened his palm to examine his finds. "I was hoping we'd find a note."

Patience Wright must have heard from across the roof. She burst into loud sobs again and ran for the stairs.

The roof door slammed open as she reached it. Patience tripped backwards, her fall surprisingly graceful.

Clasping a rough wool blanket in one arm, Michael Corbin catapulted forward as if he'd been pushed from behind.

He had. Three policemen followed him through the door. Their stiff blue and red uniforms blazed in the bright sunlight.

Daniel jammed Jude's possessions into his own pocket.

Chapter Fourteen

Becca dipped her chin and watched as two of the three officers swept past her. She recognized the one *gendarme* who had stopped to study her at the Cathedral of Notre Dame. He ran by without acknowledging her. Perhaps he hadn't taken as much notice of her as she thought. The third officer was older. His hairline, visible beneath his hat, was entirely gray, and he walked more slowly toward them.

Becca turned to search for Patience. She was gone, and Lady Augusta had taken her place. The hem of Augusta's green gown fluttered in the light breeze.

Becca's breath hitched. Augusta was strong, but Jude's death would be a blow to her mother-in-law's heart. Becca ran to block Augusta's view of the body.

"I heard Jude's name in the hallway. The police made such a clatter." Augusta strained to see past Becca.

"I'll explain everything downstairs. You don't need to see." But it was too late.

Augusta wobbled to a stop near Jude's body. Hannah grabbed her arm, but the older woman shook it free. She stiffened her spine, staring past Jude, over the rooftop to the green gardens, the river, and the distant view of Paris beyond, then sank to her knees, her wide skirt pooling round her. She reached out and swept Jude's wet hair back from his forehead.

Becca pulled Augusta away, feeling the tremors that swept through her mother-in-law's arms, despite the warmth of the day.

Becca couldn't say all would be well. It wasn't. She couldn't explain Jude's inexplicable death. She didn't understand it herself. All she could do was hold her mother-in-law's hand for comfort.

One of the officers retreated to the stairs and disappeared. A second shouted a harsh command to them.

"You are standing too close," Michael interpreted in broken English, even though Augusta was the only one on the roof who required the translation. He aimed a small gesture, the slightest shake of his head, at Hannah, as if to stop her from answering in French.

Hannah nodded.

The officer Becca recognized called to Michael, then pointed at them all.

"The *gendarmes* say to be downstairs. Stay there," Michael extended the blanket he still held in his arms to the policemen and jutted his chin toward Jude.

One of the officers grimaced and shrugged.

Michael unfolded the blanket and placed it over Jude's body.

* * *

The comforting scent of coffee met Becca at the sitting room entrance.

Benjamin Franklin and Gabriel d'Aumont huddled round a low table that held a silver pitcher and green and gold porcelain cups half-filled with the dark liquid. They rose when Becca, Hannah, and Augusta entered. Daniel stepped into the room last.

"You have been through an ordeal, I understand." The shadows beneath Gabriel's deep-set eyes suggested tension, but his lips turned up as if he still hoped for the best.

"The pastry chef told me the news. Please. Sit." Franklin's arm swept to take in the upholstered chairs surrounding the table. He appeared to have aged since the morning, Becca thought.

A servant girl rushed to serve them coffee.

Franklin nodded to Gabriel, who began. "The police came to report on certain questions Dr. Franklin raised."

That was a diplomatic way to put it. Becca's eyes slid to Lady Augusta.

She hadn't told her mother-in-law about seeing Jude at Notre Dame. She'd thought the news of his treachery would wound Augusta.

"One might say that the timing of the *gendarmes'* arrival here was fortuitous...or the opposite," Gabriel continued.

"The opposite?" Becca watched him more closely.

He shrugged in the way that only the French have mastered. The gesture acknowledged that life made little sense and that there was nothing to be done about it. "It is fortuitous to discover a murder so quickly." His expression grew sad. "It is the opposite for those who might be considered suspects in such a murder, such as you and Mr. Alloway."

Daniel stood. "Mrs. Parcell has nothing to do with this."

So, the policemen *had* recognized her and Daniel from Notre Dame. Becca's lungs tightened. She tried and failed to take a full breath. This was all her fault. Her stupid, pointless anger at the cathedral had led to this.

"Sit, Mr. Alloway," Gabriel said. "Dr. Franklin confirms that he asked you and Mrs. Parcell to go to the cathedral."

"You didn't believe me?" Daniel growled.

"Of course, I believed you," Gabriel answered. "But I must confirm facts. Though I wonder whether you can explain why this Jude Fenimore seemed to have such a strong reaction to seeing Mrs. Parcell."

Daniel shook his head. "I told you no such thing."

"You didn't have to, my friend. The policeman recalls the events of the day. He described them to me just now."

Augusta turned to Becca. "Knowing how I feel–felt–about Mr. Fenimore, you didn't tell me you saw him yesterday?"

"I am terribly sorry about Jude's death," Becca stuttered. "I thought his resemblance to Philip would make it hard for you to bear bad news about him. I thought it would hurt you to hear that Jude was helping England, that he befriended us only because we led him to Dr. Franklin. And the last thing I wanted was to hurt you."

"Jude isn't—wasn't—Philip. He was simply a young man who was kind to us and who didn't deserve to be murdered." Augusta's posture was impossibly stiff.

Becca blinked in surprise. She had entirely misunderstood Augusta.

"Am I so old and frail that you must protect me from the truth?" Augusta lowered her chin and looked up at Becca.

Becca squirmed. When someone disappointed Augusta, she raised her chin and looked down her nose at the object of her displeasure. She lowered her chin like this only when she was extremely angry.

Franklin and Augusta exchanged glances. Some understanding passed between them. "You need a cane, Lady Augusta, a sharp one. That will allow you to poke anyone who underestimates you again. There are those who underestimate me, too, because of my age." He patted his walking stick, which rested against the side of the sofa. "I have my own tricks."

"I shall search for one immediately," Augusta said.

Becca had made more of Jude's resemblance to Philip than his mother, Lady Augusta, had. And she had hurt Augusta, the last thing she intended. Her lie of omission had created distance between them. "I hope you can forgive me."

Augusta's posture relaxed by an eighth of an inch. Becca hoped that meant her apology was accepted.

"What a terrible thing to happen. This is quite upsetting," Gabriel said.

The words could have meant anything or nothing, Becca thought.

Daniel cleared his throat. "I'll answer your earlier question, monsieur. Mr. Fenimore grew close to the ladies during the Atlantic crossing. That is the only reason they invited him to share our carriage to Passy. He was merely shocked to see Mrs. Parcell at Notre Dame. Nothing more than that. Neither of us have seen or heard from him since."

"That is the truth." Becca nodded to Augusta.

"The police will be told that Mr. Fenimore's death is a matter of international concern, given that it has occurred in Dr. Franklin's house. It is quite the delicate matter." Gabriel nodded to Becca and Daniel. "You will be required to remain in France until the killer is found."

"And until then?" Becca asked.

"Until then, the police will not bother you."

"You have that power?" Becca asked. Gabriel was an assistant minister of finance.

"Certainly not." Gabriel lifted the porcelain cup to his lips and watched them over its rim. "But I have friends at Versailles with that authority. They will see the wisdom of this course when I speak to them tonight. For now, I threaten the police with the wrath of Versailles." His eyes lit with humor. "I have enough power to threaten."

"And why do the police suspect them?" Hannah leaned forward.

Gabriel sighed. "The police saw Mr. Alloway and Mrs. Parcell with the dead man at the cathedral, and today, they saw all of you on the roof with the body, even you, Mrs. Hannah."

Becca's mother blanched.

"The police must consider the possibility that one of you killed Mr. Fenimore. It is positively ridiculous. But there you have it."

"Of course, we are suspects," Becca said. "But why will you call off the police?" Becca asked.

"Call off?" Gabriel turned to Franklin.

"To make them go away."

"Ah. I see. You explain, dear doctor."

Franklin nodded to Gabriel. "I wager that once word of Mr. Fenimore's death spreads, there will be rumors within hours that Dr. Franklin's lightning rod causes death or that I myself am killing people with my 'death rod.'"

"I will not accept your bet. I fear you are correct." Gabriel d'Aumont smiled sadly. The fewer people involved now, the less chance for information about this unfortunate matter to spread."

Franklin held his hand up, palm out. "I do not mean to sound callous. The death is worse news for Mr. Fenimore than for any of us. But anything that makes me look unstable to the British, the French, or other countries, will make it more difficult to go forward with conversations about ending the war. As Monsieur d'Aumont says, a death like this will start rumors."

"It is a matter that requires great delicacy and experience," Franklin said.

He and Gabriel turned to Daniel and Becca.

She didn't like the gleam in their eyes. If there was a ship sailing for

America tomorrow, Becca would have purchased a ticket on the spot.

"No." Daniel's voice was calm. "We won't even consider it."

Gabriel frowned. "I am putting my own position at risk for you, Mr. Alloway. Hear us out."

"We don't need to." Daniel glanced at Becca. She nodded, and he continued. "You are going to ask us to find Jude's killer. With discretion. Without fuss. Because if we cause any embarrassment to our government or yours, you can disavow us and ship us home." Daniel smiled, which did nothing to soften his cutting remarks. "Unless we're killed."

"Why not ship us home now?" Becca asked in her sweetest tone.

Franklin's face tightened with irritation. "Who else can I trust, Mrs. Parcell? Providence sent you and Mr. Alloway to me for this purpose. This is clear to me."

It was not clear to Becca.

"Providence wants you to place Mrs. Parcell in danger, sir? She is here less than a month. I am here less than a year," Daniel said. "What help can we possibly give in this matter?"

"You have a demonstrated talent for uncovering secrets," Franklin said so softly that Becca had to lean forward to hear. "A British spy has been murdered in my house. Who killed Jude Fenimore? Why did his murderer place him so publicly on my lightning rod? What other trouble does the killer mean to make?"

"I came to Paris to marry, not to solve a murder." Becca shifted in her chair. *I cursed him in a church, and he died.* She pushed away the thought.

"What else will the killer do to stop us from reaching a peace that brings independence? There is nothing about American independence that is self-evident or inevitable, despite what Thomas Jefferson wrote in his Declaration of Independence." Franklin's cheeks reddened with emotion,

We hold these truths to be self-evident. Even Becca knew the words. Everyone did at home. They were read aloud in town squares throughout the colonies.

Becca dropped her gaze. She had been bored with Augusta's and Hannah's wedding plans. She had agreed to watch for the man with the red rose as a lark, an entertainment. Now that the stakes were higher, she wanted to

82

go home. But Dr. Franklin had brought the War for Independence and the ghost of Jude Fenimore into this room. She felt ashamed of her instinct to run. Her gaze slid to Daniel.

He crossed his stocking-clad leg. The rhinestone buckles of his shoes glittered in the room's bright sunlight. He leaned back in his chair, his eyes half-closed as if he were about to fall asleep.

Daniel always looked most relaxed when he listened most intensely. He was reconsidering his refusal. Becca knew the signs. "What say you, Mrs. Parcell?"

She took a relieved breath and nodded.

"All right, Dr. Franklin," Daniel said. "We shall do our best. But I am not a hero, and if there's a choice between Becca's safety and finding Jude's killer, I will choose Becca."

"Excellent." Franklin leaned back on the velvet couch as if he hadn't heard Daniel's warning. "Monsieur d'Aumont can assist you."

"My honor." Gabriel rose with a grin and bowed. "You will let me know how I may be of service."

Heavy footsteps echoed from the stairwell outside the salon. They fell silent.

"And Mr. Fenimore?" Hannah asked. "What will happen to him?"

Gabriel cleared his throat. "The police are removing him as discretely as possible."

"And then?" Hannah asked.

Augusta's face was a rigid mask. Was she trying as hard as Becca not to hear the sounds in the hall?

"The city is drowning in the dead." Gabriel shrugged. "They will find him room in one of the other cemeteries, now that Holy Innocents is closed." His face tightened as if he'd bitten into spoiled fruit. "I mean no disrespect. 'Tis only that Paris is so old, and we all rest here for eternity."

"Does Mr. Fenimore have family here or in England?" Daniel asked. "Surely they should be informed of his passing."

"Patience Wright might know," Becca said.

In the distance, she heard deep male voices, the sound of heavy footsteps,

83

an *oomph*, and a curse in French. The harder she tried not to think of the police carrying Jude from the mansion, the more she imagined their task.

"What makes you think that?" Franklin asked.

"That?" Becca said a silent prayer for Jude.

"You said Patience Wright might know about Mr. Fenimore's family." Franklin's voice boomed as if trying to erase the sound of Jude and the police passing outside the salon.

"Mrs. Wright was distressed when she saw Mr. Fenimore alight from the carriage the day we arrived," Becca said. "It was as if she already knew him. Then, on the roof, she couldn't bring herself to come closer to Mr. Fenimore. She stood as far from him as possible."

"Most people avoid murdered bodies if they have any sense. Present company excepted," Franklin said.

Slow, awkward footsteps sounded just outside the salon doors. Their conversation drifted into silence. The front door slammed, and Becca's shoulder muscles unknotted.

Daniel cleared his throat. "Mrs. Wright burst into tears and ran away just before the police arrived. She stayed on the roof until then. Something new made her run, I warrant."

Becca would share her suspicions with Daniel later. Patience Wright only reacted to the scene after Daniel rifled through Jude's pockets. There was something about the dull coin and handkerchief Daniel had removed that triggered her response.

"You'll speak to everyone, won't you?" Franklin asked. "Not just Mrs. Wright. Someone here in the house gave Mr. Fenimore access to the house. Someone here killed him."

Becca nodded. Her stomach fluttered.

"We'll speak to the servants, too." Daniel cocked his head. "What about Mr. Bancroft? I haven't seen him since breakfast."

"He left early. Business in Paris." Franklin waggled his eyebrows. "Probably a woman. But I don't ask."

"Shall we start with Mrs. Wright, then?" Becca forced herself to sound unworried. She dreaded the upcoming conversation and wanted it over with quickly. She and Patience hadn't spoken since the artist declared war on her with her drunken innuendos the other evening. Why Patience disliked her so was a mystery.

"*Bonne.*" Gabriel's cup clattered as he placed it on the saucer. They all stood. The meeting was over.

Chapter Fifteen

The heavy door swung open at Daniel's knock.

"Mr. Alloway. How could such a terrible thing happen?" Patience Wright's voice was thick with tears. When she saw Becca standing behind him, the artist tried to slam the door shut.

Daniel's arm shot out, his palm slapping the door open. What grievance did this woman have against Becca? It hardly seemed rational. "Just a moment of your time, Mrs. Wright, given this morning's unfortunate events."

Patience hesitated.

"Dr. Franklin asked us to speak to you," Daniel said in his warmest voice, "and we want to assure ourselves that you are all right."

She sniffled, then moved to allow them access to the room. Crystals cascaded from gilt-edged sconces along each gold-flocked wall and from the chandelier overhead. The ceiling moldings were sculpted in the shape of ivory-painted fruit.

The light blue velvet settee between the two bedroom windows was stacked with crumpled drawings. Sketches and books covered every surface of the room.

Daniel forced his attention away from the exuberant, wasteful explosion of paper. American printers could hardly get their hands on enough to set type for a four-page brochure.

Patience did not invite them to sit.

"Have I offended you, Mrs. Wright?" Becca crossed her arms.

Patience's lips tightened into a grim line.

"Because you have been rude to me from the moment we met."

Daniel stepped out of the line of fire. He was accustomed to Becca's direct approach.

"All right, Mrs. Parcell." Patience was almost as tall as Becca. "There's no harm in telling the truth, is there?"

"I generally find that's the best approach," Becca answered.

Daniel heard the sadness in her voice. She had withheld the truth about their confrontation with Jude at Notre Dame from Lady Augusta and hurt the woman in the process.

"You came here with Mr. Fenimore." Patience pointed to Becca as if accusing her of a crime.

"And with Mr. Alloway," Becca said.

"You dazzled both men. That was clear." Patience's expression filled with bitterness.

"I hardly knew Mr. Fenimore," Becca sputtered. "And I didn't like him very much."

Patience spun to Daniel. "Is that the truth, Mr. Alloway? Never mind. Men are the last to know how a woman feels."

"That's not terribly flattering, Mrs. Wright," Daniel said mildly. "But I don't think that Becca cared for Mr. Fenimore at all. Quite the opposite." He glanced at Becca, then away. He was ashamed to discover that he and Patience had something in common: jealousy.

Patience blinked.

"I had no interest in the man," Becca said. "Lady Augusta was the one who invited him to accompany us here."

"Truly?" Patience's forehead furrowed.

Becca nodded.

Patience wiped her eyes with the back of her paint-stained sleeve. "I thought...I thought...that you and Jude...."

Becca flushed. "Me and Mr. Fenimore and Mr. Alloway?" She fisted her hands on her hips. Offense radiated from her every pore. "That is what you thought?"

Patience shrugged. "You would not be the first woman to have more than one lover."

Best to move past this topic as quickly as possible. "You knew Jude Fenimore before he arrived with us," Daniel said.

She sniffled again. "I met him in London. " She scooped up the drawings on the couch, opened her arms, and allowed them to flutter to the floor. "Please. Sit."

Daniel watched for Becca's reaction. Her lips were still set in a grim line, but she took a seat. He followed.

"My husband is gone, and so is Jude. The old secrets can't hurt me now." She looked up at them with red-rimmed eyes. "Do not judge me. This is how it is done among the finer families. There is no break in a marriage when a couple discovers they cannot get along. Taking a lover benefits everyone."

"In short," Becca said as if to cut off a lecture on the benefits of adultery. "You and Jude had an affair."

"Not just an affair, an affair of the heart." Patience lifted a hand to her collarbone.

"But this affair of the heart didn't last," Daniel said. That much was obvious.

Patience's cheeks grew pink. "I left him in London, you know. I discovered that he had other women. I have my pride. But I knew he would come back to me one day. I always knew." Another sniffle.

"You didn't look happy to see him the day that Mrs. Parcell arrived," Daniel prodded.

"Of course not." Patience stiffened her spine. "How could I show my joy in front of all of you? It would have been unseemly. I did my best to appear disgusted."

'Disgusted' was a long way from 'joy.' Daniel studied the artist. But Patience neither looked away too long nor stared at them without blinking. She wasn't lying. She had loved Jude, and she was telling them the truth as she saw it.

"I thought he had come for me. When he left that day to go to Paris, I thought I would hear from him, that he would send a note. But there was nothing from him, and he didn't return. I hated him then. I will admit that." Patience picked at a rust-colored paint stain on the sleeve of her gown.

"When you saw him on the roof, you stayed so far away." Becca's voice was soft.

"I didn't want to see him that way. I couldn't. And you were there, Mrs. Parcell. I didn't want to see the two of you together." Patience Wright's neck was a mottled pink. "I was wrong about you. Jealousy is a terrible thing."

Daniel supposed that was an apology of sorts.

"You went back downstairs just before the police arrived," Becca said. "What were you thinking that made you run?"

"I saw Mr. Alloway take a handkerchief from Jude's pocket. He had asked for something to remember me by when we were apart. He said he'd keep it with him forever. I gave him that handkerchief. When I saw that he had kept it, I was undone." Patience sobbed. "May I see it?"

The cool dampness from the handkerchief had seeped through Daniel's breeches to his leg. "Perhaps later, Mrs. Wright. I fear you are too distressed." There was an embroidered letter on the square of ivory linen. He didn't think Patience would be happy to see it.

She sobbed, holding her hands out, palm up, in supplication.

Reluctantly, he pulled the sodden cloth from his pocket.

Patience took it from him with one hand and smoothed it with the other. There was one final sob, a hiccup, then silence. She traced the deep red embroidered *R* stitched into the linen with a pink-knuckled finger.

"*R* for Rebecca. I almost believed you." Patience balled the cloth into her fist, then flung it at Becca before turning away, hugging herself.

Becca's eyes widened. "But that's not mine." She slipped a hand into her gown and pulled a linen from her pocket. "Please, Patience. Please look. I am a terrible seamstress. I couldn't possibly have sewn that, and I sew *B* for Becca, not *R* for Rebecca."

Patience Wright shook her head, her back still to them.

"I swear on my mother's life that handkerchief is not mine."

Slowly, Patience stretched her arm back, opening her hand. She took Becca's handkerchief and held it up to the window. "I thought my embroidery skills were terrible, but yours are worse."

"I do my best," Becca said stiffly.

Daniel thought silence was the best option. The embroidered *B* on Becca's handkerchief was comprised of wavy green stitches unevenly spaced. The two semi-circles that created the *B* could have been mistaken for triangles.

"That's no proof. Your servants embroidered the *R*." Patience still faced away.

"We have one servant at home. Her name is Annie, and she is too busy for embroidery. She would laugh if I asked her to stitch a handkerchief. She would throw it at me as you did," Becca said.

Patience finally turned, the flush of anger in her expression fading. She kicked the handkerchief on the floor.

Daniel wondered who gave Jude Fenimore the keepsake handkerchief. There was no point in bringing the subject up with Patience. It would set her off crying or screaming.

"Do you know if Mr. Fenimore had any family here or in England?" he asked.

Patience shook her head. "He told me there was no one. His parents were dead, he said. Are you done now?"

"One more question, please," Becca asked. "You were at a party last evening with Dr. Franklin."

Patience nodded.

"How did you get home? Did you know Dr. Franklin was in an accident?"

Jude's death had pushed all thoughts of Dr. Franklin's accident from Daniel's mind. He was glad Becca hadn't forgotten.

Patience glowered. "I am sorry about Dr. Franklin's accident. It had nothing to do with me. And how I got home is my business. Now, will you please leave?"

Everyone had secrets, Daniel knew. And everyone lied. Everyone but Becca, he corrected himself. But the artist was shutting them out, at least for now. They'd learn little more from her today.

Chapter Sixteen

"I crossed an ocean to marry this man, and the likes of you won't stop me, even if I don't have the right papers." Becca pointed her finger at the bland-faced magistrate.

The following morning's appointment to apply for a marriage license was not going well.

The magistrate made the sign of the cross, slipped an index finger beneath the edge of his curled white wig, and scratched. "Is she a witch, do you think?" He turned to Mr. Bancroft.

"A witch? 'Tis possible but unlikely," Bancroft answered.

Becca gouged her fingers into her palms to force herself not to answer. She had picked up enough French to understand the question and the answer.

"Apologize, Becca," Daniel said.

"I don't want to apologize," she answered through gritted teeth.

"The goal is marriage. Try again." He smiled at the magistrate.

The official nodded pleasantly in return but spoke to Bancroft, as if passing time while Becca and Daniel finished their conversation. "Will you be off to Paris tonight? Will you want my coach again?"

Bancroft nodded.

Becca paid little attention to the two men. Daniel was right. Her fit of temper was a mistake. It wouldn't convince the magistrate to let them marry here. She changed course.

"You must forgive my emotional outburst. After all, I am only a woman." Becca batted her eyes at the magistrate. She had used the same I-am-only-a-woman excuse after challenging the mob that sought to drive her from her

91

home in Morristown. It had calmed the crowd.

Bancroft translated, and the magistrate smiled. His close-set eyes were equidistant from a nose as curved as a Turkish sword. His eyebrows were waxed and powdered white to match his white wig. "Ah, of course." *Bien sûr.* She is passionate, no?"

Becca bit the inside of her mouth so hard she tasted blood. They spoke of her as if she were a horse up for auction.

"Can you tell me again what other papers we shall need to satisfy your marriage requirements?" Daniel asked.

Bancroft translated his English into French.

"These are not my requirements. The country of France, sir, demands this of you." And then the magistrate spoke so quickly that Becca only half-followed what he said.

Bancroft's hooded eyes widened. "Perhaps you and Mr. Alloway would be better off returning home to marry." She thought there was satisfaction in his expression, but he blinked, and the momentary emotion was gone.

"What did he say?" Daniel asked.

"You haven't lived here long enough to be considered a resident, and only residents can marry. Mrs. Parcell must have proof of her first husband's death. She must have her parents' permission to marry. They must approve. You must have proof of your first wife's death." The magistrate, and then Bancroft, droned on.

Becca stopped listening after the fifth 'you must.' She couldn't possibly satisfy all the marriage requirements. "I doubt I can obtain proof of my first husband's death. He died on a British prison ship." She gritted her teeth. "You might have noticed that the British are not overly helpful to Americans right now.

"Daniel and I thought it would be simple." Becca wasn't certain whether she was talking to herself, Mr. Bancroft, or the magistrate. Her throat tightened round her breath.

Bancroft again translated.

The magistrate leaned back, his expression softening. "Ah. This is too bad."

"Yes, it is too bad," Becca said, not waiting for Mr. Bancroft to translate.

With a loud crack, the magistrate shut his heavy volume. His gaze traveled from Becca's chin to her toes. He winked at Bancroft. "She could become Monsieur Alloway's mistress. There are worse fates." Becca noticed a sheen of moisture on his lips.

She turned away, shame and anger curdling her stomach.

Daniel stepped up and slid the book forward until it collided with the magistrate's impressive belly, trapping him in his seat. He leaned in, his face just inches from the official's. "Look at her like that again, and I'll shove this book down your throat."

The magistrate understood his meaning, though he didn't speak English. His eyes bulged.

Daniel released his grip on the book and took Becca's arm. As they stepped into the spring sunshine, she heard the magistrate call to Bancroft. "They are both mad. On my mother's grave, I swear I will never issue them a marriage license. Never."

Becca lifted her face to the sun outside the sand-colored building. "What will we do, Daniel? Dr. Franklin said that Mr. Bancroft had arranged everything. This country is happy to leave us unmarried." The rush of anger she'd felt facing the official receded, leaving her exhausted.

"We are married in every way that matters." His voice roughened.

She felt herself smile at the simple, true statement. Why had she been so worried about a wedding ceremony? Their lives were already dedicated to each other. "But we are not married in society's eyes."

"We will tell people we are married. It is as simple as that."

"A lie. I don't want to begin our marriage with a lie." She studied Daniel's face.

Two vertical lines carved themselves between his eyebrows. "Call it a lie, if you will. We merely lack a piece of paper, a license. But I worry for your reputation. The servants must be whispering about us. And there's Patience Wright. I won't have you slandered because of our closeness."

"I lost my reputation long ago, Daniel." She placed her hand on his heart. "I would rather have you than a reputation, in any case."

"If we can't marry here, we'll go to the Netherlands or the Swiss Confederacy," Daniel said. "We might have an easier time of it in Protestant countries." Only Catholicism was recognized in France.

"We can't leave, Daniel. We won't be permitted to leave France until we find Jude Fenimore's killer. Isn't that what your friend Monsieur d'Aumont said?"

"Then we will find the killer quickly." Daniel raised her hand to his mouth and kissed her palm.

Her breath hitched, and she felt the now-customary flutter in her belly.

"Is your dance card full this evening, or will you have time for me, Mrs. Parcell?" Daniel whispered.

Mr. Bancroft cleared his throat. For a large man, he had a quiet step. "There. You've bungled that entirely." His expression filled with pleased malice.

Becca turned from Daniel, feeling her cheeks warm.

"You'll have to apologize to the magistrate if you want to marry here," Bancroft continued. "Of course, that assumes you can meet all the other requirements." He sniffed, his opinion about their chances of success quite clear. "And some of us have work to do." He gave Daniel an accusing stare, lifted himself into the gleaming black carriage, and waited for them to follow.

The coach heated quickly in the afternoon sun, but the atmosphere inside remained frosty. Bancroft scowled at the passing bushes and trees as if they offended him. Daniel leaned against the red leather seat back, studying their fellow traveler.

"Do you visit the magistrate often?" Becca began with the most innocent question she could think of.

"No." Bancroft spoke to the passing landscape. All Becca could see was the side of his face as he peered out the window.

"Do you travel often in France?"

"No." His look of distaste was unmistakable.

She controlled the impulse to stick her tongue out at the man just to see if he would notice. She swung to Daniel, raising her eyebrows.

He winked in response and cleared his throat. "Mr. Bancroft, I heard the magistrate mention Paris."

Bancroft transferred his scowl to Daniel. "What about Paris?"

Becca stifled a giggle. Daniel had pried a total of three words loose from the man, more than she had managed.

"Will you be going tonight?" Daniel cocked his head.

"Why?" His eyes narrowed.

Yes, why, Becca wondered.

"I have a business engagement in Paris this evening. I thought we might ride together."

Becca lowered her chin, afraid that Bancroft would see her surprise and disappointment. Daniel had promised to spend the evening with her.

"Where in Paris is your meeting, Mr. Alloway?"

Paris. The magistrate had mentioned Paris. She schooled her expression into a placid inattention. The magistrate had offered the loan of a carriage, and Mr. Bancroft had accepted. What was Daniel thinking?

"A restaurant. Le Procope. Do you know it? It is decidedly inconvenient, but the merchant will only be in Paris for another day, and he may have a shipment that will make my employer a pretty penny." A smile. "As you say, some of us have work to do."

Bancroft's habitual scowl evaporated. His blue eyes appeared merely tired, not distrustful, and his rosebud lips turned up at the corners.

He wasn't an ugly man, Becca realized with a start, just an unhappy one.

"Be cautious, Mr. Alloway. Le Procope is an infamous place," Bancroft said. "It draws the most radical philosophers in France. I wonder that any good, conservative merchant would want to be seen there."

"Good advice, sir. I shall be cautious. But I still need to find my way there. It is too late to change plans. I shall avoid the place in the future." Daniel smiled. "May I come with you?"

Bancroft paused, then his smile returned. "Certainly, sir. I look forward to it. We leave at seven."

Chapter Seventeen

The upstairs hallway was filled with cool shadows, a relief from the afternoon heat but not from her thoughts. Standing outside the closed oak door now, Becca listened to the muffled sounds of Hannah and Augusta laughing. Her shoulders knotted at the sound.

"Go on." Daniel touched the small of her back for comfort. "You can't put off telling them about the marriage license."

She imagined announcing to Lady Augusta and Hannah that there would be no wedding in France, that she'd uprooted their lives for nothing. "Do you think they will arrange passage home right away?" Becca asked as she pushed open the door.

The room was a jumble of linen, silk, cotton, and lace. Bed hangings puddled onto the floor from their unstable perch on a side table. Gowns and undergarments jockeyed for space on a couch. Ivory napkins and tablecloths lined up like soldiers on the shelves of an intricately carved wardrobe, her wedding armoire, at the far end of the cozy space.

"What is this?" Daniel's eyes widened.

"My wedding trousseau," Becca said.

"It is overwhelming," he said.

"They have been working on this for weeks. I don't have the heart to tell them to stop."

Hannah and Augusta faced each other on two straight-backed chairs in the midst of the hurricane of cloth. They each held needle and thread in one hand and linen in the other. They wore matching looks of surprise at the interruption.

"We didn't expect you," Augusta said.

"How lovely," Hannah echoed. She cleared her throat and nodded at Augusta as if prodding her to speak.

Augusta rose slowly. Her thin face seemed gaunt in the late afternoon light. Becca suddenly dreaded whatever Augusta was about to say.

"Can you forgive me?" Becca began as Augusta said, "I owe you an apology."

"I never should have...." both women said, then stopped. Becca shook her head in confusion. Augusta's chin rose.

"Forgive you for what?" they asked at the same time.

Hannah laughed first with a sound as pure as sunlight. Augusta's rare laughter rose next.

Becca joined them until tears came, though she couldn't say why, other than the fact that the laughter restored the warmth among them.

Not a demonstrative woman, Augusta awkwardly opened her arms, and Becca, so much taller, swept into them. She did her best not to hold her mother-in-law too tightly.

"Go ahead, Augusta," Hannah goaded. "You promised."

"In my own time, not yours," Augusta snapped.

Becca took a grateful breath. Augusta must be fine if she was snarling at Hannah.

Her mother-in-law stepped away. "I have not been myself, Becca, not since we left America, and that has nothing to do with poor Mr. Fenimore or the fact that he reminded me of Philip."

"What is it, then?" Becca shook her head, confused.

"It is you. I haven't been myself because of you," Augusta said. "You and Mr. Alloway will build a life, here or somewhere else, and I will not be part of it. This is how it is meant to be. This is what marriage means, and I find that I especially do not care for the idea that I may never see you again once you wed."

Augusta twisted, meeting Hannah's gaze.

"You are almost done," Hannah said.

Augusta lowered her shoulders and lengthened her neck, adding at least an inch to her five-foot-one frame. She turned back to Becca. "I know you only wanted to protect my feelings, Rebecca. I know that is why you didn't tell me that Jude was a spy nor that you saw him at the cathedral. And yet I was enraged. I am sorry I became so angry. It is as if I have to make myself mad enough to leave you before you leave me. Anything else hurts too much."

Augusta frowned at them all. "Hannah insists that telling the truth makes one feel better. I do not feel better at all." She clamped her lips together so tightly that her chin dimpled.

"I didn't know that leaving hurt you the way it hurts me." Becca choked the words out. "You have always been so strong." She took one of Augusta's hands. "Don't go back to America. Stay with us in France. Both of you. Stay." Becca turned to search Daniel's expression.

He nodded, but Augusta and Hannah shook their heads.

"My home is America," Augusta said. "I am too old to start over, and Mr. Mason is waiting for me there."

Becca exhaled. "Of course." Mr. Mason and Augusta had rarely been apart from the day he waylaid their carriage two years ago. He was an enigmatic thief who practiced his trade along the edge of the Hudson River. When he helped rescue Daniel in New York, Mr. Mason had earned Becca's gratitude for life.

"The only reason I am here is to see you married," Hannah said. "I never would have come back to France otherwise, my dear, and I will not be comfortable remaining here."

"You won't have to worry about how long to stay in France, ladies." Daniel stepped past the tablecloths and bed linens to stand by Becca. "We can't marry in France."

The room went silent. A white dove landed on the windowsill. It seemed to stare through the window at them, then launched itself, wings flapping.

"We do not have the paperwork they insist upon." Becca listed what the magistrate said was required.

"Then come home with us," Augusta said. "We will begin packing now." Her gaze traveled the room. She winced seemingly at the sheer volume of objects there. "You will marry in Morristown."

"And then there's the fact that we are both suspected of murdering Mr.

Fenimore," Daniel added. "We are not permitted to leave France. Not yet, at least."

"Not permitted to leave France? That's absurd," Augusta said.

"You heard Monsieur d'Aumont," Hannah said. "Daniel and Rebecca must remain here until Jude's killer is found."

"Beyond ridiculous." Augusta's cheeks flushed pink. "We shall discover who killed Jude Fenimore and find someone to slap sense into that magistrate. We will see you married."

"Well said, Lady Augusta." Hannah clapped her hands. "Where shall we start?"

Daniel stepped away from the women as if to protect himself from their enthusiasm. "Your good wishes are more than enough, aren't they, Becca?"

She didn't answer. A delicate glass bottle no taller than the height of her pinkie had captured her attention. It rested precariously at the edge of a side table and glowed scarlet in the late afternoon sunlight. A red-and-blue glass stopper protected its contents. *Perfume.*

"Perfume. That is how you can help. You will help me buy perfume." Becca suddenly felt light; the day's exhaustion lifted.

"What does perfume have to do with anything?" Daniel asked.

"You must remember. We crossed the Seine and followed Mr. Fenimore." Becca conjured up the image of their chase from Notre Dame to the neighborhood of small houses and shops. "We lost his trail just past a perfume shop on the rue du Roule. I meant to return there. We should go."

"The shopkeeper wouldn't open the door when I pounded on it." Daniel's approving smile warmed her.

"Why did she work so hard to avoid us after we followed Jude from Notre Dame? Becca recalled the woman in the window of the perfume shop. "She may know nothing of Jude. But we won't be certain until we visit."

Daniel nodded. "You have become as suspicious as I am."

She wasn't certain his remark was intended as a compliment. "I know nothing about perfume, but what shopkeeper would question my interest in his store if I arrive with Lady Augusta…" Becca added a verbal flourish to

Augusta's English title. "...and Hannah, the healer? We need new perfume, don't we, ladies?" She curtsied to the two women, who returned the gesture.

"I dislike scent that announces my presence before I arrive," Augusta announced.

"Lemon, orange, tangerine. I could bathe myself in those scents." Hannah sighed.

Augusta's eyes lit with pleasure. "I doubt that Parisian perfume is better than the English scents I recall. But I look forward to finding out. I hear the French queen spends a fortune on perfume."

"Marie-Antoinette?" Hannah tilted her head.

Augusta nodded.

"I wonder if the perfumers work with frankincense?" Hannah asked. "It has healing qualities, you know. The old perfumes were all intended to coax us back to health."

"When will you visit?" Daniel asked cautiously.

"It is too late to go today. Tomorrow morning would be best." Becca turned to Augusta and Hannah. "If you are free to join me then."

Both women nodded.

"I will accompany you," Daniel said. Before Becca could protest, he added, "But only up to the perfume shop door. Paris isn't safe. And speaking of safety, I have preparations to make for my date with Mr. Bancroft." He bowed and was gone.

Paris would be almost as dangerous for him as for her. Becca listened to the clack of his steps retreating down the marble-tiled hall and resisted the urge to call a warning after him.

Chapter Eighteen

"Chef is outside." Elbow-deep in suds, the kitchen maid lifted a dripping hand and pointed to the back door as Michael pushed through it.

"Dr. Franklin asks this morning for that pastry you make, lemon with poppy seeds," she called to him.

"I thought we had more poppy seeds. There are none left." Michael's forearms strained under the weight of a burlap bag large enough to hide his chest and face. He flung it onto the slab of marble as if wrestling an opponent to the ground, and a cloud of white flour exploded from the fibers.

The baker glowered as he slapped his hands together, casting more flour into the air. His eyes were wary when he noticed Daniel. "What do you want?"

His grim tone surprised Daniel. Michael was friendlier the other night with Hannah, Augusta, and Becca. "I must speak to you, but I can come back if you are working."

"I apologize. Now is good." Michael raked a hand through his hair, leaving behind more white flour. "This death on the roof. We are all anxious. Two servant girls have already left their positions."

The kitchen maid placed another plate on the wooden counter as she watched Daniel. Yes, they were all anxious and all suspicious.

"Let's talk outside," Daniel suggested. Within moments, the two men stood overlooking the vegetable gardens, divided by broad dirt paths and lime trees. A breeze cooled the sweat at Daniel's hairline. Even between meals, the kitchen was uncomfortably warm.

"I am not usually so rude to guests." Michael stared into the woods behind the house. "I must apologize again."

"You seem more distressed by the murder today than when it occurred," Daniel said. "Has something else happened?"

"I cannot say." Michael's severe features tightened.

"What does that mean?" Daniel asked. "You cannot say, because you don't know or...."

"Because servants do not insult their betters if they wish to keep their position." Michael's tone was bitter.

Daniel understood. His father, a shepherd in Cornwall, had trained Daniel from a young age. "'Yes, sir,' 'No, sir,' and, on Christmas Day, 'Thank you for the goose, sir.' I don't care if your hair's on fire. That is all you will say to the master."

"I am an American, Michael. We insult each other all the time. Tell me."

"Your friend, Monsieur d'Aumont, asks me if I want to move to Versailles and make cakes for the king. He thinks to steal me from this place."

"That doesn't sound like an insult. It sounds like talent being rewarded. Congratulations."

"I would starve before I agreed to feed him." Michael spit on the grass. "I say no. I am polite when I want to lift him by his collar and throw him out the door."

The baker might love liberty, but he was careless, passionate to the point of danger. Perhaps not the best choice for a partner. Was trusting Michael wise? Daniel wasn't certain. But he needed a driver tonight if his plan had any chance of working, and he didn't have a better option.

Daniel wrestled the conversation back to his purpose. "I am here to ask a favor. I need you to drive me to Paris and back tonight."

"And it is so important you reach Paris tonight?" Michael kept his head lowered, neither agreeing nor disagreeing.

"It is."

"Why ask me?" Michael pulled the beige-colored towel tied at his waist and wiped his hands.

"For one, you have tender feelings for Mrs. Hannah."

Michael scowled. "That is none of your business." A pause. "You can tell?"

"You seek her out. You want her opinion on herbs. You bring her pastries to try." Michael was a man of few words, except when it came to Hannah. He wore his feelings on his sleeve.

"And what if that is true?" The baker crouched suddenly and plucked a purple weed from the ground. He pinched the long green stem, releasing the scent of mild onions. "Chives. We have more in one of the gardens. Perhaps I'll add it to tomorrow's bread." He tucked the herb into his waistband.

"That is why I am asking this favor," Daniel said. "Because of your feelings for Mrs. Hannah."

Michael's high forehead furrowed as if Daniel made no sense.

"Take a walk with me." Why risk being overheard? "Someone close to this house may have killed Jude Fenimore. Who's to say he won't come after another of us?"

"Why would he hurt Han–someone else?" Michael's strong hands flexed, then formed fists.

"Who is to say why murderers do what they do?" Daniel shrugged.

"Someone close to the house, you say. You are following someone who lives here into Paris?" Michael asked.

Daniel nodded.

Michael frowned. "What do you require of me?"

* * *

The setting sun painted the sloping lawn and the skyline of Paris with a golden glow. Daniel pulled a stalk of hay from the collar of his linen shirt and flicked it over his shoulder.

"Any sign of him?" he asked Michael. It was seven p.m. Edward Bancroft would be driving by any minute.

"No," the pastry chef answered.

Daniel burrowed back into the cart with only a thin layer of hay to cushion the rough plank floor. Pulling the scratchy burlap tarp over himself, he asked himself again whether involving Michael had been wise.

The pastry chef hated the French monarchy, and he was inspired by the American Revolution. Was he inspired enough to kill a British agent like Jude Fenimore if it meant protecting Benjamin Franklin?

Michael was strong enough to have lifted Fenimore to the lightning rod. But Daniel couldn't think of a reason Michael would want to call attention to his crime in that way.

Michael couldn't have known Jude would arrive at Franklin's home the morning he was killed. In fact, Daniel couldn't think of a way that Michael and Jude could know each other at all.

Beneath the burlap tarp, Daniel walked through the steps he'd set in motion. The scullery maid should have run to the stable to hand Mr. Bancroft a note. *Terribly sorry*, Daniel had written in slow, careful penmanship. *But I won't be joining you tonight. The merchant I intended to meet has taken ill with a terrible migraine. Perhaps we can visit Paris together another time.*

Daniel had never intended to ride with Bancroft. He asked to accompany the man at a specific time, at seven p.m., to ensure that Bancroft left for Paris only when Daniel was ready to follow him.

The crunch of wheels on gravel grew louder. Horses whinnied as they passed the cart, and then the sounds softened. Daniel lay still, inhaling the clean, sweet scent of fresh hay.

"That was Mr. Bancroft," Michael whispered.

Daniel began a slow, silent count. When he reached twenty-five, he called to Michael. "Is he far enough ahead of us now?"

"*Oui.*" The chef made a clicking sound, and the cart's two horses pulled forward.

* * *

There is little cheer in spending hours standing behind a copse of bushes and trees while watching strangers enjoy themselves. That was all Daniel had discovered this evening. Parked several blocks away, Michael must be cursing his bad luck to be caught up in Daniel's scheme.

Candlelight, music, and the trill of women's laughter streamed through the open windows of the townhouse across the way. Edward Bancroft had entered the home hours ago. Daniel had watched from the Tuileries Garden ever since.

"Garden" was a humble name for the flowers and bushes that led to the royal palace, this Tuileries Palace. In the darkness, it was merely a hulking shadow. King Louis XIV might have loved his Paris palace, but his son and grandson had virtually abandoned the abode for Versailles.

For the first hour, Bancroft hovered by a piano near the center window. Later, Daniel caught glimpses of him framed in one window and then another, drifting from one group of guests to the next.

The male guests were interchangeable in their stiff poses and formal evening wear. Coats, waistcoats, and breeches. Silk stockings. Linen shirts with lace at the cuffs and a cravat at the neck. Through the tall paned window, they looked virtually alike. It took him more than a moment to pinpoint which was Bancroft.

Why did Bancroft need to borrow the magistrate's coach if all he intended was to make an appearance at a society party? It was a party—an innocuous party—like so many that Daniel had attended since arriving in France. Why did he need to keep this visit a secret? Was he meeting someone in particular inside the townhouse? For what purpose? Who owned the house? He wouldn't get any answers standing here tonight.

Daniel shifted his weight from one leg to the other. His attention wandered. He wore clothes like those of the men framed in the light-filled windows to blend in his new role as Mr. Barnes's agent in Paris. When Becca leaped from the carriage, she had acted as if his new clothes made him a stranger. Didn't she want him to be a man of substance? Wasn't that what *he* wanted?

Footsteps echoed nearby. One man half a block away, Daniel guessed. He pulled behind a tree trunk, the bark rough against his back.

The footsteps were replaced by the sound of a chain clinking through metal. The nighttime street darkened even more as if a curtain had fallen.

Daniel exhaled with relief. Just a street lighter lowering lamps and

105

extinguishing the candles that lit Paris. The worker passed moments later, dousing another taper just yards from where Daniel stood.

In the darkness, he admitted defeat. Dr. Franklin's personal secretary was cross, judgmental, and arrogant. That didn't make him a traitor or a killer. Why Bancroft felt it necessary to borrow the magistrate's carriage to attend a party was still a mystery. But it wasn't a crime.

And it was time to end this farce. Daniel stifled a yawn. He'd kept Michael from his bed long enough.

Which was when a dagger of light, almost long enough to illuminate Daniel, shot across the street. Daniel leaped back. Two men and a woman exited through the newly opened door. He tensed at the sound of voices. One was familiar: Bancroft's.

Two carriages pulled up to the front of the townhouse. A servant must have alerted a stable boy to have the carriages brought around.

The impatient hollow sound of horses' hooves on cobblestone echoed down the late-night street. A carriage door slammed shut. One of the two carriages pulled away.

Bancroft's voice carried. "Too much to drink. Give me a few minutes. I best make use of the king's garden before we leave."

The driver laughed.

Daniel scrambled for cover beneath nearby bushes. Lying on his belly in the moist dirt, he watched Edward Bancroft stride into the garden. His pace was steady. He didn't appear fuddled with drink. And he headed straight for Daniel, stopping yards away. The silver buckles on his black shoes gleamed in the moonlight.

Daniel tensed for the sound of buttons opening. He wouldn't manage to stay hidden if Bancroft relieved himself right here. He slid his hand silently toward the pocket where he'd secured a knife.

But Bancroft shifted direction, jogging to the tree where Daniel had spent most of the night. He crouched there as Daniel had minutes ago. One arm yanked back. His elbows pulled out as if he was working with tools or pulling at something.

What's he fussing with? Daniel couldn't tell. But when Bancroft rose, he was empty-handed. He strode back to the coach.

Carriage springs squeaked. Daniel imagined Bancroft grasping the carriage door frame as he stepped up, the coach dipping in response to his weight. Bancroft laughed at something the driver said, and a door clicked shut. The driver crooned to his horses as the coach moved forward slowly, then more quickly. The jingle of the harnesses grew faint, then disappeared.

The after-dark music of summer crickets was all that remained.

Daniel plunged forward, sweeping his hand over the ground where Bancroft had seemed to search for—something. Small pebbles scratched his fingers, and then he felt it, a string. He tugged, feeling a light resistance on the other end, and pulled again. A small glass bottle emerged from a hole within the tangle of roots at the base of the tree.

Daniel gripped the narrow-mouthed bottle and felt a trace of warmth from Bancroft's hand. In the dim moonlight, Daniel could just see a rolled page within the dark glass.

A borrowed coach. An hours-long party. All to leave a message beneath a tree. What purpose required such effort, such complexity? *What have you hidden, old man?* Daniel wedged the bottle between his right arm and his ribs and pulled out the cork that held its contents in place. He pulled out the delicate, rolled paper with his left.

A soft click, one pebble rolling into another, was all the warning Daniel had. He jammed the paper into his pocket and flipped the bottle in the direction of the sound. He could live with the embarrassment if all he did was scare a raccoon. But a satisfying *whoof* told him that the jar had found its target.

Something hit his head. Sparks of light exploded, clouding his sight. Daniel spun, leaned forward to run, and fell. The left side of his skull was numb, cold. The buzzing in his ears rose until the sound erased the world. There was no pain. Not then, and he was surprised to feel the earth beneath his belly, since all his senses told him that he was twisting and rolling toward the ground.

He flipped onto his back, triggering a wave of nausea. He'd had a knife. Where was it? Was there one attacker or three? He saw three. At least he would die facing his killer. The shadows grew larger. A hand patted his vest, his pockets. A new sound intruded, even louder than the buzzing in his head. A voice. A roar. The hand searching his clothes was gone.

And then his thoughts sank down the deep well of his mind. Daniel set the image of Becca before him, the flash of her broad smile, her half-closed eyes when they made love, the way one eyebrow rose when she was convinced he was wrong. She was as clear to him as if she stood before him in bright daylight. His vision narrowed to a pinpoint.

* * *

A dome of stars and the sound of horse hooves greeted Daniel as he woke. Where was he? He lay on a prickly blanket of hay. One stalk poked his waist. Hay? What was he doing in a hay cart in the middle of the night? Who was driving? He lifted himself to his elbows. A shot of pain and nausea forced him down again. *What's happened to me?* He lay still, panting, eyes closed as the cart slowed to a stop. He'd worry about the where, when, and why later.

The cart bounced as someone jumped in.

Daniel opened one eye.

Michael stared back. "I thought you were dead." He exhaled with relief and surprise.

Daniel next opened his eyes to find Hannah hovering over him in the darkened sitting room at Dr. Franklin's home. There was a pillow beneath his head. A blanket covered him. He lay on the floor with a rug and a sheet beneath him. He recalled his arm around Michael's shoulder, Michael's hand around his waist.

"You are a lucky man, Mr. Alloway." Hannah pressed a cool compress to the side of Daniel's head.

"I don't feel lucky," His skull was alive with pain.

"You are an idiot, sir." Becca sat near his feet. She sounded as angry as he'd ever heard her. He heard tears in her voice, too.

He agreed with her assessment.

"Will he be all right?" Benjamin Franklin asked.

"Of course, he will," Augusta said.

Their voices seemed to hover over his head, as if they stood looking down at him. From his vantage point on the floor, he caught a glimpse of Augusta and Dr. Franklin seated on the nearby couch. Michael stood behind them. Each heartbeat pounded his skull. He raised his head to speak again and felt the earth spin.

Hannah's voice was closer. "It is too soon to tell how long it will take you to recover. Your mind has been rattled."

He tried again. "Rattled as a general matter or just at the moment?" His voice sounded rusty to himself. There. Speaking didn't make the pain worse, and, besides, hearing his voice might remove the panic he saw in Becca's red-rimmed eyes.

"You're talking. That is a good sign," Hannah said with satisfaction. "Can you tell us your name?"

"Really, Hannah," Augusta said. "Why would you ask that?"

"Really, Augusta," Hannah replied. "Patients with a head injury can be confused." She turned back to Daniel. "Please answer the question."

"My name is Benjamin Franklin." There had to be some humor in all of this.

The group gasped.

"Or call me anything you like, even Daniel Alloway." Daniel shifted to study Becca. She let slip a smile. At least he'd succeeded in that.

Hannah's hand pressed on his shoulder. "Best lie still for now."

"Who did this to you, Daniel?" Becca asked.

His memory was a thin, tenuous thread. A thread. A string. He clutched at the memory of a string, but nothing came. He didn't know what it meant. "I stood across the street from a townhouse."

"You were searching for...." Dr. Franklin prompted

Hannah interrupted. "That won't help. Let Mr. Alloway remember."

"We left here to follow...." Daniel struggled for the name. "To follow Mr. Bancroft." The recollection made him feel as if he'd won a race.

"Bancroft? You didn't mention you were following Mr. Bancroft," Franklin said with surprise.

"You told us to…." Daniel stopped. Fenimore was dead by the hands of someone with access to this house. Franklin and Gabriel d'Aumont asked them to investigate. He remembered that much, at least.

"And then?" Becca asked.

"And then…." A thick curtain of emptiness separated his memories of before and after. "And then, I was here."

"You don't remember." Michael's voice was weary.

"No." Daniel supposed he should be upset, but the accident had dulled all his emotions, even anger.

"Mr. Alloway's memory may return," Hannah said.

"You are not certain?" Franklin asked.

"Memories of the time just before an accident sometimes return," Hannah added.

"And sometimes don't?" Franklin pushed.

Hannah shrugged.

"They are coming too close, too close entirely," Franklin muttered as if he'd forgotten there were others in the room.

"Who are 'they,' Dr. Franklin?" Becca asked. "What aren't you telling us?"

It was hard enough to breathe around the pain in his head. He would worry about why he couldn't recall who slammed his skull another time.

The clock struck four a.m.

Michael sighed. "I must go. The bread cannot wait."

"I can't thank you enough for bringing Mr. Alloway home." Becca lifted her hand to her heart.

"It was the bread, you see." Michael stepped around the couch. He crouched near Daniel's feet.

Daniel appreciated the effort. It was easier to watch the baker this way. "The bread?" His tongue felt thick in his mouth. It took effort to speak. Hannah was right. His brain was rattled.

"You followed Mr. Bancroft to the Tuileries Palace," Michael began. "You tell me to park away but not too far, and you will come soon. You do not come. I watch the moon move across the sky. At one, I think, if we don't go now, I will get no sleep tonight because of the bread. I am up at four every

110

day to make the bread." Michael stopped as if waiting for Daniel to say, "I recall."

But he didn't recall. It was the oddest feeling to hear what he'd done just hours ago, as if it had happened to a stranger.

"It is bad in Paris late at night. I walk quietly to hear if anyone follows. I see you. But it is not you. It is a man in a cloak. There is a half-moon. He has a club. A long stick. You are on the ground."

Franklin leaned forward. "The man with the club. Who was he?" The deep shadows beneath his eyes looked carved from stone.

"I tell you this already, sir," Michael said. "I could not see. I yell. I run at the man. I am aiming low to make him fall, not looking at his face. His feet come up. He almost falls, but then he runs."

Becca asked quietly, "What about his feet, then? Do you remember anything about his shoes?"

Her logic was impec…impec. Daniel couldn't remember the rest of the word. Her logic was very good. Where had his mind gone to hide, he wondered, and would it come back?

"Leather. He wore leather shoes." Michael stares at the corner of the ceiling as if the man's feet would materialize there. "I hit him low and feel leather against my shoulder. Shoes with a buckle. Something metal. It tears me when I hit him." Michael corrected himself. "Scratches me."

A flash of memory rose like smoke. Bancroft stepped out of a house across a street, Daniel recalled. He'd pressed behind a tree. Daniel's thoughts thinned and evaporated. He struggled to remain awake.

"You weren't moving. I thought you were dead," Michael continued. "And then I lifted you over my shoulder. At least I knew you are breathing. I am glad you are alive, sir."

"I wish I could erase that memory for you," Daniel said. Some things were better forgotten.

"And I wish I had come before, earlier." Michael rubbed his shoulder with one hand, stretched his neck. He examined his palm and frowned.

Hannah stood. "I'll look at your shoulder."

"But Daniel needs you," Becca protested.

"I will return soon. All we can do is watch Mr. Alloway for now." She stood gracefully and strode to the sitting room entrance, waiting for Michael.

"Chef," Franklin called.

In the doorway, Michael turned.

"After you finish the bread, take the day off." He paused. "And be careful."

"Harm can come whether one is careful or not," Michael said as Daniel's eyes fluttered shut.

Chapter Nineteen

Becca tucked her linen shift over her shins again and tightened the belt of her robe. She watched Daniel's chest rise and fall as he slept in the sitting room. She'd watched the night sky glow pale peach, then brighten to clear blue. In the other room, a grandfather clock chimed the hour: ten a.m. Hannah didn't want Daniel moved yet, and so Becca had kept vigil all night.

Last evening, she had waited for the sound of his footsteps in the upstairs hall, the click of her bedroom door opening, the flicker of candlelight that pushed away the darkness when Daniel came to her. Sometime after midnight, her eyes had closed despite herself.

She came fully awake sometime later, disoriented, cocooned in the soft featherbed, her heart pounding in her chest. The frightened bellow came again.

She'd kicked away the thin summer quilt and scrambled out of bed, grabbing the summer robe at the foot of her bed. There hadn't been time to search for her bedroom slippers in the dark. She raced down the stairs barefoot, feeling the cool wood beneath her feet. Her feet were still bare. She certainly wasn't going to leave his side because society dictated that a woman wear shoes in public.

Now, his breathing was steady, his forehead cool, and he lay on a fine beige linen sheet that covered the red and blue Turkey rug beneath it. The pillow still lay beneath his head.

"Please," Becca whispered. "Please." She'd repeated the one-word prayer from the moment she'd raced down the stairs to find Daniel in Michael's arms. What she meant was, *Please don't take him. Please let him be all right. Please give us more time. Please give us forever.* Putting any of that into words would bring her fear to life, and so all she whispered was, *Please.*

Footsteps creaked on the floorboards above as the house came to life and the servants prepared for the day. They passed the sitting room silently, their voices rising once they passed the doorway.

Hannah came by twice this morning, nodding to Becca as she studied Daniel. In pantomime, she offered to take Becca's place. Becca shook her head both times and shooed her mother away.

Augusta, Michael, Dr. Franklin, and even Patience Wright had stood at the door whispering good wishes for Daniel's recovery.

If Becca had been home in Morristown, she would have pushed Annie out of the kitchen to make soup for him. She would have changed sheets and washed floors, brought in fresh flowers from the meadow to set near him, as if that, any of that, would keep him alive. It was the fairy tale women told themselves. If they worked hard enough to make a comfortable home, nothing truly bad could ever happen.

But the truly bad thing had happened, and she was not home. There was nothing she could do but sit cross-legged on the floor next to Daniel, willing him to keep breathing.

Her eyes burned, and she closed them tight. This was the problem with love, she thought, which should be avoided at all cost. It made loss—even the thought of loss—unbearable.

She opened her eyes to find Daniel contemplating her. "Will you forgive me for sitting out this dance?"

Becca caught the sob of relief in her throat before it escaped. Even the few hours of sleep had done him good. His skin had lost its pallor. "Don't jest." A pause. "How do you feel?"

"As if I've been run over by four horses and a carriage."

"Should I call for Hannah?" Daniel was speaking in full sentences. That must be a good sign.

"No. Not yet."

Footsteps slowed outside the sitting room. Becca ignored them until someone cleared his voice. "Is he…will he…." Edward Bancroft's eyes flicked to Daniel, then away, as if his weakness were an embarrassment. He hovered in the doorway.

A wave of revulsion choked Becca. Daniel would be fine if not for this man. She pushed forward to stand.

"Thank you for asking, sir. I can't say that I'm well yet, but I am sure I will be." Daniel gripped her wrist with one hand.

His intent was clear. He was capable of speech this morning, and he wished to lead the conversation. She settled as comfortably as she could back onto the rug-covered parquet floor.

"You were attacked in Paris?" Bancroft stepped into the room.

"I'm told that I was."

"Told? You don't recall?"

"No. I don't," Daniel said. "Take a seat, Mr. Bancroft. Given the difference in our stature at the moment, that would make us a bit more equal."

Lines formed between Bancroft's thick, gray eyebrows as if he feared whatever Daniel would say next. He searched the room as if he'd never seen it before, then sat on the yellow silk couch nearby. "I am glad to see you improved. When I awoke, I heard you were injured, and I see it is true." He paused. "But why did you go to Paris at all? You told me that your plans were cancelled."

Becca studied Bancroft more closely. He was not a loquacious man, and those few sentences practically constituted a speech.

"Did I say that my plans were cancelled?" Daniel laughed.

"No. You had a note sent."

Well, I'll be damned. I don't recall." Daniel turned to Becca. "Do you know why I was in Paris?"

His tone was lighthearted, but Becca's heartbeat roared in her ears. "Even that memory is gone?" When he arrived home, he knew he'd gone to Paris to follow Mr. Bancroft. Now, he didn't. His mind was weakening, not strengthening.

"I am afraid so. But didn't I tell you anything?" His hazel eyes widened. The change in his expression was hardly noticeable. Neither was his slight nod.

She recognized the wide-eyed trick to make a lie sound like the truth. He was lying. And he wanted her to lie, too. Which meant he did recall that he'd gone to Paris to follow Mr. Bancroft.

She was going to kill him for scaring her. No, she wouldn't kill him. But she would hurt him very badly once he was well.

"I was with Lady Augusta and Hannah last night." Becca put as much concern into her voice as she could. "You didn't tell me where you were going, Mr. Alloway." She widened her eyes, too.

"Just so." Daniel's lips curved into a small, half-smile. Her performance had pleased him. "I didn't want you to worry."

"Not worry? Am I sitting here all night begging your lungs to keep breathing because I'm not worried?" She wasn't playacting now. "I should have gone back to bed when you arrived half-dead last night. Is that it? You addlepated nincompoop. You...you blockhead. You...."

"*Ow melder.*" *My love.* Daniel interlaced his fingers with hers. His grip was strong, stronger than she expected. His palm was warm. She swallowed past the lump in her throat and stopped. She thought she would lose him, and anger was less terrifying than grief.

Moments passed in silence. Bancroft cleared his throat. "Don't you recall anything, Mr. Alloway, about where you were or who attacked you?" He leaned forward, elbows on his knees, hands clasped as if in prayer.

"Ms. Hannah says that those memories may be gone forever." Daniel rubbed one hand against his forehead. "I might as well be fuddled with drink. Nothing stays straight in my head. The last thing I remember is eating breakfast yesterday morning. Leftover pork from dinner. Sweet rolls and...and eggs." Daniel smiled as if remembering the eggs was an accomplishment.

"I remember something else before breakfast." Daniel asked. "Are you well, Mr. Bancroft?"

"Very well. Why?" Bancroft's expression was wary.

"I could have sworn that you and Dr. Franklin had an accident on the way home from a party the other night." Daniel looked with confusion from

Bancroft to Becca. "Was that a dream?"

"I heard about Dr. Franklin's accident," Bancroft said. "A terrible thing."

"But you were not in the carriage with Dr. Franklin?" Becca asked. "You must have left the party much later."

"And your interest in my affairs?" Bancroft's face reddened.

Becca wondered why he was as unwilling as Mrs. Wright to talk about that night. She would press him a little harder. "An affair of the heart, sir?"

"Your affairs are your affair, sir. It's chivalrous of you not to identify the lady." Daniel flashed Becca a warning look.

"Precisely my point, Mr. Alloway," Bancroft said.

Becca had been too direct with Mr. Bancroft. But Daniel's question about the night Dr. Franklin was hurt told her his mind was still intact. Her spirits rose.

Bancroft slapped one hand on his thigh. "Well, then." He stood, looking positively cheerful. "It does sound as if you are mending, thanks be to God. I'll leave you to rest. If I can help at all, please don't hesitate to call on me."

What is he hiding, Becca wondered. Why is he so relieved?

The sound of his footsteps receded, and Becca hissed, "How much do you truly recall?"

"More than I said but less than I wish."

She swept his hair back from his forehead, letting her palm linger on his skin. "No fever. Another good sign." She paused. "You truly don't know who hit you?"

"It could have been anyone, even a natty lad."

"A pickpocket?" Becca considered the possibility. "Don't they run when caught? This one fought back."

"All I know is that it wasn't Mr. Bancroft. He doesn't have the speed or the strength."

Daniel's voice thickened and slowed. His eyes fluttered shut.

* * *

Daniel woke to the sound of a quill pen scratching paper, to the sight of a single candle on the desk across from his bed, and to Becca, who sat hunched over her ledger book. The pain clawed at the back of his head, but its power was ebbing.

Sprawled in a featherbed, he supposed he should be grateful for that. Featherbed. He was in his bedroom. "How did I get here?" He kept his voice steady. He didn't recollect climbing the stairs. Didn't remember tumbling into bed. Pain had stolen his memory. His heart sped, pounding to the same rhythm as his throbbing head.

A chair scraped the floor. The ledger thumped decisively shut. Becca was there in a moment.

He hated the look of fear she wore.

"How did you come to France, you mean?"

"No. How did I come to be here in this room." He almost laughed. "And is it day or night?" He couldn't tell. The velvet curtains were entirely closed.

"Two of the servants used the sheet to create a stretcher after the midday meal. You slept through the trip upstairs." As if she guessed his thoughts, Becca added, "You didn't awaken at all."

He let himself sink back into the bed, his heart slowing. "Then my mind hasn't slipped away, not entirely, at least."

She poured water from a pot that stood on the black lacquered end table nearby. Tapping a folded paper over the drink, Becca watched as a gray powder spilled out, clouding the water before it cleared. "Here. Hannah said to take this when you awoke."

"What is that?"

"My mother said it is a relaxing tea to help the pain."

Daniel inched himself back until he half sat against the bed's blue velvet headboard. He emptied the cup in seconds, then held it out for a refill. "Or you can hand me the entire pitcher. I'm that thirsty."

Becca poured but didn't add more gray powder. "Do you hear a ringing in your ears?"

"No. Should I?" He emptied the second cup.

Becca studied him with the intensity of an eagle. "If I lift my hand, how many hands do you see."

"One hand." He grinned. "Is this a game?"

"Can you repeat 'Lucy Locket lost her pocket' three times?"

"Lucy Locket?" He searched her face. "You are serious?" Perhaps Becca's brain was as addled as his.

"As serious as can be. My mother insists I report your answers to her. Now, sir, Lucy Locket lost her pocket."

Intrigued, Daniel repeated the phrase three times.

"Well, your tongue still works," Becca said with satisfaction.

Daniel thought it best not to share his thoughts on that subject.

She strode to the windows and stopped so suddenly that her blue-and-white gown swayed like a clanging bell. Staring back, she pulled the curtains open.

Daniel winced, then blinked and grew accustomed to the light. That answered his other question. He had managed to sleep through the remainder of the night, despite his head injury. The strong sunlight suggested he'd slept through most of the morning.

"Hannah said that if you could do all those things, and if the light did not overly bother you, you would soon be well. 'Of course, he will be well,' I told her. I never doubted it." Becca wiped her eyes with the back of a hand. "Are you well enough now to change? I never want to see those clothes again." Her face tightened with distaste.

Daniel examined his jacket and winced. Blood, his blood, pockmarked the collar and sleeves in dark brown splatters. It was ruined.

"If you are comfortable, I'll call the servants to assist," Becca said.

"No," he barked. "'Tis not time." *Not time?* Becca was wrong. His mind was still unmoored.

He'd developed a distaste for uncleanliness while he was imprisoned on that disease-infested prison ship in New York Harbor. He should have been eager to don clean clothing.

A memory flickered to life. Pebbles digging into his knees. His hands in dirt. He pulled at something. A string? A string in the dirt? He had been searching for something.

"Are you all right?" Becca rushed to him. Her hand cupped his cheek.

"I was looking for something. I was digging."

Her fingers shivered against his skin. He was scaring her, and that wouldn't do. "I'm fine. The pain is less already. What was that powder you gave me?"

"Hannah said it would soothe the pain. Michael gave her some of the poppy pods he uses for cakes soon after we arrived. She crushed them into powder. But you were remembering, weren't you? You were remembering last night?"

Digging. A string. A bottle. Then, a flash of pain. A bottle. String. Paper. Memory assaulted him.

"I remember, and I'm hungry." He took her hand and kissed her warm palm. "I do not deserve you."

"Probably not." She leaned over to kiss him properly. Her lips were soft, and the kiss not nearly long enough.

"Why so gentle?" he scraped her bottom lip with his teeth as she shifted to pull away.

"Less gentle later." Becca paused. "What do you remember?"

"Won't you feed me first, or are you torturing me on purpose?" Becca's curiosity cheered him. Her fear over his injury was receding.

"Don't tease," she protested. "Tell me who did this to you."

"And you will hunt him down?" Now, he was teasing.

But she wasn't. "With my last breath." It was an oath.

"I don't know who attacked me. I didn't see him." Daniel swept away the light summer quilt that tangled round his legs and swung his feet to the floor. He waited for the room to stop spinning. That was better. He stood cautiously, then slipped his left hand into his pocket, feeling for the paper he'd jammed there last night. Was it just last night?

"Bancroft hid this in the Tuileries Garden. I was too focused on retrieving it from a bottle hidden in the ground. T'was my mistake. I didn't hear anyone approach from behind. We were right. Mr. Bancroft is hiding something."

Becca reached for the paper, smoothing it on the table by Daniel's bed. He sat, and she rushed to retrieve the lit candle still sitting on the desk.

Daniel inhaled the scent of the sweet beeswax taper in the silver candle-holder as she read aloud:

As I sit here, pen in hand,
I cannot help but think of you,
My beloved.
I cherish each visit
And pledge my loyalty to you,
As always.

"Why did you stop reading?" Daniel asked.

"Because there's nothing more." Becca handed the letter back.

"I risked my life for a badly written love letter?" Daniel exhaled a disgusted breath. "How ridiculous." He rubbed his thumb over the letter, feeling the slightly nubby texture of the finest quality paper. "What a waste of good paper. 'Tis a great expense for such a brief message. There is enough space between each line to write a message three times as long."

"Why hide a lover's note in the Tuileries Garden at all? It makes no sense to me," Becca said.

"Mr. Bancroft's lover might be married and live near the garden. They might think it's romantic," Daniel guessed.

Becca *hmmfed.* "It is too businesslike a love letter for my taste, and what woman would think it romantic to dig in the dirt for a message?" She moved to the bed. Her hand rested on his thigh, her right arm against his left.

He interlaced his fingers with hers, lifting her warm palm to his lips.

She sighed with pleasure and rested her head on his shoulder. "Do you think Mr. Bancroft was meeting this woman the night Dr. Franklin's wagon overturned?"

Daniel smiled. It was hard to distract Becca from a puzzle. "I forgot about the neighbor's party and the accident," he said. "You think Mr. Bancroft refused to tell us where he was that night to protect this woman's reputation? I don't see him as a chivalrous knight, but I suppose it is possible."

She stood with another sigh. "I best find you a meal."

Daniel smiled, "And a change of clothes."

Chapter Twenty

Becca and Daniel sat in the shade of a linden tree behind the mansion on a hot, windless afternoon. The servants had brought out a table and wrought iron chairs with their lacelike curves. Moisture beaded on the two cut crystal glasses of lemonade sitting on the table. Thin slices of cut lemons decorated the side of the glasses. Becca's account book sat there, too.

"I have a list." Becca dipped her quill pen into a pot of black ink and tapped it against the edge of the squat glass bottle.

"Of course you do." Daniel looked up from the *Journal de Paris*, the four-page French newspaper he read daily to improve his language skills.

"You can read without a headache?" Becca asked.

Daniel growled, retreating behind the newspaper.

"All right," she laughed. "I will stop asking how you feel." He had improved so much in the three days since the accident. There were moments now when she forgot how close she'd come to losing him.

"I have a list," she began again, "of all the things we do not know about Mr. Fenimore's death."

"I suppose that's all the entertainment I can expect today." Daniel folded the newspaper and set it down on the table.

"We do not know how he died." Becca lifted one finger.

"A lightning strike, according to your mother," Daniel said.

"But we do not know why or how he allowed himself to be tied to the lightning rod." Becca put a check next to the questions she'd written.

She lifted a second finger. "We don't know why he ran toward the perfume shop when he escaped the police." Becca would have gone to visit the shop two days ago but wasn't ready to leave Daniel's side then.

Daniel nodded.

A third finger. "Did Mr. Fenimore conjure the letter to Dr. Franklin, or is someone else involved?"

"Another question," Daniel said. "Mr. Fenimore was tied to the lightning rod with a rope. Where did the rope come from?"

Becca lifted her pen from the page. "Did the police leave it here?"

"I'll find out," he said.

A drop of her iridescent ink splashed onto the paper. "Patience Wright had a cut on her hand the morning we found Mr. Fenimore. She could have sliced her hand cutting a rope." Becca made a note. "But she was so upset when she found him dead. It doesn't make sense to think she killed him."

"Unless she saw the body and discovered that she didn't like thinking of herself as a murderer," Daniel said.

Becca made another note.

"What about Edward Bancroft?" he asked.

"I don't like the man. I wish he would leave Paris." She placed her pen in the ink bottle and sipped the tart cool lemonade.

"Don't be too hard on Mr. Bancroft. He is a doctor and a scientist, a well-known one at that. But he lives in Dr. Franklin's shadow. It has made him bitter, I think."

Becca thumbed through her account book and plucked a loose page from it. "I brought his love letter with me. There's something more to it, isn't there? There has to be."

Daniel tilted his head, staring at the lemon slice in his drink. He leaned forward, scooping up a handbell and ringing for a servant. He plucked the lemon slice from the drink, threw it in the air and caught it, then began to laugh.

The servant's face puckered with confusion at the request, but minutes later, he returned, carrying a tin lantern with a lit candle on a black lacquered tray.

"How did you learn this trick?" Becca stood over Daniel's shoulder,

123

watching as he lifted the conical lid.

"General Washington mentioned 'sympathetic ink' one night in Morristown. I waited until he'd left and asked Alexander Hamilton what the phrase meant. Ink that is invisible, he said. It is a way of sending secret messages, so long as the person receiving the note knows how to do this."

Daniel waved Mr. Bancroft's badly written love poem over the flame. He kept the expensive paper close enough to the candle to heat the note but not so close as to singe it. "This will work if the message is written in lemon juice. But there are other formulas." His voice faded. "We should know in a minute."

It was magic, Becca thought. Thin brown letters, spidery thin, one then the next, formed themselves into words between the lines of the poem. *A death here. Jude Fenimore. The Cathedral of Notre Dame.* Becca's name was mentioned. So were Daniel's, Hannah's, and Augusta's.

"What good news," Daniel drawled.

"I don't see anything good about it," Becca said. "Who was to receive the letter?"

"Not France," Daniel said. "Gabriel d'Aumont must have reported all of this to Versailles. Most likely, England. We can't be certain."

Becca swiveled to study the elegant white mansion with its soaring columns and high windows, its secrets, and its murder. "I wonder how often Mr. Bancroft reports on what is happening in this house."

"And I wonder if the message was meant for the person who played ground billiards with my head." Daniel blew out the candle and closed the lantern. "Dr. Franklin needs to know."

"Doctor Franklin is gone to Versailles," the servant outside the sitting room told them moments later. "No, I do not know when the good doctor will return. But Lady Augusta is asking for Mrs. Parcell," he reported. "She and Mrs. Hannah, they wonder about the perfume." The servant's face creased with confusion. "They would not tell me what it is about the perfume that requires your attention."

"You don't mind, do you?" Becca asked. "I know you meant to come to the perfume shop with us, but that was before your attack."

CHAPTER TWENTY

"Go," Daniel said. "I shall be as tame as a lamb here. And if Dr. Franklin returns, I'll wait until we can talk to him together to give him the news about Mr. Bancroft."

Chapter Twenty-One

Servants in red, blue, and black livery jockeyed for position, waiting for packages to be brought out from a backroom. Women in shimmering silk gowns and delicate lace wafted from one counter to another, lifting a pair of perfumed kid gloves here, a bottle of *eau de toilette* there.

Becca eyed the storm of activity that buffeted this jewel box of a perfume shop on the rue du Roule. How could Jude Fenimore possibly have hidden in a place like this?

A portly man with light brown hair sprinkled with gray applied face powder and dabs of rouge to a woman standing before him as if her face were a painted canvas. "This color would make you look ill at Versailles. It is meant only for the quality of light found in a garden." He shook his head. "I will not sell it to you."

A woman behind the counter held out her index finger to display a small black circle of taffeta to a customer who bent over the artificial beauty mark as if it held the secret to happiness. "Place this at the corner of your mouth, and the men will know you would like a kiss," the saleswoman instructed. "Or here by your eye if you merely wish to flirt."

Floor-to-ceiling mahogany shelves were filled with pomades, potions, and powders. The walls of the perfume shop were lacquered a luminous, pale blue that reminded Becca of the sky at first light.

She had no doubt that Jude had fled toward this store in particular when he ran from the Cathedral of Notre Dame. But the shopkeepers certainly would have barred his way if he'd attempted to enter this place. His clothes had been wet once he climbed back over the bridge and began to run. Where else could he have hidden? What drew him here?

She exhaled a frustrated breath. "I might as well be invisible," she said to Hannah and Augusta. No one, neither customer nor this shopkeeper, had looked at them in the half-hour or more since they'd arrived. She still needed to talk to the shopkeepers. "We could return when they are less busy."

"It won't make a difference when we arrive," Augusta answered. "They have decided we are not worthy."

"Worthy?" Hannah sputtered.

"Worth their attention. We are neither fashionable nor wealthy enough, it seems." Augusta raised her chin.

Becca swept her hand along the side of her day gown. It was four years old, practically new, and the finest dress she owned, even if its flower-and-stripe print seemed outdated compared to the complex, winding flower patterns the customers wore. Their bodices were much lower than hers, too. It was a miracle their breasts didn't spill out of their gowns whenever they leaned forward.

Becca hated the idea of making a scene. She hated even more making herself the center of attention. But she didn't see an alternative. "We may not be fashionable or wealthy, but we have one thing every French woman seems to want this year."

"What on earth is that?" Augusta asked.

"We have Benjamin Franklin," she turned to Hannah. "I know I promised not to call attention to ourselves. Do I have your permission?"

Hannah nodded cautiously.

Becca lifted her chin and spoke loudly enough to be heard throughout the room. "Dr. Benjamin Franklin assured us that this was the finest perfumery in Paris. I will be sorry to disabuse him of that notion."

Hannah translated softly to Lady Augusta.

The buzz of voices faded, and the whispers began. Dr. Franklin's name echoed throughout the room. The man who painted women's faces and the middle-aged woman behind the counter smiled at the Americans as if they hadn't ignored them for the last half hour. Customers stared with curiosity at the trio of American women.

"Well done. Now turn as if we're leaving," Augusta said.

Becca pivoted so quickly that she stepped on her hem.

Augusta took one of Becca's arms and Hannah the other, although whether their gesture was intended to ensure that she didn't fall on her face before reaching the door or to comfort her, Becca would never be certain.

The two shopkeepers materialized, blocking the path to the door. "It would be an honor to assist you today. I am Monsieur Fargeon and this is my wife." He bowed, still holding a cosmetic brush in one hand.

"We meant only to give you time to enjoy the wares before asking to assist you." Madame Fargeon curtsied. Her face was powdered a translucent white, and her hair was covered by a white mobcap with a red ribbon. She smelled of violets.

Becca, Hannah, and Augusta introduced themselves.

"Do you wish me to prepare something for Dr. Franklin?" Monsieur Fargeon asked.

"However did you guess?" Augusta asked.

Hannah coughed to suppress a grin.

"Is there a place we may talk privately?" Becca asked.

The Fargeons exchanged a look, the type of silent conversation long-married couples share, and madam nodded. "Émil and Renée can watch the store. I shall call them."

Moments later, the couple gestured the three Americans toward a narrow door at the rear of the store.

Bitter orange. Soft violet. Dignified rose. Calming lavender. Base notes of musk. A wall of scent embraced Becca as she crossed into the storeroom. She gagged. Augusta lifted a lacy handkerchief to her nose. Hannah gasped with delight.

"We have the finest scents in France," Madame Fargeon said.

The right side of the storeroom was lined with narrow worktables featuring bowls, pots, potions, funnels, bottles, and a rainbow of flower petals. Hannah swept past them, heading for the tables. The left side of the room held unpainted pine shelves overflowing with large and small boxes, gloves, fabric squares, and more bottles.

This was where monsieur created his perfumes, Becca surmised.

"What matter requires such privacy? Does Dr. Franklin wish me to create a perfume for him?" Fargeon's tone was light, but lines of concern crossed his forehead. He seemed to know that a request for a new perfume would not come in this manner.

His wife's gaze followed Hannah, who was inspecting every pot and bowl displayed on the tables along the wall. She lifted her head from a glass bowl, holding damp cotton balls and delicate white flower petals. "How did you find jasmine so early in the season? The petals open only at six p.m. and must be picked immediately."

"You know of it? It is delicate work." Fargeon's face lit with pleasure, or was it relief at the change in subject?

"Who does not know the jasmine that grows in your country?" Hannah lifted her hand to her heart. "It is remarkable."

"Do not flirt with my husband, madam, not while I stand before you." Madame Fargeon snarled.

Becca's hands twisted into fists. "Flirting? My mother is not...."

"My apologies." Hannah interrupted, dipping a small curtsy.

Had she been flirting? Becca studied her mother.

"I should have directed my flattery at both of you. What you have created is miraculous." Hannah shook her head in wonder. "I have never seen the like. You have hundreds of flowers and herbs. They are my business, too. I am a healer."

"There are times I also consider our perfumery a miracle. It is unmatched in France, which means it is unmatched in the world." Fargeon's chest expanded with pride.

Hannah lifted her face, her attention captured by other ingredients along the wall. "I smell apple, but not apple. What is it?" She peered into a reddish-brown clay pot and lifted a knob of some dark root. Her winged eyebrows rose. "Mandrake root? You use that in your perfumes?"

The Fargeons' attention was entirely on Hannah now. Becca scanned the workshop space. Jude could have slipped in through the door along the back wall. It led to an alley or a yard, she guessed. There was another door on the wall to her right. It was half open, and she spied stairs. They probably led to the couple's apartment. Would Jude have had the nerve to invade the Fargeons' home? If they were friends, he might have.

Monsieur Fargeon nodded. "But of course. The root lends a green freshness to a scent. Add some birch root, a bit of citrus bergamot…."

Madam interrupted, looking fondly at her husband. "You would share all our secrets to anyone who'll listen. And we must get back to our customers. The nobility is not known for patience." She pursed her lips into a tight smile.

Becca would thank Hannah later. Her interruption had relaxed the shopkeepers. Conversation would come easy now. She would start by assuming that Jude had stopped here. If he had, the couple might think she knew more than she actually did. "We are hoping you can tell us about Jude Fenimore and how you came to know him."

"Who is this Mr. Fenimore? We don't know anyone by that name, do we?" He spoke to his wife.

She shook her head.

Chapter Twenty-Two

"**M**adam. Monsieur. A servant has come for Princess Elizabeth's packages." A young woman with light brown hair severely pulled back beneath a mobcap slipped into the room. She wore a navy gown and a simple white apron.

"One moment, Renée," Madame Fargeon snapped.

The servant winced at the rebuke. She hovered near the door.

"Perhaps Mister Fenimore used another name here," Becca said. She didn't have much time left. The couple would want to get back to their store in moments. "He was this tall." She lifted her hand halfway up her forehead. "He had blond hair. A pleasant face. He was an American who lived in Paris. Did he come into your store a week ago? You would remember him. He'd fallen into the Seine. His clothes were wet."

"Why would I let a man like that into my store?" Madame Fargeon pushed back. "We would lose customers. Do you think I am stupid?"

"Of course not, madam." Becca kept her voice low and even. She was not here to fight. "Could he have stepped into this room without you knowing?"

"No one of that description came into our store. I would never have let them in," Madame Fargeon said. "I am sorry we cannot help."

"There was that one afternoon last week." Monsieur Fargeon rubbed the side of his nose as if it would improve his memory. "You begged me to come to church with you to pray for your aunt. We were gone two hours."

"That day, we left you and Émil in charge. Did you see a young man run through the store?" She asked Renée with amusement, as if the very idea was preposterous.

Becca supposed it was.

"Of course not, madam." Renée curtsied, then dragged the back of her wrist along her forehead. The servant's face was pale, which highlighted deep purple shadows beneath her wide-set green eyes.

"Of course not." Madame Fargeon said. "Is he dead, this Mr. Fenimore? Over and over, you speak of him in the past. You say, 'he was.' He 'had.'" She made the sign of the cross. "Am I right?"

From the corner of her eye, Becca watched the servant take one deep breath, a second. She swayed.

"I am afraid so, madam. He is dead," Becca said.

"Dead?" Renée whispered. Her knees buckled. She sank to the wood floor.

Hannah reached her first. Renée's navy skirt puddled below her knees, exposing knitted pink wool stockings with delicate embroidered flowers. Her eyes fluttered open by the time Becca reached her.

Renée struggled to stand, but Hannah gently pressed her shoulder to keep her seated. Augusta smoothed the young woman's skirt over her shins.

"That was your man, Renée? And you let him into our store?" Madame Fargeon's voice rose. "You lied to me?"

Renée shook her head again and again. "I would never. Not in the store." She paused. "Behind it."

Renée seemed little more than sixteen years of age. But Becca had never seen those exhausted shadows beneath the eyes of a child. Crouching near her now, Becca gauged that they were close in age, despite the servant's round cheeks and childlike, perfect skin.

Hannah twisted to Becca and Augusta. Speaking in English, she said, "It's not good for her to stand all day in such warm weather. She is with child."

"Mr. Fenimore's child?" Augusta asked.

"We don't know," Becca said. "She hid Jude behind the store, though." A twinge of sorrow tore through Becca. Three years of marriage to Philip without a single pregnancy proved she was barren. Her inability to bear a child hurt more now that she'd found the man she loved.

"Do you have cider or ale? Even water will do," Hannah called to the shopkeepers.

Monsieur Fargeon scooped a ladle of water from a clay pitcher on the wide-planked floor. He poured it into a chipped tea cup and passed it to Renée.

Hannah cupped her palm beneath the servant's shaking hands to steady her.

But Renée didn't drink. Her brown eyes spilled with tears. "I knew he would die soon. I expected it. It was the shock of hearing the worst had happened."

The fine hairs on the back of Becca's neck rose. If she had just learned of Daniel's death, would she have spoken her grief in soft, articulate sentences? No. She would have burst into flame until there was nothing left of her but ash or until she'd hardened into bitter salt like Lot's wife. Renée did neither. She wasn't surprised by the news. How did she know Jude Fenimore was going to die?

"I need your help." Becca pulled Augusta away from Renée. She didn't have much time.

"Whatever I can do, I will." The older woman reached for Becca's hand.

Across the room, Hannah's voice rose and fell. Renée answered in one syllable when she answered at all.

"Renée may not speak openly to us about Jude with her employer listening. I need the store owners to focus their attention on you while I talk to her."

"But what can I do?" Augusta's light eyebrows rose.

"I am certain the Fargeons would love to brag that English royalty purchases their perfumes."

"Royalty? Me?" Augusta released Becca's hand in surprise.

"Even at home, everyone calls you Lady Augusta."

"I am no longer English." Then Augusta's face softened. "I hardly remember the rules of decorum. Her voice trailed off. "But it might be...amusing."

Becca couldn't recall whether Philip's father had been fifty-seventh or seventy-fifth in line for the throne. Either way, he had gambled away his estate, died, and left Augusta and young Philip to deal with the consequences. They fled England just steps ahead of her husband's creditors.

"I'll tell the Fargeons that you only agreed to come to prove that French scents were much inferior to London perfumes," Becca cajoled.

"That is close enough to the truth." Augusta smiled, then transformed the grin into a pinched expression suggesting that she found little to her liking here. "There. I am ready. Also, tell them that the trunk containing all my cosmetics and powders was lost on the ship and that I require superior replacements."

"That is brilliant. Anything else, m'lady?" Becca curtsied.

"Just one thing. Tell them to send the bill to Dr. Franklin."

Becca clamped her lips together to suppress a smile.

By the time Becca referred to Augusta as *Lady* Augusta for the fifth time, mentioning for the third that the bill should be sent to Dr. Benjamin Franklin—*the* Dr. Benjamin Franklin—the Fargeons confessed that they had rarely seen as noble and elegant a lady as Augusta. They begged to show her their finest wares.

Madame Fargeon lingered for a moment. "Rest for a quarter hour, no longer, Renée," she cautioned, then slammed the door shut behind her.

"You knew that Mr. Fenimore would die? That is what you said?" Becca restarted the conversation.

Renée nodded. "He could hardly eat for a year. I saw the way his stomach grew, as if he were growing a baby. He said he spoke to the doctors who charge a lot of money, and there was nothing they could do. His stomach malady killed him." Her gaze traveled from Becca to Hannah, then back more quickly.

Hannah grabbed the cup as Renée's hand opened. "It wasn't his stomach. I can see in your faces." Renée scrambled to her feet. Red blotches bloomed across her neck. "What happened to him? Tell me."

"He was murdered, *ma petite*," Hannah said.

"How did he die?" Renée's hand went to her belly.

"Struck by lightning," Hannah added.

Renée's eyes filled with tears. "It was God's kindness, then, so my Jude wouldn't suffer any longer. That is not murder."

"Someone left him where he could be struck by lightning during a storm.

They meant him to die." Becca's stomach twisted at her lie of omission. She didn't say that they were looking for Jude's killer because she and Daniel were suspects in his murder. She didn't tell Renée that the murder occurred at Benjamin Franklin's home. Dr. Franklin wanted to keep his name out of this, if possible.

"Left him?" Two vertical lines formed between Renée's blue eyes. "What do you mean?"

"It seems he was not awake when it happened," Hannah said.

"Who are you?" Renée's face tightened with suspicion.

"We met Mr. Fenimore on board the ship from America," Becca said.

Renée's eyes widened. "Jude told me about three women on the ship. He said you were angels, you two and the lady. He told me that he rode with you and that he met Dr. Franklin. I did not know whether to believe him." She turned from Becca to Hannah. "What he said was true?"

"All of it," Hannah said.

The mistrust and doubt in Renée's eyes faded. "I will help, then."

Becca's shoulder muscles relaxed. Maybe they would still learn something more about Jude. "Mr. Fenimore told you he saw Dr. Franklin. Did he hate Dr. Franklin?"

"He never said."

"Did he tell you about writing any letters to Dr. Franklin?"

"No."

Becca was asking the wrong questions. "What did he tell you when he came to you last week stinking of the Seine River and running from the police?"

Renée closed her eyes for a moment as if to see the memory. "I know what you're thinking. I thought the same. A man like him couldn't care for someone like me. He knew so much. He was educated and kind. And me?" She shrugged. "He said I made him feel at peace. He said I didn't ask anything of him."

Her lips quivered, then tightened. "His health was worse when he came back to Paris. He talked of dying for the first time. On that day you ask about, he came to the back door.

"We met here, you know." Renée smiled for the first time. There was a small space between her two front teeth, which made her look even younger. "He was buying perfume for another woman and asked my opinion. No one asks my opinion here."

Becca didn't interrupt. Daniel had taught her that everyone had a story to tell if one gave them time to tell it.

"He said it would be better if I didn't know what he had done. He placed his hand on my stomach." Renée cupped her slightly rounded belly. "My Jude said he had found a way to take care of me even after he was gone. He said I would not have to worry about the babe. But that day you speak of…." Renée's voice filled with grief. She stopped to collect herself. "He told me that he had been blind to the harm."

"Blind to the harm? What did he mean?" Becca asked.

"I didn't know. He didn't say."

"Was there anything else?"

"He said he would make it right. 'I am not going to let it happen,' he said." Renée looked from one woman to the other. "That was all. It was the last time I saw him."

"Did he find a way to care for you?" Hannah asked softly.

Renée's gaze slipped left. "Perhaps."

The door to the shop squeaked open. "Renée. We need you now. Customers are waiting. Wipe your eyes and come." Madame Fargeon stood in the doorway.

"Can we speak to you again? There may be something Mr. Fenimore said, something you thought was of no importance, that could help us." Becca's words tumbled out.

"There was nothing else." Renée smoothed her skirt. She tucked a loose strand of blonde hair back into her cap, then wiped her eyes one last time with the back of her hand.

"We will meet you here." Becca walked her to the shop door.

"Not here. Madam doesn't like it. You can see that, yes?"

"Then where do you live? At least tell us that."

"I tell you only because you will not leave me alone, and I must work now."

Renée gave Becca an address. "Come to tell me who killed my man. That is all I want from you." She stepped back into the shop. Hannah and Becca followed.

Augusta and Monsieur Fargeon stood in the center of a flock of young women. He lifted his brush and bowed. Three of the women applauded.

Augusta was barely recognizable. The shop owner had transformed her, lightening her complexion, emphasizing her elegant bone structure and high cheekbones. She reminded Becca of the carved figurehead—the cool, stern wooden sculpture of a woman—on the bow of Captain Roberts's ship. She's meant to lead sailors to safety," he'd explained.

"You must use carmine such as this, a lighter rouge, during the day." Monsieur Fargeon instructed the crowd as he examined Augusta. His arm shot back. He lifted a jar of lotion on the counter behind him. "And do not forget the lotion of sweet almonds to remove the powder." He pantomimed the action of dipping a hand into the lotion, then rubbing his face.

The ladies murmured their appreciation. A few applauded.

Renée returned to her station behind one of the counters.

Augusta pointed to the jar and nodded.

Fargeon grinned and handed it to his wife, who wore an identical joyful expression.

No wonder the shop owners were joyful. At least twelve small wrapped boxes sat on the counter. Dr. Franklin was not going to be happy when he received their bill.

Finally, Fargeon handed Augusta a mirror. She lifted her chin, examining her reflection. "Do I look absolutely ridiculous?"

"You look lovely," Hannah said, and Becca nodded.

The Fargeons stood on the sidewalk and waved as the three Americans left, followed by two servants carrying thirteen boxes.

Their carriage was parked down the street, less than a block away. The women lifted their skirts to avoid the mud, garbage, and even more foul-smelling objects at the curb.

"Did you learn anything about French scents?" Hannah asked as they walked beneath the three- and four-story buildings on the street. They moved from sun to shadow.

"Only that several make me sneeze. But I made the acquaintance of a lovely woman. She speaks English, and she has invited me to visit her," Augusta said. "In fact, she has invited us all. She is especially curious about you, Becca."

"Who is she?" Why did Augusta sound nervous, Becca wondered.

"She is a princess, and she lives at Versailles."

"No. I am not going to Versailles. I will be awkward. I do not know their manners. I will embarrass Daniel. I will embarrass Dr. Franklin. It is out of the question."

"And I accepted her invitation to visit at the end of the week," Augusta said.

Becca increased her pace as if to outrun the invitation.

Chapter Twenty-Three

"It is out of the question," Becca repeated as they stepped from the carriage later that afternoon. "Not another word about the party," she begged Hannah and Augusta as they entered the great hall with its shining marble and stone.

"I think the saffron ballgown can be completed in time." Hannah leaned forward, past Becca, to talk to Augusta.

"I will find a hairdresser who can come the afternoon of the ball," Augusta answered. The two women took each other's arm and climbed the stairs together, heading toward their rooms. "Find us when you are done with Dr. Franklin," Augusta called.

"Or hide from you," Becca called back. "Any more talk about the party, and you may never see me again."

But Augusta was right about one thing, Becca admitted. She needed to find Dr. Franklin and Daniel to tell them what she'd learned from Renée. She followed the sound of familiar voices into the sitting room.

"There you are, Mrs. Parcell. You are in time for hot chocolate." Dr. Franklin raised a delicate white-and-gold porcelain cup to her. He sat across from Gabriel at a chess table in the center of the sitting room.

Franklin swept his free arm toward another table against the long wall. "Monsieur d'Aumont has brought us this treat. He whisked an egg into the drink, just the way the last king, Louis XV, preferred. You must stop spoiling us."

Gabriel merely smiled. The French official had visited each day since the attack on Daniel, bringing small gifts to entertain him. Cantal cheese from central France, which dated back to the ancient Gauls, he told them, and, now, the hot chocolate.

Finding kindness in the world was a rare thing, Becca knew, and it undid her in a way that confrontation and anger never could.

Daniel sat across from the two men. In green breeches, a green and yellow striped vest, and a starched white linen shirt, he was the picture of a French gentleman. After living this luxurious life here, could Daniel ever be happy returning to America?

He had been reading *The Wealth of Nations*, one of his favorite books, Becca knew. Now, he slid the book onto the nearby table where his hot chocolate waited. "Did you learn anything at the perfume shop?"

"Were you out seeking new gloves or scents? I hope you visited a reputable establishment." Gabriel studied Becca with amusement.

"Quite reputable. We met a princess." Becca stepped to the sideboard and poured herself a cup of chocolate from the silver pitcher.

"A princess? You must have gone to the perfumery on the rue du Roule," Gabriel said. "It is one of the queen's favorite establishments."

"The queen?" Becca's stomach dropped. Would the queen attend the party at Versailles? "I think it is Lady Augusta's new favorite place, too." She took a sip of the chocolate, savoring the complex, sweet flavors. She drifted over to Daniel's chair and whispered, "Did you mention Mr. Bancroft to Doctor Franklin?"

He shook his head. "I kept my promise."

Becca smiled with gratitude. Daniel hadn't told Dr. Franklin about Mr. Bancroft's love letter. He'd waited for Becca, as he'd promised. And Becca would add what she'd learned from Renée. Mr. Bancroft's connection to Jude seemed obvious to her now.

"We'll need some privacy, Monsieur d'Aumont, for a bit of business. I know you'll understand," Daniel said.

"Anything you can say to me, Monsieur d'Aumont can hear." Franklin frowned.

So did Becca. Dr. Franklin was as careless, it seemed, about who heard news as he was about who read his papers left on tables and chairs around the house.

When Daniel hesitated, Franklin pounded his fist on the chessboard. A small, white tower rattled and fell off its rectangle. "France would never have approved so many gifts and loans to America without Monsieur d'Aumont. We have no better friend in this country. Now, what is this business of yours that cannot wait?"

Daniel shrugged. "You are a cautious man, Dr. Franklin, and so am I. You asked me and Mrs. Parcell for a favor. You had some questions about the household."

"Just say what you mean, sir." Franklin paused. His eyes lit with understanding. "Ah. You have said what you mean."

Franklin had asked Daniel and Becca to share any evidence that members of the household were spying for the British.

"You found nothing. That is what you told me," Dr. Franklin said.

"That was true until the night I was attacked," Daniel answered. "I told you that I was following Mr. Bancroft. I didn't tell you that I saw Mr. Bancroft leave a letter in the ground. He hid it in a bottle. I retrieved it just as I was hit."

d'Aumont's chair creaked as he shifted. "It was dark. You are certain?"

"Yes." Daniel leaned forward, resting his elbows on his knees, clasping his hands together.

"Why didn't you tell me this the night it happened?" Franklin pushed away from the chess table.

"I didn't remember then," Daniel said.

"The note appeared to be a love letter. It was none of our business and certainly not worthy of bringing to your attention," Becca said.

"You tell us now. Why?" Franklin scowled.

"Because this morning, we discovered a note written in sympathetic ink between the lines of his love letter. You were at Versailles, or we would have told you then," Daniel said.

Franklin sank back into the chair.

d'Aumont threw his hands in the air. "Did I not tell you, Dr. Franklin? Have I not warned you about this man?"

Becca's chest tightened. She strode to the sitting room doors, yanked them shut, and whirled around. "You knew Mr. Bancroft was a spy, and you let him stay?"

"My enemies are right. I am too old for this work." Franklin raked his hand through his thinning gray hair. His voice was raspy. "I have known Mr. Bancroft for so long. I could not make myself believe you, Monsieur d'Aumont." He turned to Daniel. "That is why I asked you and Mrs. Parcell to study the household. I could not be objective."

A servant's footsteps clattered on the hallway's marble tile. Outside the window, a crow called *kraw-kraw*.

Finally, Franklin sniffed, then turned to Becca. His cheeks were flushed, his eyes cold. "What did the message say?"

"It described Jude Fenimore's death on the roof," she answered. "It mentioned me and Mr. Alloway."

Franklin turned his attention back to the chessboard.

Becca waited for an outburst, for Dr. Franklin to demand to see Mr. Bancroft. Instead, he placed the white chess piece that had fallen back on its square.

"Aren't you going to send Mr. Bancroft home or have him arrested?" Becca demanded.

"Of course not." Franklin moved a pawn. "Enemies can be as useful as friends."

"Enemies can kill," Becca said.

"Will one of you gentlemen explain to Mrs. Parcell?"

Daniel grimaced. "Dr. Franklin will make sure Mr. Bancroft finds more information to report, but it will not be accurate."

"He will change a number, a date, on some official-looking paper that he will leave on his desk," Gabriel added. Mr. Bancroft will pass along the misinformation on troop strength in Virginia, perhaps a ship's location, a plan of attack. None of it will be true."

"Who will receive the information?" Becca asked. "England?"

"Most likely England," d'Aumont said. "Maybe it will go to the Dutch or the Austrians."

Franklin slid the tower forward on the chessboard. d'Aumont contemplated his move. Daniel picked up *The Wealth of Nations*.

Pressure squeezed Becca's chest. They were speaking of lies, murder, and spies. How could they be so calm? Was something wrong with them or with her? Perhaps this news would rattle them enough to do something.

"Mr. Bancroft's crimes extend beyond spying to murder." She had their attention. "Jude Fenimore said that he hadn't understood the harm in the days before he died. "He said 'he would make it right,' and that, 'he was not going to let it happen.' He came here to warn someone. Jude arrives here and is killed. Who else but Mr. Bancroft could be guilty?"

The three men spoke at once. "Warn who?" "When?" "How do you know?"

Becca described her conversation with Renée at the perfume shop. "'Tis obvious that Mr. Bancroft is part of this scheme, whatever is intended by it. He is a spy. He must have killed Jude Fenimore the night of the lightning storm to stop him from warning one of us."

"Warn us about what?" Daniel asked.

Becca didn't have an answer.

Monsieur d'Aumont shivered. "I was here the morning you discovered Mr. Fenimore's body. I did not see anything amiss."

Nothing amiss but murder, Becca thought.

Franklin seemed to be sleeping. With eyes closed, he said, "The fact that Mr. Bancroft is a spy does not make him a killer."

"You defend him?" Daniel asked with surprise. "Because he is your friend?"

"Was. He was my friend." Franklin stood. "I suspected, but I couldn't make myself believe," he murmured. "You will forgive me, Monsieur d'Aumont, for leaving before we complete our match. I find that I am tired." He shuffled to the door, seemingly years older than when he welcomed Becca to the room.

"I almost forgot," Daniel called. "Becca and I were thinking of spending a day in Bougival with a merchant friend. Has your carriage been repaired, Dr. Franklin? Might we borrow it tomorrow?"

This was the first Becca had heard of the trip or the friend. Daniel barely shook his head in her direction, but it was enough. She sat back in her chair to the extent her stays allowed. She would seek an explanation when they were alone.

"No. I'm afraid the carriage is still at the neighbor's. It should be ready soon." At the entryway, Franklin turned a last time. "They are coming closer, aren't they, Mrs. Parcell? Mr. Fenimore's death, then the attack on Mr. Alloway."

In a fluid motion, Gabriel d'Aumont stood and strode to Daniel. "My friend." His sharp features softened. "I am sorry you are caught up in this matter." His gaze slid to the door, as if to assure himself that no one stood listening in the hallway. "I can arrange to have the police look the other way if you and Mrs. Parcell wish to voyage home."

"Mrs. Parcell will go," Daniel answered. "I have goods on a ship leaving from Le Havre in a month." He turned to Becca. "You will be on that ship."

"I think not." Her voice rose with surprise and hurt.

He raised one finger as if to count. "We'll never be able to marry in France. The magistrate swore to prevent it. I'll come back for you as soon as I can."

He raised two more fingers. "I have already been attacked, and another man—Jude Fenimore—has been killed here.

"More important. *Most* important...." He pointed at Becca. "I will worry about you every moment until we leave this place." Daniel's slightly down-turned eyes filled with grief. "Thank the Lord we are not married."

Thank the Lord. The sentence didn't register for a moment. Then, her heart fractured into a thousand sharp pieces. She wondered whether Daniel had heard the sound. "Yes, thank the Lord." She slammed the cup of chocolate on the side table so hard that its contents spilled. "This is how you tell me that you don't wish to marry me? You thank the Lord that it's not possible for us to wed?" She would not cry. Not here. She clamped her lips shut.

Heels clacked in the hallway. A giggle. A second voice *shushing* the other. How many servants had passed by outside the room? How many had heard her outburst?

"I did not intend to cause a lover's quarrel." Gabriel's hand rose to his heart as he stood. "Consider my offer, *mon ami.* You will be coming to Versailles in two days, yes?" He turned from Becca to Daniel.

Daniel nodded. Becca drifted away, turning her back on both men. Her limbs were stiff with anger.

"We will continue our discussion at Versailles," d'Aumont said. The door softly clicked shut behind her.

"I shall return home to Morristown," she said. What had just happened? How had her life changed course in the space of a breath?

"Quite sensible." Daniel's smile was approving. "Tell everyone that you will be going home. It will be best if we say that we have come to our senses and realized that we will not suit," he said as they were discussing an unwanted dinner invitation.

She stood, her limbs wooden and clumsy. If she ever made the mistake of falling in love again, she would force herself to recall these words: *Thank the Lord we are not married.* She couldn't catch her breath.

"Becca?" Daniel sounded confused.

But she would never make the mistake of falling in love again. Of that, she was certain. She strode to the door and flung it open.

He shot across the room, blocking her exit. "What is it?" He took her hand, and she shook it off.

Her eyes filled. "You are an addlepated blunderbuss. A muttonhead. A, a clodpate. And I am, too, for thinking you meant...."

He kicked the heavy door shut, then drew her into his arms. His kiss was fierce, and she returned it, despite everything.

"Only for your safety," he whispered into her ear. "You couldn't think I mean to break our engagement." He pulled back. His forehead furrowed. "How could you believe that?"

"Because you said so." Numbers were so much easier to understand than words, she thought, not for the first time. Numbers were exact. They meant the same thing every time. Words could mean almost anything or nothing at all.

You said it was a blessing we weren't married." She poked him in the chest. "You said we'd tell everyone we don't suit. How am I to know when you don't mean what you say?" She poked him again.

He grabbed her hand. "Of course we suit. What does it matter if we don't get married here? I wasn't certain you'd even arrive to marry me until your ship docked in Nantes."

"You weren't certain? You didn't tell me," Becca said.

"How many times did you decline my proposals of marriage?"

"I didn't count," Becca admitted. She never thought to marry again. Never *wanted* to marry again.

"You count the clouds in the sky but didn't bother counting my proposals?" His hand rose to his chest in mock reproof. He pulled her away from the door. "Jude's murderer is one of us, one of the people living here. Perhaps Mr. Bancroft. Perhaps not. He or she will guess that you and I share confidences. They'll guess your questions are intended to find them out. That makes you as much his target as I am."

"And I am just as capable as you of protecting myself." She placed her hand on his chest.

"You might be more capable." He acknowledged, sweeping his arm round her back.

He was right. She was more capable, given her skills with knife and gun. But Becca didn't think it was the time to point that out, not when she was losing herself in his arms.

"I still think you, Hannah, and Augusta should return to America." His warm breath against her cheek made her shiver. "But for now, you should be safer if everyone thinks you want nothing to do with me, that you have discovered I am a rapscallion."

"That you have behaved badly." She echoed his thought. "And so everything you said?"

"How could you think I didn't want to marry you?"

She would consider his question later. She had assumed he was pushing her away, as if that were bound to happen. But for now, she leaned forward and lifted her lips to his, a quick, warm kiss. He tasted of chocolate.

"Let us make sure the entire household hears of our broken engagement," Daniel said.

"Shall I start?"

"Ladies first." He nodded.

Becca cleared her throat, then roared, "I meant every word. You have deceived me from the moment I landed in France. Perhaps from the first day we met."

"Well done," Daniel whispered. "Now, my turn."

He bellowed, "I am not responsible for your assumptions, Mrs. Parcell. We are not wedded, and if there are other women...." Caressing the line of her jaw, Daniel whispered, "There will never be other women." His voice rose again. "If there are other women, you have no call to chastise me."

"How will we meet if we are so estranged?" Becca whispered.

"There's still the door between our two rooms." He swept one finger along her bottom lip. "We'll meet after dark as we do now." He paused. "Shall I deliver the final *coup de grace*?" He opened the door to the front hall. "There is only one way to make this right. I ask you to release me from our engagement."

On the stairs, footsteps slowed, then stopped.

"I do." This was not how she expected to say *I do*. "I do release you. Nothing would make me happier."

Words had power. Daniel was play-acting, but a sudden sadness settled over her, as if speaking of a broken engagement could attract bad luck.

His half smile reflected her foreboding. In a loud, angry voice, he added, "As soon as I can acquire tickets for you, Hannah, and Lady Augusta, I will see you safely away from here."

He leaned in and whispered, "I mean that about the tickets. I need to know you are safe. I want you on the first ship sailing from here." His kiss was quick, and then he was gone. His voice echoed in the hall as he muttered a sprinkling of French curse words.

Shouldn't she be relieved, Becca wondered. She *was* relieved that Daniel's feelings were as steadfast as her own. But she wouldn't be dismissed for her own safety, not by Benjamin Franklin and not by Daniel Alloway. She stormed from the room.

A male servant passed her near the staircase. She nodded, ignoring his doleful look of pity. It wouldn't take long for the entire house to learn of her fight with Daniel.

Fine. Her spine straightened as she climbed the stairs. All she and Daniel needed to do was find Jude's killer. Then, somehow, they would marry. And if playing the humiliated, embarrassed former fiancé of Daniel Alloway helped her get answers, all the better. She was not leaving.

Chapter Twenty-Four

Becca contemplated the leftover bites of tender beef in red wine on her plate. She had asked to have the midday meal brought to her bedroom, as if she were too distraught to bear other's company. She'd forced herself to leave more behind on her plate than she ate.

She didn't understand how some women lost their appetite at the slightest upset. Strong emotion had the opposite effect on her. She swirled the last piece of crusty bread through the beef gravy and popped it into her mouth before sliding the silver tray to the side of her bedroom desk. She hoped the servants would spread the word that Mrs. Parcell was so upset that she hardly touched her meal.

Augusta and Hannah were spreading the word, too. They had burst into her room within an hour of her *faux* fight with Daniel yesterday.

"Tell me it isn't true," Hannah had said.

Augusta's hand had risen to her mouth. "Oh, Rebecca, I never would have thought Mr. Alloway could betray you. I knew we never should have come to this awful country. We shall all leave immediately."

Becca had reached for their hands. "You must not hate Mr. Alloway. I can explain." And she had.

Now, Becca scanned the list of Dr. Franklin's guests she'd penned in her ledger. She added notes about Mr. Bancroft's love letter and continued down the list. She was most curious about Patience Wright, whose heart seemed to have been broken by Jude Fenimore. With her quill pen, she placed a checkmark next to Patience's name before closing the book and leaving the room.

Becca turned left into the far hallway, interrupting two servants. Both held stacks of newly dried sheets that still smelled of sunshine and fresh air. One was blonde with hair rigidly pulled back beneath a starched white cap. The other was a redhead with curls as unruly as Becca's. She could have sworn she heard them whisper Daniel's name.

The blonde servant blushed. The redhead stared at Becca with eyes wide. "Can you tell me how to find Patience Wright's studio? I have not been there before."

The red-headed servant pointed down the hall, lifting three fingers as if to say, "Count three doors."

The two girls' whispers followed her. Good. They *had* been gossiping about her and Daniel. Word was spreading. She would be free to snoop as much as she wanted without raising suspicion, at least for a few days. The entire household would assume that her attention was entirely consumed by her estrangement from Daniel.

The third door on the left, like all the others, was bordered by rectangles of gold-painted molding. Becca's fist rose to knock, then fell limp by her side. Just beyond Patience's studio was the door that led to the roof. Becca recognized it. She had raced there just days ago to find Jude's body tied to the lightning rod.

She turned away, rapping on the studio door once, twice. Becca held her breath, listening. The hall was silent. So was the studio.

She slipped into the room, and her hand rose to her chest. The walls were filled with rough sketches of Jude. Slashes of black chalk. Lines of red paint. There were images in profile and full face. His features were little more in some drawings than a suggested line or circle. But all seemed to stare at her. A few painted canvases with his image in heavier paint lined the floor.

The slashing lines suggested speed, anger, and obsession. If Jude hadn't already been killed, Becca would have suspected Patience of wishing him dead. *Only wishing?* The door to the roof was so close to the artist's studio. She could have met Jude there without anyone noticing. Becca inhaled the sharp scent of linseed oil.

And then? Patience seemed strong enough to have lifted Jude.

Becca scanned the rest of the room. She expected it to be similar to hers. It wasn't. The bedroom furniture had been replaced with a few chairs, a red velvet settee in one corner, and a wooden box near the north-facing window, just large enough to hold the partially-finished bust of Dr. Franklin.

The white wax sculpture shone in the afternoon light, and Dr. Franklin's sightless eyes seemed to follow her round the room. Becca stooped to study the first canvas. Her striped gown pooled round her as her mind focused on the puzzle of Patience Wright. The artist had appeared outraged when Daniel showed her the handkerchief bearing Renée's initial. But what if Patience were play-acting? What if she already knew that her former love had taken up with another woman?

Becca inched over, studying another painted image of Jude. She pulled it forward to peek behind at a second, smaller canvas and found herself staring into the painted eyes of Daniel's friend, Gabriel d'Aumont. She stood, holding the smaller canvas up to the cool light of a north-facing window.

Patience might be a renowned sculptress, but she also had a real talent for painting. She had captured Gabriel's sharp chin and slightly-too-long nose. There was humor and calculation in his gaze, the same expression Becca had noted on more than one occasion. Patience had painted him with his chin slightly lifted, emphasizing an arrogance that reminded Becca of Alexander Hamilton.

Becca had detested Mr. Hamilton, at least at first. She smiled at the memory. They were friends now.

The sound of footsteps just outside the door snapped Becca's attention back to the present. It was too late to leave, and there was no place to hide.

"Do not think too much," Daniel would whisper if he were here. "Especially when there is no time."

As the door opened, she slipped the portrait of Gabriel behind one canvas and picked up another.

"What are you doing here?" Patience's voice was angry.

Becca held up the portrait of Jude. "Are all men like your Jude Fenimore?" she asked, as if she and Patience were continuing a conversation about men who strayed. "I think they are all alike."

"I asked what you are doing here." Patience stepped toward Becca, who placed the portrait back where she'd found it.

She wanted both hands free, not that she expected the artist to attack her. "Are you the only one in the household who hasn't heard?"

Patience's thin eyebrows rose. For the first time, she saw compassion in the woman's expression. The sculptress reached Becca in four steps and patted her awkwardly on the shoulder. "You poor dear."

Becca forced herself not to flinch. Her broken engagement was practically old news, it seemed. Everyone knew.

"Is that why you came to find me? For comfort?" Patience asked.

Tell as much truth as you can when you lie, Daniel had taught her. "We have not been friends, Mrs. Wright. I don't expect comfort from you." That was the truth. "And that is precisely why I came."

Patience's close-set eyes widened with surprise.

"The last thing I need is someone who will smother me in comfort and make me cry."

"You have your pride," Patience said with approval.

"Apparently, that is all I have now," Becca said bitterly.

Patience's laughter was jarring. She headed to a cabinet on the far wall. "One must keep men at a safe distance. But I am no expert in defining what distance is safe. We shall be friends now, m'dear."

Some women only extended friendship to those whose hardships matched their own, Becca thought. Patience Wright was one of those women.

The artist removed two rounded goblets and swept a half-filled bottle from one of the cabinet shelves. "Here. This will soften the harsh words I hear Mr. Alloway threw at you." She poured amber-colored Madeira into one and then the other glass.

Becca took the tumbler from Patience's outstretched hand. She turned from one side of the studio to the other as if examining the sketches for the first time. "You must have loved him very much." Whatever Patience felt for Jude, it wasn't love.

"I thought I loved him, then I thought I hated him." She looked shrewdly at Becca. "You will feel the same about your Mr. Alloway."

"I have had enough of love," Becca lied. She swallowed a larger sip of Madeira than she intended. It was sweet and burned her throat. She would love Daniel until the day she died. This was as unchanging as the fact that two plus two equaled four.

"The only cure for love is more love, or at least the illusion of love." Patience's gaze skittered to the painted image of Gabriel d'Aumont.

"You and he?" Becca hoped her shock wasn't evident. "Monsieur d'Aumont?" That would explain why the Frenchman seemed to practically live here.

"Why? Do you want to try him out?"

Becca gasped at the coarse question.

"He is fine in his way, but not as lively as your Mr. Fenimore, God rest his soul."

Becca widened her eyes. Daniel had taught her this trick when she wanted to appear most credible. "But could you tell he was a man who could betray the people he loved? Did you know at the start?"

Patience's expression settled into sadness. "He was a man of impulses. He said 'yes' to every opportunity that arose. He said yes' to me, and 'yes' to the next woman, 'yes' to one business and to the next. And he was always short of funds." The artist shook her head, turning to Becca. "Do not think he was evil. I never saw evil in him."

Had Jude said "yes" to someone who offered him cash in exchange for playing the role of the 'man with the red rose'? Was that how he'd found money to take care of Renée?

"Then who would do this to him?" Becca didn't mention the macabre manner of Jude Fenimore's death. She didn't need to. Patience had seen him on the roof.

Patience shook her head.

"Who tied him to the lightning rod? You must wonder," Becca prodded.

"I must wonder, must I?" Patience tilted her head. "Are you wondering whether I killed Jude? I did not, but I could have. When I've given my heart, being lied to makes me angry." Patience seemed carved from stone, all hard angles. "If I killed Jude. I would have stood close enough to watch his face until he understood what I was about to do, and then I would shoot him. But no, I did not kill him." The artist threw her head back and swallowed, finishing the Madeira.

Becca winced. She imagined each sketch of Jude begging for mercy.

Pity was the only emotion Becca felt now. But Patience was not a woman who would want sympathy. The most compassionate thing Becca could do was answer in kind with a tone as icy as the artist's. "Well, Mrs. Wright, 'tis obvious you had nothing to do with Mr. Fenimore's death."

Becca lifted her chin as she had seen Lady Augusta do countless times. "I do not relish the idea of living in the same house as a murderer." She forced her forehead to furrow. "Surely, not Mr. Bancroft? He and Dr. Franklin are such old friends."

Her questions about the murder were too pointed. Best to act the part of the heartbroken former fiancé. "My apologies. Now, I sound like Mr. Alloway. He pays no attention to me." Becca swallowed hard. "If this is what our marriage would be like, I am better off. He spends the day asking questions to which no one has answers. 'Tis a horrible habit."

Patience strolled to the bust of Dr. Franklin in the center of the room, tilting her head one way, then the other as she inspected her work. "Well, Mr. Alloway is not asking about the servants."

Becca lifted the glass to her lips to hide her surprise. "How could any of the servants know Mr. Fenimore?"

Patience plucked one of the wooden-handled blades from the table. "Ask Michael the baker."

"Why should I bother?" Patience was teasing her, drawing out the story for her own amusement. Becca didn't appreciate it.

"Something woke me in the middle of the night before we found Mr. Fenimore." Patience squinted, then peeled a minuscule shard of wax from Franklin's left earlobe with the blade. "I was to begin sculpting Dr. Franklin the next morning."

"And?" Becca pressed her nails into her palms to hide her impatience. Becca knew—everyone in the household knew—that Dr. Franklin had been sitting for Patience Wright when they looked up and saw Jude's body on the roof.

"A noise. There was something. It was not the storm that woke me. This was before the thunder began. Sometimes, it is hopeless to go back to sleep. You will see when you are older, Mrs. Parcell. Then, I will get out of bed and draw or go to the kitchen. When I return, sometimes then I fall asleep.

"That night, I got up and lit a candle. I decided to go to the kitchen for some bread and cheese." Patience stepped away from the bust and frowned, judging her work. "I was barefoot. When I neared the kitchen, I heard Michael's voice."

"You recognized his voice?" Becca asked with surprise. "How often have you heard him speak?"

"Often enough. He was angry. Loud. He was speaking to someone else."

"You heard them both?"

Patience shook her head. "The other voice was too soft. But Michael would yell, then pause and yell again. Perhaps he was talking to a woman." Patience studied Becca with the same intensity she'd shown the sculpture.

"What was Michael saying?" Becca asked.

"To stop coming by. That he didn't want to do business anymore."

Becca tried to make sense of it, tried to imagine how and why Jude Fenimore and Michael Corbin could have known each other. Had Jude paid Michael for information about Dr. Franklin?

"Did you hear anything else?"

Patience shook her head. "I took a few steps back. I don't like sneaks. I cleared my throat and must have scared them away. That's what I intended, at least."

"Why didn't you mention this to anyone after Mr. Fenimore was killed?"

"It didn't seem to matter." Patience picked up another tool and smoothed Dr. Franklin's wax nose. "And then, of course, there is your mother."

A pulse beat beneath Becca's right eye. She waited for more. When the artist didn't continue, Becca crossed the room and set her glass on the cabinet with a thump. She wouldn't be Patience's cat's paw. The woman would have to find someone else to torture. "Thank you for your hospitality. I am afraid

I must go."

"Your mother, Mrs. Parcell." Patience whirled, her eyes curious. "Your mother and Michael. I have heard the two of them come and go on their way to the roof. I've heard both of them as clearly as if they came through my door."

"That's ridiculous." Becca's hands tightened into fists. Her mother and Michael seeking privacy on the roof? "Even if your story is true, it proves nothing. Whatever unhappiness you need to spill out into the world, Mrs. Wright, keep away from my mother."

"Ridiculous, am I? I told no one about Michael out of respect for Mrs. Hannah." The artist shoved her arm toward Becca. Where there had been a bandage before, now there was a faint reddish-brown scar about two inches long. "I never asked. She came to me with a salve for the cut on my arm.

"But now?" Patience swerved past Becca. "At the window, she craned her neck, smiled with satisfaction, and pointed far to the right. "Oh, my. I didn't know the servants were permitted to have picnics on the grounds. And isn't your mother having a grand time."

Becca wouldn't give Patience the pleasure of seeing her ruffled. She slow-walked her way to the window, then stretched her neck and peered down. On the grounds, at the far edge of the house, her mother, Michael, three dark-haired women and one man sat talking on a large blanket. Michael clapped the man on his back. Hannah threw her head back and laughed at something one of the women said.

Becca's lungs emptied of air. When had she last seen her mother so happy?

"I tell you this out of friendship, Mrs. Parcell. Warn your mother to stay away from the baker." Patience called as Becca flew down the stairs, her footsteps echoing in the massive hall.

She stuttered to a stop at the sight of Lady Augusta in the back hall.

Augusta shot away from her perch before a small, square window. She blushed as if she'd been caught eavesdropping. Which she had.

Augusta grabbed her arm as Becca reached for the door latch. "You knew about them? Hannah told you about Michael?"

It was true then. Michael and her mother. "Why do you know about

CHAPTER TWENTY-FOUR

Michael and I don't?"

"It isn't like that, Becca," Augusta said.

Becca shook off Augusta's arm and slammed the back door open.

Chapter Twenty-Five

Thin poplar trees swayed in the yard. Leaves rustled on the branches of the oaks. The wind was rising, and the air smelled fresh and alive. A thunderstorm was coming. Becca strode toward the lawn party, swiping away a strand of hair blown loose by a sudden gust.

Hannah, Michael, and their guests sat at the northwest end of the property, out of sight of the road. Their delighted voices carried on the breeze.

Michael and Hannah saw her and climbed to their feet. The four strangers stood, too, seeming to drink in the sight of her.

Hannah stepped forward, her face joyful. "Come. Here is good news. Meet your family."

"Family?" Becca stepped forward cautiously. The three women had the same black, unruly hair as Hannah. The same dark, winged eyebrows. Similar broad, high cheekbones. The three could have been cousins.

Becca glanced at her mother. Not three cousins, four. She touched her own cheekbones. Five. Becca's smile grew as large as her mother's. Two years ago, she had been a recent widow with no family, other than Lady Augusta. Now, she was a woman with a mother and so much more.

The new relatives spoke at once, introducing themselves and naming an ocean of nieces, nephews, cousins, and great-great-grandparents. A great aunt had been a healer like Hannah. A third cousin didn't bear a child until the ancient age of thirty. A nephew had moved to South Carolina. "Is that close to Morristown?" one asked. They spoke so swiftly that Becca had trouble following.

"Michael arranged this all," Hannah said. She and Michael shared a look that left no doubt of their affection.

"How did you manage it?" Becca asked him. Curse Patience Wright. Because instead of enjoying her new family, Becca was also wondering whether Michael had talked to Jude the night he died. She couldn't make herself believe that Michael would hurt her mother.

"Simple. A friend from our village works nearby. He was going home. I ask him to tell everyone about you and Mrs. Hannah. Of course, they come to meet you. You are family."

A man who would go to such lengths to bring a family together could not possibly be a murderer. Becca tried to reassure herself. Whatever Patience thought she'd heard had nothing to do with Jude's murder. *Hannah is safe with him. He would never hurt her.*

"It is a shame that they cannot stay long," Hannah said. "Despicable, really."

Becca's smile dimmed. "What is despicable?"

"Didn't you tell her?" the man, her cousin Sebastien, asked Michael.

"The police still look for us. We hear this from friends," Michael said.

"Whatever happened was long ago. The police can't still be chasing you," Becca argued.

Sebastien and Michael exchanged a furtive glance.

"It was long ago, wasn't it?" Becca asked slowly.

Both men avoided her gaze.

"Your country's freedom is what we seek for ourselves," Sebastien said. "The nobles take and take. And what does the king give us? More taxes. If he won't give us what we need, then we must act."

"You cannot speak thus," another cousin cut him off.

"We spread the word of freedom. Mostly, that is all we do," Michael said.

"Talk changes nothing. Talk is not enough." Sebastian's mouth settled into a grim line.

"You shouldn't have come if it is not safe for you," Becca said. In America, revolution was patriotism. Here, it was treason. Hannah needed to stay away from Michael.

"Of course, we came. You are family," one said. The others nodded.

"Where will you stay tonight?" Becca asked.

"We have a wagon," a cousin said.

"And a tent and food," said another.

"And the best desserts in all of France." The third woman looked fondly at Michael. They all laughed.

A sudden chill swept away the last dappled bit of blue sky. The birds grew silent. The first cool drops of rain smacked Becca's shoulder.

One of the cousins folded the blanket quickly. Another scooped up the battered picnic basket. The women brushed off their skirts.

The cousins bestowed quick kisses on Hannah's cheeks, then Becca's.

"Why not stay here? Cook will be happy to give you a meal. At least you will be dry." Becca hated saying goodbye so soon.

"Such a kind offer." One of the cousins curtseyed. "We are safer in the woods. We shall return for a longer visit tomorrow." They jogged toward their wagon, half hidden within the grove of oaks.

Becca turned to Michael. "Isn't it safe here?"

"French officials arrive at Passy at any time of the day or night. I do not call that safe."

"Are you speaking of Monsieur d'Aumont?" Becca swiped a few droplets of rain from her brow with the back of her hand. "He is not a *gendarme*. And he is the mildest of men. He is a friend of liberty."

"He is a friend of liberty who works with the police and protects the king." Michael watched his friends climb into their cart.

Sebastien took the reins and clicked his tongue twice. The horses pulled forward.

Michael, Becca, and Hannah dashed to the back door as the light mist thickened to a steady downpour.

Michael bowed to Hannah. "You should enter the house without me."

She should return to America without you before her heart is broken. "Thank you for bringing our cousins." Becca curtsied. What could this kind, sweet criminal offer her mother? Heartbreak, was all.

Michael nodded with a shy smile, then strode away.

Becca dashed after him. "I heard you had an argument the night Jude Fenimore was killed." She'd almost forgotten Patience Wright's accusation.

"I am in the kitchen early, before it is light every morning. We argue all the time there." He quickened his pace.

"No, not before dawn. In the middle of the night." Becca lifted the front of her skirt. It was soaked now, and she didn't want to trip on the hem. "A different argument in the kitchen. Before the thunderstorm." She ran to keep up.

"I don't recall," Michael said.

"You said 'stop coming by,' and you 'didn't want to do business anymore.' What did you mean?" Becca slid on a patch of mud near the kitchen door.

Michael caught her arm. "You think I have something to do with Mr. Fenimore's death? Is this why you ask? I never see him in life. I swear that to you." His wide mouth curved into a scowl. "Or you are looking for reasons to prove I am not good enough to court your mother? I know that I do not deserve her." He flung the kitchen door open, stepped through, and slammed it shut.

That had gone even worse than she expected. Becca retraced her steps and found Hannah and Augusta waiting for her inside the back door.

Pots clanged and rang in the nearby kitchen. The cook's voice rose in complaint about a fire not tended well enough. The scent of chicken cooking in white wine perfumed the hall. For now, the three women seemed to be alone.

Augusta held out an embroidered cotton towel. Becca pulled her soaked mobcap off and dabbed at her forehead. She was soaked to the skin.

"Why didn't you tell me about Michael?" she asked her mother.

"I meant to tell you that we were growing close." Hannah flushed. "But the time was never right, not with Mr. Fenimore's death and the attack on Mr. Alloway. Not with the magistrate refusing to let you marry or our adventure at the perfume shop."

"And you would have noticed," Augusta said, "if you weren't so distracted." She gestured for Becca to lean forward and whispered, "Mr. Alloway asks to see you. He says it is important. Go to his room when you can. He says he will wait."

* * *

Becca held her arms straight out as the maids pinned and tied her into a dry gown. Petticoats, then stays. A stomacher, then a bodice. She eyed the connecting door that joined her bedroom to Daniel's. How much longer would this take?

"Shall I dress your hair, too," the blonde maid assessed Becca's loose, damp hair as the redheaded maid scooped up her wet clothes.

"I am sorry to have made more work for you. You have done more than enough, both of you." Becca exhaled with relief as their footsteps faded down the hall. She slipped into Daniel's room.

He sat in a yellow upholstered chair by the window and rose when Becca entered. There was no lace at his wrist, no brightly-colored embroidered jacket today. He wore a simple linen shirt, navy wool breeches, and leather shoes without buckles.

The rain had passed quickly. The afternoon sun streamed into the room.

"What's happened?" She wondered whether her expression was as grim as Daniel's.

He brought his index finger to his lips. "Whispers only. We have broken our engagement, after all. Someone might overhear us."

"Making believe I hate you is wretchedly hard. I don't like it."

At least that drew a smile. Daniel pulled Becca onto his lap, his arm around her back, her arm around his neck. She placed a line of kisses along the side of his jaw but pulled away when he didn't respond. "Is it that serious?"

"Doctor Franklin told us that his broken carriage was still at the neighbor's house. They insist on fixing it."

Becca nodded. "That was gracious of them. It wasn't their fault, even if the accident happened on the way home from their party."

"There are too many coincidences. The bribery letter. Jude's death. The attack on me. And Doctor Franklin's carriage. It is all of a piece, at least it seems so to me." Daniel said. "Too many coincidences means that none are coincidences."

"Which means you wanted to examine the carriage." Becca kissed Daniel

162

quickly before removing herself to a matching chair near the window. "Did you call on the neighbors?"

"In a manner of speaking. I called on their stable hands this morning. But first, I went looking for Michael."

"Why?" Michael again. Becca bit her bottom lip to stop herself from interrupting with her own news about the baker.

"I thought he might know servants in the other great houses in town. I told him what I wanted, and I asked him if I could use his name as an introduction. I went straight to the stables instead of the entrance." Daniel's lips curved into a lopsided smile. "I changed into my old clothes. They mark me as a tradesman at best. I fit in at the stables."

"I like your old clothes," Becca said. "They mark you as an American."

Daniel shrugged and continued. "Having Michael's name was the key. The stable hands grew up with him, they told me."

"That is what I heard, too," Becca said.

"What you heard?" Daniel's eyebrows rose in surprise.

"Just a while ago from Michael. I will explain, but not until you've finished."

Daniel nodded. "The stable hands are fixing Dr. Franklin's carriage. One of them told me what they found. The carriage's rear axle was cut. Sawed. Just enough to let Dr. Franklin begin the ride home that night. But any single bump would crack it and did. It was no accident."

"You are certain?"

"Yes. The carriage is parked behind the stables. They pointed the damage out to me. I saw it."

"Dr. Franklin could have been killed." Pressure built in Becca's chest as if she'd heard a brown bear roar, ready to attack.

Daniel nodded.

"But why doesn't Dr. Franklin know about the damage?"

"The servants are afraid to tell their master. They think they'll be blamed for the act." Daniel paused. "You knew that Michael's friends worked at the great house nearby. How?"

"He told me." Becca recounted how the baker's friends had played a part in bringing her newly discovered cousins here today.

163

"That's wonderful," Daniel grinned. "Your family is growing by the month."

Becca combed both hands through her still-damp black hair.

"Meeting family is wonderful, isn't it?"

"It is. But I do not trust Michael, though I wish I could."

"Is it something he's said? Something he's done?"

She shook her head. "Michael fought with someone in the kitchen late the night Jude was killed just before the thunderstorm. Patience told me she heard the argument."

"She would know if she heard Jude's voice," Daniel said. "Was she certain he was fighting with Michael?"

"No. She said Michael was loud enough that she recognized his voice. The other man spoke too softly to hear. I asked Michael about it. He claimed not to remember the fight."

"The timing of the fight makes you question his actions," Daniel said.

Becca nodded. "The timing and that he is so close-lipped about it now."

"It could have been about anything, and there is still nothing to show that Michael ever met Jude Fenimore," Daniel said.

"That is true." Becca sighed.

"You're worried for Hannah," Daniel said.

She nodded. "I don't want my mother hurt. What if Michael and Jude were working together and fought?"

"He practically worships American independence," Daniel said. "Michael would never hurt Dr. Franklin."

"What if he thought that Jude was going to hurt Dr. Franklin? How far would Michael go to stop it?" Becca asked.

They were both silent.

"Will you tell Dr. Franklin that his carriage accident was no accident?" Becca asked.

"You mean, the attempt on his life? Yes, I will." Daniel's jaw tightened.

"And the truth about us? Will you tell him that we still plan to wed?"

He hesitated.

"You don't trust Dr. Franklin? I can see that you don't."

"I trust him with large secrets," Daniel said. "Matters of state. Questions about the war. But I won't trust him with secrets about you. Those are the most important of all."

She yanked him forward. He tumbled into the chair, squeezing next to her, and that ended their conversation.

Chapter Twenty-Six

"Y ou called for me, Dr. Franklin?" Daniel strode into the library the next afternoon in a foul mood. He'd returned from a long morning with one of Mr. Barnes's customers to find his room empty.

The servants had transferred all his clothes, papers, and goods to a new bedroom far from Becca's. The baby-faced butler had the decency to look pained. "Dr. Franklin ordered the move," he'd said. Daniel supposed his host wanted to maintain the proprieties now that his betrothal to Becca was supposedly ended.

God's blood, he missed her already. The connecting door between the two bedrooms made their false separation easier to bear.

Franklin sat behind an elegant white desk with fine curved legs. It was weighted down with a mountain of papers, some so old that their edges had curled. A wide window behind him displayed the lawn at the rear of the house.

Not for the first time, Daniel wished that Franklin would lock away his correspondence instead of leaving it out for anyone to read.

"Am I late? I apologize." Becca floated into the room. She wore her blue-and-white striped day dress with light blue slippers and froze at the sight of Daniel. "Please excuse me. I didn't mean to interrupt. I can return later."

What was Franklin doing bringing the two of them together? Daniel tensed even as he admired Becca's playacting.

"I apologize for calling you both here," Franklin began. "I know it must be uncomfortable. But we thought it best to free you both from the obligation we imposed on you to find Mr. Fenimore's killer."

166

We? Franklin never spoke with the royal 'we.' His decisions were his alone.

"That will allow you, Mr. Alloway, to spend your last days in France finishing up your business for your employer, Mr. Barnes. And you, Mrs. Parcell. You will have all the time to prepare for the party at Versailles tomorrow."

"Preparing for a ball at Versailles is a full-time job," Gabriel d'Aumont bowed to Becca.

Daniel whirled. Gabriel and a familiar-looking stranger rose from an overstuffed red silk couch in the shadowy far end of the room.

The stranger wore a serviceable navy blue coat with a border of simple white embroidery and a matching vest and breeches. He studied them in silence.

Daniel wore navy as well. But his jacket was of dark blue silk with a gold ribbon border. For a moment, he was jealous of the man's simpler clothing.

"I didn't recognize you without your uniform," Daniel said. "You were at the Cathedral of Notre Dame to arrest Mr. Fenimore. You were here the day that we found him on the roof, too."

Gabriel interpreted for the officer. He nodded with a tight smile.

"May I introduce Captain Charron of the Paris Police Prefecture," Gabriel said.

Captain Charron had the austere features of a monk and a thick lower lip that suggested perpetual disappointment. His jet-black eyebrows set into a straight line at the sight of Becca.

Gabriel listened to the captain's French. "He says it is a pleasure to formally meet you."

Franklin's eyes slid to Gabriel, then back. "We thought...*I* thought that it was time to bring in the Paris police, since you will both be leaving for home soon."

"I haven't agreed to leave France." Daniel widened his stance. What game were they playing?

"The police will continue the investigation of Mr. Fenimore's unfortunate death. It would be best if you would pass along whatever you have learned," Franklin said.

"You said we couldn't leave because we were suspects." Becca crossed her arms.

"I should never have urged Dr. Franklin to involve you and Mrs. Parcell in this." Gabriel opened his arms to them. "I should have insisted from the start that the Paris police take on the unfortunate matter of Mr. Fenimore's death. *Pardon.* And no one is or will question your innocence. Do not worry."

Gabriel was an assistant minister in the French government; at least, that was his title. How did he have the power to order the police to do—or not do—anything, Daniel asked himself.

"They are the largest police force of any city in the world, and they employ more than three hundred spies." Gabriel's chest expanded as if he were responsible for all three hundred.

Why bring up spies, Daniel wondered.

"They are more than capable of discretion," Gabriel continued.

"You said the opposite about the police when you asked for assistance," Daniel said. This was no conversation. Franklin and Gabriel had decided Becca and Daniel needed to leave the country. Gabriel had merely suggested they leave other night. Now, they were being ordered to go. It made no sense to him, which only meant that Daniel was missing some important piece of information that would explain their decision.

"Let us begin with your observations of the residents and servants," Dr. Franklin said to Daniel.

He launched into a description of the little he and Becca had learned. "Is there more?" Daniel asked Becca. But she'd turned her back to him and closed the distance to the window. He saw nothing there other than the lush green lawn and a small herb garden.

Captain Charron whispered to Gabriel, who shrugged, then nodded. "Captain Charron asks where you were born, Madame Parcell."

"What does that matter?" Becca stepped toward the window.

"She is American." Daniel tensed. Why the question?

"It would be best to answer." There was steel beneath Gabriel's gentle tone.

"I was born in the colony of New Jersey," Becca called back, distracted.

CHAPTER TWENTY-SIX

The yard still held her attention.

Daniel saw it then. A large shape, slightly darker than the shadowy forest, was just visible in the thick copse of trees at the edge of the property.

"You mentioned the baker. His name is Michael?" Gabriel asked.

"Yes." A week ago, even an hour ago, Daniel would have answered with more than one word. He would have teased Gabriel for his faulty memory. Because the Frenchman knew Michael's name. Gabriel had offered him a job in the kitchen at Versailles, Michael had said. Why was Gabriel making believe he didn't know Michael now?

"And your mother, Mrs. Parcell, she speaks to this Michael often?"

"We all talk to Michael." Becca's expression remained placid, but Daniel practically saw sparks of tension radiate from her.

"Would you care to tell us what this is about, Dr. Franklin?" Daniel asked. Why was Gabriel gathering information about Michael?

Franklin nodded to Gabriel.

"We have been looking for this man calling himself Michael for a long time," Gabriel said. "His baking is what gives him away. As soon as word spreads of the miraculous pastries in another province, we hunt for him, and he moves on. He urges rebellion everywhere."

"Zadkiel." The captain spat the name.

Gabriel nodded. "This Michael goes by the name of Zadkiel, the archangel of freedom and mercy. He travels from one province to the next, telling farmers not to pay taxes to the king."

"Some people don't have enough money for all the taxes." Daniel kept his voice mild.

"The government raises taxes each time the king loans America money to beat the English. Would you have me protest?" Gabriel's answer was sharp.

This was how America's revolution began, Daniel knew: an argument with a different king over taxes. He heard the imaginary hiss of a cannon's quick match as if the sound already filled the room. The explosion would come here in France as it had in America. Not now, but soon.

"We come for Zadkiel," the captain said.

Becca whirled to face the captain as if to tell him what she thought of him.

169

That would not end well for Becca. Daniel interrupted. "Dr. Franklin, as the American ambassador to France, all members of this household are under your protection and our government's. Isn't that true?" Daniel didn't know whether that was case, but it sounded as if it should be.

"Now, Gabriel, my friend." Franklin's tone was pleasant, but his hands lay fisted on his desk. "Inform your colleague that the household is under my protection and the protection of the American government."

Gabriel tapped the captain on his wrist. The small signal was enough.

Charron stiffly sat back on the couch, glowering. The policeman's hands, like Franklin's, were fisted.

Daniel took a relieved breath. He wondered again how a mid-level government official like Gabriel d'Aumont had the power to call off a police captain. Whatever the answer, Daniel was grateful for it.

But the détente didn't last.

Charron sat forward, cursing under his breath. His attention careened from Becca to something he saw out the window.

Daniel followed his gaze. So did Becca, who gasped.

Hannah flew across the yard, aiming for a rough dark green wagon as it pulled from the woods into the early afternoon light. Michael, wearing his white chef's hat, followed more slowly.

A stocky, dark-haired man jumped from the driver's seat. He slapped Michael's back as the baker took the reins of the two horses from him. Becca's mother turned her face to Michael and laughed.

Charron sprang from his seat and ran from the room.

"You can't catch him," Daniel called to Becca, but she was gone, following the police officer.

Daniel scrambled past Franklin, shoving open the window. "Run. *Vite.* Quickly."

Michael jerked around, searching for the danger.

Daniel couldn't see Charron in the yard, but Michael didn't hesitate. He grasped Hannah by the waist and hoisted her into the wagon.

"Stop. *Arrêt.*" Charron's voice boomed in the yard.

Michael leaped into the driver's seat and cracked the reins. The dark-haired man jumped onto the other side of the driver's bench as the wagon pushed forward slowly, then more quickly, until the trees surrounded it, and they disappeared.

Charron sprinted toward the forest's edge, slowing as he reached the trees, as if he recognized he couldn't catch them. He leaned forward, hands on his knees. His back rose and fell with the effort to catch his breath.

At the window, Franklin, Gabriel, and Daniel contemplated the police officer.

"I don't think Captain Charron is going to be happy with me," Daniel said.

"Leave now, Monsieur d'Aumont." A breeze reached through the open window, ruffling thin strands of Franklin's gray hair. "Take your captain with you. You have made a terrible mistake bringing him here."

"Captain Charron is dedicated to the monarchy, as am I. I would do anything to preserve this nation." Gabriel stood at the window like a sea captain staring into a dangerous ocean instead of the great, deep woods behind the mansion.

"Of course, you would do anything for France, my friend." Franklin clapped d'Aumont on the back. "But you will leave my friends alone. Is that clear?"

"I will leave alone your friends, but not France's enemies. And Michael is no longer part of your household. He has run, and we will add kidnapping to the charges against him, since he has taken Mrs. Hannah."

Franklin exchanged glances with Daniel. By running, Michael had given up the protection of Dr. Franklin's household.

"I will discuss all of this with the captain, and I will see you at Versailles tomorrow." Another bow, and d'Aumont was gone.

Franklin sank into his leather chair as Becca burst back into the room. Her eyes were red. "How will you get my mother back?"

"I am certain your mother is safe enough for now," Franklin said.

"Safe enough? How safe is that?" Becca demanded.

Franklin gnawed on his bottom lip. "She is safe because Captain Charron and Gabriel d'Aumont are after Michael the baker, not your mother."

"Whose idea was sending us home?" Daniel asked.

"Yours." Franklin's eyes opened wide.

Daniel knew the trick. Franklin's expression was intended to add credibility to a half-truth. His throat tightened with anger. "The subject of traveling home came up the other night. There was no final decision."

"I thought it was a capital idea when Gabriel suggested it." Franklin shifted in his seat. You had been attacked. I worry for your safety." He turned to Becca. "And I think that you and Mrs. Parcell might reconcile without the strain of searching for Fenimore's killer."

"You have been attacked, too, Franklin. Or have you forgotten already?" Daniel had told Franklin last night that his carriage accident was intentional. "Are you ready to leave France, too?"

Franklin's neck turned a mottled red. "I may be leaving France whether or not I'm ready. I should hear in weeks whether I remain America's ambassador here."

Mourning doves cooed outside. Servants walked overhead.

Daniel pulled back his anger. "May we go now, sir?"

Franklin nodded. His scowl matched Daniel's

Augusta met them in the hallway outside Franklin's office. "I heard the commotion. Hannah is more resourceful than you give her credit for. And I doubt very much that Michael kidnapped her."

"He lifted her into the carriage as if she had no choice," Becca argued.

"As if she trusted him with her life." Augusta corrected.

Chapter Twenty-Seven

Blue stripes. Yellow flowers. Gleaming satins. If Becca couldn't fling rocks to satisfy her anger, dresses would do. She grabbed another armful of new gowns from hooks along the wall and flung them onto her desk chair and, then, her bed.

She should be out searching for her mother. But where would she begin? Where would she go? Becca was trapped here. Trapped in this room. She pulled open the weathered black trunk that sat at the foot of her bed, thankful that she'd resisted the servant's attempts to remove it.

"It is not pleasing to the eye," one maid explained. Well, it was pleasing to Becca's eye. It was plain and exactly what it appeared to be, unlike the rest of the mansion. Living within these painted, shining walls, Becca felt as if she had eaten too many sweets. Virtually every surface was decorated.

Good riddance. She scooped up a pair of silk stockings with flowers embroidered at their heel, threw them into the trunk, and stopped. She and Daniel would leave for home once they found her mother.

Becca flung a blue silk slipper into the trunk and heard a satisfying thump as it came to rest. What if Hannah wanted to stay? Of course, Hannah would come home to Morristown. Who would want to live here in a country at war with itself?

Never mind that, she told herself. As many Americans opposed independence as supported it, even after all these years of war. Especially after all these years. Becca threw the second slipper against the wall with even more force. A small plaster chip flew into the air.

Did Hannah go willingly with Michael or not? Michael saved Daniel the night of the attack. He brought Hannah's French family together to meet her. Could a kind man also be a killer? The question gave her a headache. She wanted clear answers, and there were none to be had.

Tossing clothes round the room was less soothing than she'd anticipated. So Becca settled herself at her desk, sweeping her arm across it to clear the surface. From a drawer, she pulled out her ledger, pen, and ink. The familiar activity brought her a rare moment of peace. She began with a column labeled 'Suspects.'

Michael. She underlined his name.

Loves America's fight for freedom. Hates the king. Would he kill to protect Dr. Franklin? Did he know Jude? Her pen hovered until a blotch of ink marred the page. *Does he love my mother?*

Becca pressed a blotting sheet to the smudge, then moved on to the next name, underlining *Patience Wright.* She raised her gaze to one of the tall windows, recalling how the artist's face had lit with joy the day they arrived with Jude, then the hatred when she saw the handkerchief with another woman's initials. Becca refilled her pen.

Loved and hated Mr. Fenimore. Did Patience lure him here to kill him? But how? Strong enough to lift him to the lightning rod and tie him there. What about Dr. Franklin's carriage accident? She lived in England for years and was beloved by all the gentry, even the king and queen. Is she here to hurt Dr. Franklin at the king's behest?

There was only one name to add: *Edward Bancroft.* Be fair. Be especially fair, because you do not like him. She took up the quill pen again.

A spy who is jealous of Dr. Franklin. Jealous enough to cause the carriage accident? Met Jude the day we arrived. Has lived in France for a while. Did he meet Jude earlier, before his trip to America?

Becca took a deep breath. Her rib cage pressed against the boned stays beneath her dress. She didn't have many answers. But making a list gave her the illusion that life was as well-ordered as the accounts she kept at home in her ledger. She loved a good list.

The sun had shifted, creating new shadows in the bedroom, darkening a corner of the floor strewn with stockings, highlighting the bed with its

174

mountain of gowns.

"You made this mess. You'll clean it up, missy." That's what Annie would have told her at home in Morristown. The thought put a small smile on her face. It would take Becca at least twice as long to return the objects to their hooks than it had to create this chaos. She might as well begin.

But standing by the desk, on impulse, she added one more name to the list of suspects: *Gabriel d'Aumont.*

Is he having an affair with Patience? Loves American independence and the French king. As talented a liar as Daniel. Why wait to bring the police to arrest Michael today when Monsieur d'Aumont already knew Michael was here?

That would have to be enough for now. It was time to straighten up.

"May I come in?" Augusta called. Her voice on the other side of the bedroom door was muffled.

"Of course," Becca called.

Daniel slipped through first.

Augusta's eyes lit with humor as she followed, whispering, "I haven't snuck into a bedroom like this since a weekend party in Mayfair before either of you were born."

"I think I know where to find Hannah," Daniel said.

"Where?" Becca's spirits lifted.

"The stables next door. Where else can he go safely for now? The police will be looking for him."

"Have you been there yet?"

"I shall go tonight. Come with me."

Becca closed the gap between them, then disentangled herself as Augusta cleared her throat.

* * *

Daniel waited for Becca at the back corner of the mansion's lawn. In the distance, a chorus of crickets sang, and the church bells rang the hour. Ten p.m.

Becca appeared moments later. Her tread was silent beneath the light of the waxing moon. He nodded, and they headed toward the neighbor's place.

"They could be anywhere," she whispered minutes later. "They could be on their way to the Swiss Confederacy for all we know."

Benjamin Franklin mentioned that mountainous country often enough. One of his grandsons was at school there, Daniel knew.

"Or they'll want to go to ground nearby until they know whether the police are blocking the roads to search for Michael," he said. "And he and your family know the stable hands."

"I only want my mother back," Becca said. They fell into silence again.

"There," Daniel said a while later. He recognized the long, narrow stable where he'd talked to the worried servants the other day.

A dark shape hurried toward the stables, holding a tray almost as wide as he or she was tall. Daniel could just make out the shape of a pitcher. It glistened in the light of the moon. But he was too far away to see whether the tray held food.

Daniel scanned the back of the house before stepping forward. The windows appeared dark and empty. Either the family had gone to sleep or was out at a party. He and Becca crept forward.

Two men separated themselves from the darkness of the building. One held a pitchfork, the other a scythe.

Daniel held his arms out to let them see that he carried no weapon.

Becca gasped, "Sebastien," then pulled up the front of her hem and ran.

Daniel approached more cautiously. They waited for him.

The taller, stouter stranger gestured to come round the far side of the building. Daniel and Becca followed, entering through a small door round the back of the stable. The sweet, earthy smell of a well-kept stable greeted them.

So did Michael, Hannah, and their three female cousins.

Daniel nodded at the man holding the dinner tray. He was one of the stable hands. They'd met when Daniel came to talk about Franklin's carriage.

Becca glared at Michael and rushed to her mother.

Michael placed a finger over his lips in warning.

"Eat first," Daniel whispered. "We'll talk after."

Yeasty bread, tangy cheeses, cold ham, and ale made up the late-night meal. After they ate, the cousins hugged Becca, then retreated. They spoke softly to each other as they made up beds comprised of piles of hay. A single candle cast a wobbly light on four sleeping horses in the five stalls.

Michael tore off another piece of bread. Without looking up, he said, "I thought I saw Captain Charron."

"So, it is true, what we heard?" Daniel sat next to him on the hay-covered floor.

"It depends on what you've heard." The baker shrugged.

"That you are the scourge of France and travel the country convincing peasants not to pay taxes," Becca said.

Michael flashed a smile. "I wish I were the scourge of the monarchy. But it is not too far from the truth. Did you know the nobility pay no taxes here?"

"Doesn't sound terribly noble," Daniel said.

"It is getting harder to hide." Michael gave Hannah a worried look. "I wish you had stayed behind. This isn't a safe life for you."

"You didn't force my mother to come with you?" Becca asked.

"He couldn't stop me." Hannah's smile was sad. "I cannot lose him so soon."

Becca's face tensed with trepidation, as if she foresaw her mother and Michael without a home, running from the police like foxes before hounds.

"But it's not Charron who worries you." Hannah reached for Michael's hand. "It is Monsieur d'Aumont."

Daniel's attention sharpened. d'Aumont had given the police officer orders. Even Dr. Franklin took the young man's advice. Who was he? "He's a pleasant enough fellow." Daniel leaned against the stable wall. "d'Aumont may have a secret or two. Who doesn't?"

Michael shredded the crust between his fingers as he spoke. "Would you be surprised to hear that d'Aumont has known for weeks that I go by Zadkiel?"

"Yes, I would be surprised," Daniel drawled. The more intrigued he was by a conversation, the less interested he appeared. Becca teased him about it on occasion.

"Do you recall the lemon and poppy seed pastry Michael made our first week with Dr. Franklin?" Hannah asked.

Becca and Daniel nodded.

"Monsieur d'Aumont told him he couldn't believe his luck that night, sitting at the table with us. He said that Michael's extraordinary creations are what gives him away each time he moves to a new province." Hannah smiled at the baker with pride.

"He did enjoy that lemon poppy tart," Michael said.

"Why didn't he have you arrested then?" Becca asked. "Why wait?"

"He offered to make the charge of treason go away." The baker's eyes were cold. "I would only need to provide the names of those who think as I do about our need to end the monarchy. I would be a spy." He spat the word as if it were a curse.

Becca and Daniel exchanged a quick glance. They had been spies, too, spies for liberty.

"Michael said no, of course," Hannah explained.

"Over and over, I say no."

Becca's eyes lit. "You had a fight the evening that Jude Fenimore was killed. Someone heard. Who did you fight with?"

"A fight?" Michael frowned. "Yes. That was the night I fought with Monsieur d'Aumont. I am in the kitchen early, even for me. He finds me there.. He says I must decide then and there to accept his offer or not." The baker waved his hand as if shooing away flies.

"Be a spy or be arrested. Before then, he would say, 'think about it. I will come back.' But that night, he says, 'you will tell me now your decision.' I say 'no.' You are there the day Monsieur d'Aumont and the captain come to take me."

"It is dangerous to be right in matters where established men are wrong," Daniel said. "That makes you a dangerous man."

"An American who quotes Voltaire?" Michael's smile brightened his face. "You yelled to warn me about the police. I am grateful to you forever, my friend." He reached out his left hand to Daniel, who shook it with his left.

The gesture cemented their friendship. Few people took Daniel's injury, his frozen right hand, into account with such ease.

The candle was worn to little more than a nub. Hannah's eyes were fluttering shut.

"And now you must go with your daughter," Michael said to Hannah.

She blinked herself awake. "I said I would stay with you. I meant it."

"You will become a criminal. You will be hunted as I am, and you will never be safe. Do you know what that will do to me?"

Hannah's eyes pooled with moisture.

Michael knew her well for the little time they'd spent together, Daniel thought. Becca's mother couldn't tolerate the idea that she was the source of pain in the people she loved.

Becca reached to hold her mother's hand. "Dr. Franklin says that anyone living in his household is safe from the police, even you. Michael. Can you come back when the police stop looking for you here?"

"Hannah and I were separated as children. We will never be apart again, will we, my dear? I will be back for you in days." Michael forced cheer into his voice.

"Of course you will. All will be well." Hannah didn't seem to notice the tears running down her cheeks.

Daniel tensed at the phrase. He was surprised to see it had the same effect on Becca.

They said their farewells and stood outside, giving Hannah and Michael a few minutes of privacy before leaving. Alone in the dark, Becca leaned against him, her back to his chest. "Will they ever see each other again, do you think?

"All will be well," Daniel said.

Becca twitched as if she'd been shot through with some of Dr. Franklin's electricity.

Chapter Twenty-Eight

The thought woke Becca in the early morning darkness. She nuzzled Daniel's neck. He stirred but didn't wake. She exhaled heat onto the sensitive skin between his ear and jawbone and waited. "We have been asking the wrong question."

"What?" Daniel's voice was muzzy with sleep. His eyes still closed, he scooped her into his arms. "Talk morning," by which he meant, she thought, "For the love of all that is holy, Becca, can't this wait 'til daylight?"

Daniel was right. There was nothing to be done now. She melted against him, letting herself savor the feel of his chest against her back. If he hadn't found his way to her room this evening, Becca told herself, she would have gone to him.

The grandfather clock struck two. His breath slowed.

Her mind raced.

His lips curved into a slight smile in sleep.

Wasn't he even the slightest bit curious about her conclusion? Her teeth clenched as the clock chimed the three o'clock hour. His breathing hitched once, then settled back into the slow rhythm of slumber. Becca's heel struck his anklebone. By mistake.

"Did I wake you?" She planted her palm on his warm skin. Perhaps her hand shook his hip. Just a bit. He stretched and reached for her. Her hand skimmed his rib cage.

"All right, how have we gone wrong?" he mumbled.

With the world reduced to the circumference of her four-poster bed, Becca said, "We have been asking which of the residents knew Jude? Who could have let him into the house secretly, then killed him?"

"Those are sensible questions." Daniel's hand caressed the curve of her back.

She purred. "We need to start with Jude and why he came here."

"Why what?" He traced kisses along her neck.

"Renée said that Jude wanted to warn someone. Was he here to warn the man that killed him or to warn Dr. Franklin?"

Daniel lifted his lips from her skin long enough to murmur, "Jude's lover. You intend to see her again."

"With you. Come with me." Becca said before a kiss ended the conversation.

Sometime later, the house still dark and quiet, Daniel rolled from the bed. "How are we to travel together when the household believes we are not on speaking terms?"

"I will request a cart to pick up last-minute things for the ball tonight." She'd had hours of wakefulness to devise a plan. "You can tell everyone that you have a business meeting in town. We shall meet at the perfumery where Renée works. We'll leave here separately. No one here will know we are meeting in Paris."

He kissed her one last time. "I will see you there at eleven." Then he was gone.

* * *

"And she hasn't come to work for two days?" Becca asked.

"Madam, I cannot do my best work if I am answering your questions." Monsieur Fargeon dabbed a powder puff at her cheek with a staccato tap.

This is how a tree must feel when a woodpecker attacks it, Becca decided. She coughed as the loose powder threatened to choke her. But agreeing to pay for the cosmetics Fargeon applied was the only way he would answer her questions. Daniel had retreated to the carriage once it was clear that Renée was missing.

His eyes gleamed with triumph. Fargeon grabbed the nearby hand mirror and held it up with a flourish. "I have not seen Renée since you were here, not for two days."

Becca didn't recognize the woman who stared back in the looking glass. Her face was snowy white. Her eyes were rimmed in black kohl, her cheekbones rounded by red circles of blush, and her lips brightened to a scarlet red. She raised her fingers to her jaw. The figure in the mirror raised her hand, too.

"Just a few more minutes, and I will be ready for you." Monsieur Fargeon called to three women waiting to be transformed by his magic.

The ball at Versailles was to begin before sunset, and the shop was mobbed.

Becca cleared her throat to call his attention back to her. "Did you or madam send someone to see if Renée was all right when she didn't come to work?"

"I worry about her, yes. But you see the crowd here?" He waited for Becca to scan the busy store.

"It has been like this for days, and without Renée, my wife and I can only leave here for a few minutes at a time." Monsieur Fargeon's hand hovered over the brushes on the nearby table. His long fingers plucked up a narrow one with fine bristles.

"Your eyebrows cannot disappear entirely," he murmured, dipping the brush into a pot of black, then mixing the pigment with brown from another pot.

The bristles tickled her skin. "Before Renée disappeared, did she say anything that surprised you? Did she act any differently?"

Monsieur opened a small box and scrutinized its contents, pulling out a quarter-moon-shaped beauty mark. He applied the same scrutiny to Becca. "Yes. This one is right for you. Renée did act differently. I've never heard her argue with my wife before, not until two days ago." A small, proud smile. "Few people argue with my wife."

"Do you know what the argument was about?" Becca inhaled the store's rich scents of violets, roses, jasmine, and musk.

Fargeon jutted his chin toward madam. She sat behind the counter, fenced in by customers. "You must ask her." He applied a spot of glue to the small black taffeta moon and applied it to her cheek. "You are perfection, Madame Parcell. You will be the talk of Versailles tonight."

"I certainly hope not." Becca thanked him and wove through the crowd toward Madame Fargeon.

"There was no argument." She shot her husband a disapproving look across the shop.

"Well, was there a disagreement with Renée?"

The confident, pugnacious madam aged in the course of a single breath. The lines on her forehead and those from nose to chin seemed etched more deeply. "I told her that she was a fool in her condition to give up her position. That no good could come of it. I said she was wrong, that whoever had given her this baby had left her. That there was no treasure."

Madame Fargeon's gaze swung to the new customer, then her husband. She stood on tiptoe to stretch across the counter and whispered. "Renée will be back soon. I know it. I have not told my husband that she has quit. I know I am very stern. Everyone thinks so. But I worry for her. Where can she go? I will save her position for another week."

"This treasure Renée spoke of," Becca prodded. A small bell at the front door chimed. From the corner of her eye, she watched two new customers enter the shop. "Did she say what this treasure was?"

The bell chimed again. Three more customers. Madam wouldn't give her more than another minute.

"Only that there was money and a secret. A young girl's fairy tale." Madam spun around as two women approached the counter. She smiled broadly, ignoring Becca. "How may I help you beautiful ladies?"

Becca burst from the store minutes later, muttering to herself. "A treasure. Of course, there is a treasure." Had she ever been young enough to believe that treasure existed and could change her life? She inhaled the much more pungent smell of the streets.

Becca counted seven carriages outside the shop. Their colors and markings differed, but all gleamed in the bright light of the day. Some drivers brushed their horses. Others set out water or feed pails.

Daniel leaned against the third carriage in the row, monitoring the entrance to the store. His eyes noted her presence but moved on.

She was only eight steps away when his eyes widened. He pushed himself away from the carriage and frowned. "What did they do to you?"

"Am I so horrible?" Becca lifted the bag of cosmetics she had purchased. "This was the only way I could convince the Fargeons to answer my questions.

"You are different." Daniel fumbled for words. "And beautiful. But you were beautiful before, and I don't know about this change."

Becca would have laughed if she was certain that her make-up wouldn't crease. "I was just as shocked when I first saw you in your fine French clothes. I felt as if I were seeing someone I didn't know."

"But I was still myself," he argued.

"And beneath this mask, so am I." Becca curtsied.

"Have you become accustomed to the clothing I wear?" Daniel lifted an arm. The lace at his wrist wafted in the breeze.

"No matter what costume you wear, I know you." She touched his chest lightly, where she thought his heart lay.

"And beneath those cosmetics, I trust that you are Becca." Daniel's grin was the one he saved just for her.

She allowed herself to enjoy the moment, then recounted what the Fargeons said about Renée. Finally, she said, "Too many people are being hurt. I'm worried."

"Renée gave you her address," Daniel said. "Do you have it with you?"

Chapter Twenty-Nine

"She's gone. Gone for days." The voice on the other side of the door was muffled.

The dark third-floor hallway smelled of mold and waste. There were days when the British prison hulk where Daniel had been imprisoned smelled just like this and days when it smelled worse. For a moment, he heard the boat creak, felt the rolling motion at anchor in New York Harbor. He steadied himself.

Becca touched his arm, her expression filled with concern.

Daniel nodded to her, shaking off the memories, then pointed to the stairs, as if to ask, "Should we leave?"

Becca shook her head.

Leaving would be the prudent thing to do. With Becca in her court make-up and Daniel in fine cotton clothing, they stood out in this neighborhood. They'd be marked for theft or worse. The sooner they returned to Franklin's mansion, the better.

But who was to say that the woman behind the door was telling the truth? Renée might be gone. She might not.

Even if Jude's lover thought she was safe and could care for a babe, a woman with child needed all the friends she could find. Everyone knew that, especially Daniel. Childbirth was the most dangerous moment of a woman's life.

He shallowed his breath, listening closely through the door.

He heard a bird trill, then a woman's sob. But the sound of her tears was gone so quickly that he wasn't certain he'd heard anything but his own memory. Was the woman who answered them standing on the other side of the door holding her own breath? Was she struggling to hear him?

"Can we talk to you then? We are friends of Renée, the best friends she could have."

Silence.

He wasn't ready to give up on the pregnant woman he'd never met. "Jude Fenimore would want to know Renée was taken care of."

The door protested with a squeak. It opened into a one-room apartment barely larger than a kitchen larder.

The young woman behind the door with light brown hair held a wooden stick in her right hand. Her left eye was swollen shut. Her cheekbone and jaw were a mottled mix of blue and purple, and she held her left arm against her side as if it hurt to move. She was alone.

"Renée? What happened?" Becca rushed through the door.

The woman raised the wooden stick, ready to strike. "I don't know you."

"I know I look different," Becca said. "Your Monsieur Fargeon had his way with me, or, at least, with my face."

Renée *hmmfed* and stepped back, allowing them entrance to the apartment. "You look like all the others now. I recognize you. Tell me what you came to say and go." She leaned the three-foot-long dowel against the wall.

A small yellow bird stared back at Daniel, ruffling its feathers in protest at the intrusion. It resided in a wire bird cage that hung near the only window.

A beige day gown, wet from waist to hem, hung from a hook on the back wall. A blanket the color of light tea was curled like a cat onto a lumpy straw-filled mattress. Low, uneven shelves teetered against the left wall. Another small table held a bowl with water for washing and a brush with a porcelain handle decorated with painted roses.

The elegant brush was so out of place that Daniel knew it must have been a gift from Jude or another admirer. Something drew his gaze back to the side of the bed. A reddish-brown bloodstain. Several bloodstains.

Becca noticed them, too. She took Renée's arm. "You should be sitting. When did it happen?" She pointed to the stains. "Was it because of whoever did this to you?"

It? What had happened?

Renée shook off Becca's arm as she sat on the bed, tugging her tired beige gown away from the blood. Her chin puckered with the effort not to cry.

"Are you all right?" Becca kneeled before the woman, raising her face to Renée.

"How could I be?"

"The baby?"

Renée wrapped her arms around her belly, rocking forward and back.

"Were you alone when it happened?" Becca whispered.

"You lost the baby," Daniel finally understood.

"The landlady heard me crying two days ago. She came." Renée's eyes pooled with tears.

Words came easily to Daniel, but he didn't speak now. There would be no comfort in telling Renée that it was God's will she'd lost the child or that there would be others, or that, as a woman alone, she was better off without a babe. Sentiments such as those could leave permanent scars. He still bore some of them from the misguided kindness of neighbors after the death of his wife and son.

"Who did this to you?" Daniel couldn't offer comfort, but he could promise justice. That might console her in the future. "If what happened to you was no accident, someone should pay for the harm they caused."

"Who are you?" Renée studied him.

"It's Jude's killer we're after," Daniel said after introducing himself. "Mrs. Parcell told you that, I know."

Becca yanked at the single small window in the room until it popped open. It was stiflingly hot. The room reeked of perspiration and the sharp scent of vinegar. That was vinegar, not water, in the bowl, Daniel realized. Vinegar to clean bloodstains from the miscarriage.

A small carafe of wine, a heel of stale bread, and two mugs without handles stood on a shelf. Daniel poured a half cup of the wine and brought it to Renée.

She gripped it with both hands, sipped, and exhaled. "An accident. I think an accident."

"When?" Becca asked.

"Two days ago."

Becca said that Renée had quit just two days ago. That left her with no reason to let the Fargeons know she was hurt.

"I walk home each night. This neighborhood is not a safe one. I think someone is following. A woman has that sense. Isn't that true, madam?"

"Women have that sense when they are paying attention," Becca agreed.

"I pay attention. But I did not see anyone paying attention to me." A shrug. "I hear footsteps running. Running footsteps do not alarm me. I hear them often enough. My neighborhood is full of beggars and thieves who find reasons to run. The Court of Miracles they call this place, this slum. Parisians have a sense of humor."

"But?" Daniel prodded.

"But this time, the running man pushed me. Did he bump into me by mistake? Did he shove me? I think one thing, then the other, monsieur." Renée gulped air, her chest rising and falling.

"Did you see him?" Daniel asked.

She shook her head. "I lose my footing. My arms go over my stomach, and so I cannot stop myself. Into the street, I fall and fall." She closed her eyes. "My cheek and shoulder hit the side of the carriage. The driver didn't stop."

"Do you remember anything about the man who pushed you? Daniel asked.

She kneaded her hands, staring down at them. "He was not tall, not like your man here."

"How do you know?" Becca asked.

"I do not know. I have a sense. A shape moving. Hands straight out to push, not reaching down at me."

Becca and Daniel exchanged another glance. That wasn't enough to help identify the man.

"Madame Fargeon said that you left your position. You quit," Becca said.

The bird sang again.

Tears leaked from Renée's eyes. "Jude promised to take care of me, and

he did. At least, he tried to. He left money for me and the baby in this box."
Renée pointed to the shelves. A small, narrow pine box sat open there.

"I crawled out of the street. I don't know how long it took. When I made
my way home, I found someone had been here. I hurt too much to clean
up their mess until this morning. They took the money Jude left me for the
baby. Now I have no baby, no money, and no work."

Daniel kept his thoughts to himself, not wanting to scare the injured
woman. He might, just might, believe that a man unthinkingly shoved Renée
into the street. But the attack had come with a side dish of robbery. Neither
event was random.

Three steps brought him to the shelves. The floorboards creaked with
each footfall. Daniel studied the narrow, empty wood box. Almost empty.
It contained a narrow, untied blue ribbon, the type used to keep currency or
letters neatly bound.

Daniel wondered where Jude had come by the money. Patience Wright
had said he was a gambler and always short of funds.

"The thief took Renée's money. Perhaps that was all he wanted." Becca
said doubtfully.

"On the same day, Renée is pushed into a speeding carriage?" Daniel asked.
"A fine coincidence. It is more likely that the thief pushed her to give himself
more time to arrive here and search for something. He took the money to
make this appear to be a simple theft."

"Or he pushed her because she knows something that is dangerous. But
what does Renée know?" Becca asked in English.

"Do you have family who can take you in for a while?" Becca switched to
French

Renée shook her head furiously.

"She can't stay here alone now," Becca said to Daniel.

"No." He studied the small yellow bird fluttering against the thin bars of
its cage. "Can you pack quickly?" he asked Renée.

"Pack?" She tightened her arms round herself. "To go? Go where?"

"To come with us." Daniel wondered what type of greeting they'd receive
at Passy, with Benjamin Franklin practically pushing them out the door.

Renée's stare combined pride, insult, and distrust. "To come with you? You want to take me to the place my Jude died? No, monsieur. I do not know you. I will not."

"To the perfume shop, then," Becca jumped in.

"Madam hates me."

"She does not hate you." Becca crouched next to Renée. "She is worried. She cares. She is holding your job for you."

"My job? How do you know?"

"She told me so this morning."

"You spoke to her?"

Becca nodded. "Madam will want you safe. Come with us to the perfume shop."

Renée's face brightened. "My bird. The box from Mr. Fenimore. I have little else. I will be ready in moments." She handed Daniel a square of cloth. "Alphonse will sleep if you place this over his cage, monsieur." Then she turned back, chatting with Becca and plucking a blouse from one hook, a skirt from another.

"You seem happy enough, Alphonse," Daniel said to the bird. "Any word on who broke in?" Alphonse turned his head left, right, and back. "No help there." Daniel shook the cloth out as his eyes skimmed the cage's base. He dropped the cloth and went still.

Becca's forehead creased. "What have you found?"

He pointed to the paper at the bottom of the cage.

"Oh, that," Renée swept her hand out as if shooing away a fly. "That is to keep the cage clean."

Daniel and Becca studied the yellow bird as it ruffled its feathers, expressing its indignation. Renée had ripped some paper to protect the bottom of the cage. One piece lay atop the other. Those were torn bits of English words at the bottom of a French bird's cage.

"Is that Mr. Fenimore's writing?" He pointed to the strips of paper.

Renée nodded. "Business letters, Jude tells me." She jutted her chin in the direction of the box he'd left her. "Under the money, there were letters." She shrugged. "He left a few folded under the money. He said to keep them there until he returned." Her voice caught. "I do not read English or French. And since my Jude won't need them, I put them to good use."

Daniel cocked his head to make out whatever words he could. But Renée had torn the pages vertically. His gaze skimmed down one strip, and he read: "*Red rose; me a thousand; one-third; not countenance.*" A second word strip read: *Notre Dame; more than; He works for;* and, *told him not.*"

"A confession?" Becca stepped forward, contemplating the paper.

"It mentions Notre Dame. But it's impossible to tell." Daniel switched to French. "Mademoiselle, did Mr. Fenimore talk more about these papers when he gave you the box?"

"How did you know?" Renée's eyes widened.

"Because the correspondence must have mattered to him a great deal if he gave it to the one person he trusted." It was flattery but also the truth.

She nodded. "He said that if anything happened to him and someone came for the papers, I should say that he could not go through with it. That is what he wanted people to know." Renée recited the words as if she'd carefully memorized them.

Becca hugged herself and switched to English. "What a reckless, foolish man. 'Tis one thing to risk his own life. But there is no excuse for risking Renée's. What if Jude's killer came asking for the letters?"

"Jude's killer probably did come. He pushed her into a carriage first to make sure she wouldn't interfere with his search." Daniel's voice was dry.

Renée raised her face to Daniel, then Becca. "Do you know what my Jude meant? I asked, but he wouldn't say. What couldn't he go through with?"

Daniel struggled to keep his frustration at bay. "May we take the letters? We'll return them." Perhaps the answer was there, protected by Alphonse.

Renée shrugged. "What do I care about letters with Jude gone? I can't even read them. Take the ones that are left."

Becca froze. "Left? There are others?"

"There were." Renée winced. Her hand rose to cover her stomach. "But when Alphonse dirties the paper, I do not leave them there, madam. I throw them out. Some letters are gone." She sank onto the bed, her voice growing faint. "I must sit now." Her pale skin shone with perspiration.

Becca rushed to the shelf. Lifting a chipped terra cotta pitcher, she poured a cup of cider and brought it to Renée. "We need to get her to Madame Fargeon," Becca called to Daniel. "The letters will have to wait."

She looked so pained by the thought of delay that Daniel almost laughed. But damn it, she was right. He swept the ragged paper strips into his broad hand, trying not to think about the souvenirs Alphonse might have left there.

Chapter Thirty

Renée sat with her head against the cushion, eyes closed, as the carriage swayed along the cobblestone streets. She shared the seat with Alphonse to one side and, to the other, a large, lumpy square of brown cloth knotted together at its ends containing her clothes and keepsakes.

Becca's hand covered the pile of paper they'd saved from the birdcage. "I hate to wake her now," she whispered. "But I have other questions."

"The poor bird," Daniel said.

"Alphonse?"

"No, I meant Renée," he said. "Wake her. We may not have another chance."

Becca touched Renée's knee.

The young woman came awake gasping. Becca wondered if she'd had a nightmare or forgotten for a moment where she was.

She waited to give Renée a moment to collect herself. "Did your Mr. Fenimore ever talk about Dr. Franklin?"

"He told me they met. I did not believe him at first. I told you that the day you came to the perfume shop. Sometimes my Jude exaggerated." Renée's smile was fond, as if she treasured even his faults now that he was gone.

"Mr. Fenimore was telling the truth. I was there." Becca hesitated. "Did he speak of anyone else he'd met at Dr. Franklin's house?"

"No. No one else." Renée angled her gaze toward the window, drinking in the view of narrow townhomes and shops. "I am happy you woke me. I have never ridden in a carriage before," she said shyly. "I feel like the queen of France."

"It is special, isn't it? I remember my first carriage ride, too," Becca said, and the two women smiled at each other.

The carriage swerved, and their driver growled a stream of curses at the coach lurching by them in the opposite direction.

Daniel asked. "Did Mr. Fenimore mention visiting Passy?"

"Oh, certainly." Her eyes focused on the passing streets. "He had business there. Three times he went." Her forehead creased. "Perhaps three."

"Who did he see?" Becca held her breath, waiting for the answer.

"I do not ask. It was business," Renée sniffed.

Becca wasn't surprised. Most women wouldn't think to ask men about their business.

"After he returned from Passy, did he tell you anything about his visits?" Daniel asked.

Becca gifted him with a small smile. "What did he tell you?" was a better question than "Who did he see."

Renée cocked her head. "After the first visit to Passy, he said he would be able to take care of me and the baby. He was excited, the way he used to be when he won *cavagnole*."

Becca looked sharply at Daniel for an explanation.

"A game of chance. Italian, I think," he said.

"Someone offered Jude the chance to earn money. It must have seemed simple. All he needed to do was stand at a certain spot in Notre Dame holding a red rose," Becca said. She turned back to Renée, switching from English to French. "What about the other meetings? Did Mr. Fenimore say anything to you after he returned?"

Renée's face darkened. "After the second meeting, he said his business partner had lied to him. He was a dangerous man who could not be crossed. He said he didn't have any choice. But he wouldn't tell me anything else. I remember that day."

"Why do you remember it," Daniel asked.

"Because it was the day I found Jude in the back of the perfume shop." Her lips tightened into a grimace. "He smelled like the Seine River, and his stockings were wet. His stomach pained him. I was scared for him. I begged him to stop whatever he was doing."

"How did you know he was returning from Passy?" Daniel said.

"He told me so."

Jude had lied to Renée, Becca thought. He had run from Notre Dame, not Passy.

"He said the Americans would not understand." Renée kneaded her hands together. "At the front of the store, there was a man who must have been chasing him. He pounded on the front door. He would not stop, and Émil—I work with Émil—said to lock the door. I left Jude in the back and ran to do as he said." Her gaze lifted to Daniel, then sharpened.

She lurched back, shimmying as far from him as she could. "That was you. I closed the shades in the store. I saw you. You were chasing my Jude. You were the one." Her eyes were wild with fear and anger. "You tricked me. Both of you tricked me." She rammed her shoulder against the carriage door. It swung open. Her possessions tumbled out. Renée dove to follow.

Becca lunged, catching Renée round her waist and pulling her back. "I'm sorry, I'm sorry," Becca repeated. "It wasn't a trick."

Alphonse batted his wings against the cage.

Renée batted her fists against Becca's shoulders. Becca held tight. Renée's punches were so weak they barely counted as an assault. The young woman burst into tears, twisting away from Becca.

"We didn't run after Jude to hurt him," Daniel said. "We ran to question him. And I told you the truth. We will find his killer."

The carriage rocked to a stop a few doors from the perfume shop.

Renée pushed away from Becca. "I do not trust either of you, and I need my things back before they are stolen." She wiped her eyes with the back of her hand.

Becca called to the driver and whispered the request when he jumped from his seat. He nodded with a scowl and jogged back the quarter mile to retrieve Renée's pack.

"You don't have to trust us," Daniel said. "You said that Jude went to Passy a third time. What did he say to you after that meeting?"

Renée exhaled an aggravated sigh.

"You will be rid of us soon enough. What did he say?" Becca hoped that Renée would be rid of them soon. What would they do if the Fargeons turned Renée away?

"Not after. Before. He talked to me before he went to Passy. He was calm. He said he was going to cut ties with his business partner, and it was for the best. What does this 'cut ties' mean?" She shrugged. It didn't seem to matter to her any longer. "He said, 'I know what I must do,'" Her eyes welled again with tears. "That was when he gave me the words to say if someone came looking for his letters. That he could not go through with it."

"And then he was killed," Daniel said in English.

"Because he was coming to warn someone at the mansion," Becca guessed, "about something that was planned but hasn't yet happened."

"Possibly," Daniel said. "But what was the warning, and who needed to receive it?"

"With each answer, the questions grow." Becca shook her head and leaped from the carriage.

Daniel stepped down, then raised his hand to assist Renée. She turned her back and waited for the driver to help her. The look she gave him would have sunk a frigate.

"Aren't you coming?" Becca called to Daniel.

He shook his head. "I'll stay here and try to make sense of Fenimore's notes."

Becca felt the same curiosity, the same tug to read the dead man's message. But Renée looked impossibly weak. "Oh, bullocks," Becca muttered. She took Alphonse and his cage from Daniel, then led Renée to the shop door.

* * *

Daniel watched until the shop door closed behind the two women. They were safe for now. He casually swiveled to take in the length of the entire street. A woman holding a straw basket waddled away from him, then turned a corner. A young boy kicked his way out of a butcher shop and threw the two pails of entrails he held onto the street. He leaped back to

196

avoid the splatter.

Daniel's gaze rose to the upper-story windows of the perfume shop and nearby buildings.

Staring back was the gray, grizzled woman he remembered.

He laughed with delight and bowed as deeply as he could, sweeping his arm forward and back as if greeting a member of the royal family.

The woman smiled a toothless grin in return before sticking her tongue out and slamming the window shut. She'd thrown a pail of slops at him the day he and Becca chased Fenimore from the Cathedral of Notre Dame. At least he'd stayed dry today.

Daniel contemplated the closed shutters and the woman who seemed to spend her day keeping track of the neighborhood.

The papers would have to wait. He climbed the worn wooden stairs three at a time to the top floor. The woman in the window stood in the doorway, a cleaver in her hand.

She lowered her weapon at the sight of him and grinned again.

Ten minutes later, he descended with a half slice of Madame Auclair's brioche, the slightly sweet egg-and-butter enriched bread he'd come to love in France. The old woman had insisted he needed a good woman to feed him.

Less tasty was the word picture she'd drawn of the man who followed Renée from the perfume shop the day she was attacked. The description was not detailed, but it supported Renée's story. "The hat was broad-brimmed. It was black." Madame Auclair scratched her nose. "Others walked by him. He was shorter than some and taller than others. So medium height."

"You see the people who walk into the perfume shop. Was he dressed like them? Was he well-to-do?"

She scratched the side of her jaw. "Now that you ask this, he was dressed well. He wore clothes with embroidery."

"You are brilliant, madam," Daniel said.

She blushed.

"Just one more question. Where was this man standing?"

"He was not hiding, not at first."

"Not at first? But he tried to hide while you could still see him?"

She nodded. "When that girl from the shop turned around, he jumped between two houses down the block. That is how I knew he was following her. I would have yelled. But she was too far already. I worried when I did not see her the last few days. I was glad to see her just now."

Back on the street, Daniel tipped his head back. There she was, the guardian of the street. Daniel blew a kiss, and Madame Auclair nodded like a queen.

In the shadowy coach, Daniel scooped up the paper strips and spread the narrow, torn sheets on the cushion as if they were a deck of cards.

He plucked one from the bunch with his good hand, testing its rough surface with thumb and index finger. Fenimore had employed a poor-quality paper for this last will and testament.

He lay the scraps out, moving one, then the next, to see where he could make words form. He had the impression that he was looking at pieces of separate pages, though most of the strips seemed to belong to a single page.

Letters became words as he joined the strips. Words became sentences. "Life is a cheat," Jude had written, "...a Game of Chance that we are Bound to Lose. I am Sorry for One Thing only, that I shall not Survive to see my Child. The Pain is worse, and I will not let the Doctors bleed me any longer. Their Cure weakens me...."

Daniel felt Fenimore's sorrow in each pen stroke. Becca was right. Jude believed he was dying. He had left behind a confession, a confession or an apology.

He kept reading: "But when I was offered money for a simple jest, how could I...." It ended there. What jest? Frustration tightened Daniel's shoulder muscles. There was more. There had to be.

The poor sod. Jude was dying. Someone offered him money to play a jest. It was an odd jest, certainly. Daniel imagined the conversation. "Go to Notre Dame and stand there with a red rose for an hour." The amount of time hardly mattered. In exchange, Daniel was certain, Fenimore was offered a large sum of money. And it was money he wanted for Renée and the baby.

Fenimore must have thought the police who surrounded him in the church were actors, too. When they bundled him out of Notre Dame, he must have been stunned, then scared. No wonder he ran.

Jude Fenimore wasn't a villain. He was a careless, impulsive man who'd trusted the future to take care of itself. But when he knew he was dying, he took on a job that gave him money to support Renée, the woman he loved, when he was gone.

But what job? And what threatened "harm" made Fenimore back away from his deal with the devil?

"Who did you come to see at Dr. Franklin's house? What made you climb to your death on the roof?" Daniel tossed the paper to the cushion in disgust. How much of Fenimore's confession had Renée discarded?

The day's heat pressed against him in the carriage. A litany of suffering had followed Franklin's receipt of that blasted bribery letter. Fenimore murdered. Franklin hurt in a sabotaged carriage. Renée's miscarriage. And the back of Daniel's head was still tender from the anonymous attack in the Tuileries Gardens. What had Jude Fenimore gotten himself into? What had they all gotten themselves into, and who would be next?

Daniel lifted the remaining scraps of paper and let them tumble to the cushion. Maybe he would be able to make out a few more words if he began again. He pushed one strip to the left, others to the top or the right, until a series of letters caught his attention–*klin*. Franklin. This had to be about Dr. Franklin. Daniel leaned forward, his fingers shifting paper with new urgency.

Minutes later, Becca exited the shop alone, her face lit with pleasure. "Success. The Fargeons are taking in Renée," she called as Daniel vaulted from the coach to escape the message he had just pieced together.

Chapter Thirty-One

"Nonsense." Dr. Franklin shoved Jude Fenimore's torn word strips back toward Daniel and Becca. "This proves nothing."

Daniel shuffled through the strips, plucking another one from the bouquet of paper and shaking it at Franklin. "Someone intends to kill you, and Jude Fenimore came to warn you. This proves it."

Daniel and Becca had barged into his study as soon as they arrived.

The vertically torn strip read:

Never intended
Trusted, and I trusted him
a thousand francs
Saw it all. But I will not
kill Benjamin Franklin, and I
I am no traitor.

"I am a dangerous man to trifle with," Franklin said. "I have the king's ear and the love of all of France. There is no one here—not one person—who would dare to harm me."

Daniel's temper rose with his voice. "Your carriage was sabotaged. Someone's already tried to kill you."

"And those with a connection to you have been harmed," Becca said. "The man with the red rose is dead. The attacks all lead back to you and to the letter you showed us."

"The letter?" Franklin shifted, moving an inkwell an inch or two, straightening a pile of papers.

"The letter attempting to bribe you into reconciling America and England."

Becca's eyes widened as if confused by Franklin's memory lapse.

Franklin did not exhibit nervous tics. Not ever. Not until this moment. "What have you done, Dr. Franklin?" Daniel asked.

Franklin raked his hand through his thinning hair. He sagged in his chair.

The pulse in Daniel's neck beat an alarm. "What have you done?" he repeated.

"I wrote that bribery letter. I practiced a handwriting that was unlike my own. I had the letter delivered to myself. I made up the entire story, and I made up the man with the red rose."

"And yet you asked us to find the man with the red rose at Notre Dame." Daniel stood, leaning over the desk.

"How did you know he would be waiting at Notre Dame holding a red rose?" Becca added.

"I didn't," Franklin said. "I wanted a witness who could swear that he hadn't arrived if the letter was made public."

"You must have been shocked when we told you we saw him," Becca said. Franklin nodded.

Daniel's anger exploded. "Find the spy, you said. Go to Notre Dame, you said. We risked our lives for you, for nothing, for a lie."

"Sit down, Mr. Alloway," Franklin said. When Daniel remained standing, he added, "Please."

Daniel reluctantly took a seat.

"It is the easiest thing in the world for a man to deceive himself." Franklin stared past Daniel and Becca as if to avoid the judgment he expected to find in their eyes. "I wrote that, you know."

"Yes, we do know. Your daughter Sally quotes you all the time," Becca said.

"I told myself that no one would be harmed by my letter," Franklin said.

"A man is dead because of it," Daniel said. "You could have died because of that letter."

"Why? Why did you write it in the first place." Becca's voice was gentler than Daniel's.

"Congress is ready to replace me with some young rapscallion who will blunder his way into the French court and offend everyone, just as John

Adams has." Franklin looked away again. "The Congress needed a reminder that I still matter, that I can do as much for the country as I have ever done, perhaps more. What would it hurt if the reminder came as news of a letter asking me to reconcile our country with England?

"I deceived myself into believing that the letter I wrote was necessary. It was for a cause greater than myself, a lie for independence."

"A righteous lie. Is that it?" Daniel struggled to control his temper.

"Why didn't you tell us about the letter when Jude Fenimore died?" Becca asked.

Franklin seemed to shrink inside his plain brown suit. "Because it would make me appear to be a desperate old man, which, it seems, I am."

Floorboards creaked overhead. A gardener called to a child not to step on the flower beds.

"You lie when it serves your purpose." Daniel's voice was raw. "You lied to your brother all those years ago. How did you sign the letters you wrote for his newspaper?"

"Silence Dogood." Franklin's eyes lit with humor.

"You disguised your handwriting then, too. You bragged about it." Franklin had shared that story with Daniel over a tankard of ale.

"Those letters hurt no one." Franklin frowned.

"And in London before the revolution began?" Daniel accused Franklin. "You wrote a letter supporting the American cause and signed it 'An Edict by the King of Prussia.' The London papers believed you. They published it that way. That was one of your drinking stories, too."

Becca laughed, then covered her mouth.

"Call it an imitation letter, not a lie," Franklin winked at Becca.

Daniel stopped himself from growling. Franklin and his damned charm. Even Becca wasn't immune.

"There was another instance." Daniel closed his eyes to avoid watching Franklin flirt with her. "It was quite a scandal. You wrote a letter to make the Hessian soldiers in America think that their officers wanted them dead."

"No one was hurt." Franklin's lips tightened.

"You didn't keep your bribery letter a secret. Edward Bancroft carried the letter into the house. You told Gabriel d'Aumont about it, too. Half of Paris must know of the bribe by now."

"I am counting on it." Franklin's tone was sharp. "I needed everyone to know about the letter. I needed word to travel to London, Versailles, and, yes, all the way to Philadelphia. How else could I make my point to the Congress?"

Daniel imagined letters about the bribery letter crossing from one continent to another in just a matter of weeks.

"I not only told Monsieur d'Aumont about the letter, I sent him my response." Franklin's lips curled into a proud half-smile. "I expressed great indignation that anyone would think I could be persuaded to betray my country. My indignation would have been real, if the letter had been genuine, of course."

Daniel felt the urge to punch something. He eyed Franklin's jaw.

"But then Jude Fenimore died," Becca said.

"When he disappeared, I chose to put the entire matter out of my mind."

"You put the image of Mr. Fenimore tied to your lightning rod on your roof out of your mind?" Daniel scoffed.

"I thought his death put an end to whatever game was being played." Franklin's gaze shifted left, then returned to Daniel.

"You can't believe that," Becca said. "Mr. Fenimore's killer placed him on the lightning rod to make a statement. It was meant to tell everyone who saw him there that the murder was about you."

Franklin winced. "All right, Mrs. Parcell. The truth is that I shall never forget the sight of Mr. Fenimore on the roof. It was cruel. His death haunts me. And, yes, I understood that it was a warning, though I have the damnedest time understanding what that warning means."

"And we haven't found the killer." Daniel's voice was flat.

Franklin leaned forward, beseeching them. "You and others have been hurt, Mr. Alloway. That is why I agreed when Monsieur d'Aumont suggested you both go home. Go home and be safe."

Patience Wright's voice boomed from the front hall. "Can't anyone here find my wrap?"

"Don't you have another, Patience?" Edward Bancroft called.

Patience? Daniel turned to Becca and wondered if he looked as surprised as she. Only the closest of friends used each other's first names.

Franklin sighed, splayed his hands on the desk and pushed himself upright. "We can't be late for the ball."

"You're not thinking of going?" Becca's forehead furrowed. "You shouldn't be in a crowd of hundreds of people. Whoever killed Mr. Fenimore may make another attempt on your life. Jude Fenimore died because he wanted to warn you."

"Hundreds? There could be thousands of people at Versailles," Franklin said, "and I'll be perfectly safe. Besides, if I am to be killed, I would prefer to die while drinking French champagne."

"*L'idiota*," Daniel muttered under his breath.

Franklin scowled. "I understand enough Italian to know you've insulted me."

"Then don't insult us, Dr. Franklin. Don't tell us you're willing to risk your life to drink champagne."

Franklin sighed. "I am attending the ball at Versailles because I am the American ambassador to France and because the royal family will be insulted if Dr. Franklin cancels at the last moment.

"France has paid for our revolution. They have bankrupted themselves to give us a chance at freedom. Ask Monsieur d'Aumont if you want proof of that. So, no, Mr. Parcell, I will not insult America's only friend by staying home tonight."

Franklin turned to Becca. "You have an hour to dress before the ball, Mrs. Parcell. I pray that is sufficient."

* * *

Humming under his breath, the hairdresser teased Becca's hair over the small pillow that gave her strands more than a foot of height. She sat in the drawing room on the third floor, facing a full-length mirror.

She was a hostage to the hairdresser for a while longer and let her thoughts drift to the afternoon's return to the perfume shop.

Madame Fargeon had burst into tears at the sight of Renée, shocking her husband and the customers into rare silence. Becca had left the two women in a narrow bedroom on the third floor.

She smiled at the memory. The stern, cold Madame Fargeon berated Renée as she dabbed her forehead gently with a wet cloth that scented the room with cloves. Love, like flowers, it seemed, grew in many shapes and colors here in Paris.

A sharp pin poked the back of Becca's skull. She lurched forward to avoid the pain.

"If madam will sit without moving, *shhil vous plait.*" He spoke through a mouthful of hairpins, that turned the S into a snakelike *shhhh*. "I am very gentle with my clients, but you give me a challenge to finish in so little time."

"*Pardon,*" Becca murmured.

"I have given you a canvas, madam, one as magnificent as the surface of any painting." he lectured. "Do you wish your hair to reflect your delicate emotions? Then we will decorate to express those sentiments. Perhaps there is an event you would care to commemorate with your hairstyle, a *pouf à la circonstance*? Your country's great signing of the Declaration of Independence, perhaps?"

She'd had enough. "We leave for Versailles soon, and I am horribly sad that I must cut your time short." She peered into the mirror to assure herself that Augusta still guarded Jude Fenimore's strips of paper. Becca and Daniel had asked her to keep them safe.

She nodded, patting the lumpy linen bag resting on the couch. She'd fanned out the skirt of her lavender and silver ball gown along the bench to avoid wrinkles. Her skin was whitened with cosmetics, her hair powdered white and festooned with lavender silk ribbons and purple silk roses.

"But I am not finished." The hairdresser's expression filled with horror.

"Yes. Yes, you are finished," Becca said gently. "If you will add that one decoration, we will be done." She pointed to the end table next to her chair.

He glared at the small furry object that lay there. "No, madam, this will destroy my reputation."

"We will, of course, pay an additional fee for your masterful work," Augusta said smoothly.

The hairdresser's Adam's apple bobbed as avarice warred with pride. Greed won. "As madam wishes." He picked up the miniature version of Dr. Franklin's famous round fur cap with two long fingers.

His eyes narrowed as he studied Becca's hair. Then he nodded to himself, pinning the hat at a tipsy angle above her forehead.

"Do you really like it?" Augusta asked Becca.

"It is the best surprise. I will stop and tell Hannah how grateful I am." Augusta had sewn the miniature cap, but it was Hannah's idea to create it. Becca paused. "I wish she were coming with us tonight."

"She is adamant." Augusta shook her head. "She says that she would not feel safe there."

"She must wish she'd stayed in Morristown." Becca sighed.

"No," Augusta sighed. "She will never regret this trip, no matter how it ends."

The two women exchanged glances in the mirror. Augusta was talking about Michael. Hannah would never regret their reunion. Becca hoped he was safe.

The hairdresser's eyes lit. He leaned toward the floor, fishing in a large canvas bag that held combs and powders. He pulled out three long pheasant feathers that gleamed brown and black. In the mirror, Becca watched him pin them in a fan shape behind the miniature hat. "Now, it is art," he said solemnly. "I give you a tableau of America's natural world."

Becca bit the inside of her cheek to stop herself from laughing at the hairdresser's grave pronouncement. But viewing his creation in the mirror, she revised her opinion. "I quite like it," she said with surprise. "It suits me. Thank you."

Lady Augusta shepherded the man to the door.

Becca stood, examining herself in the mirror. She felt like an overdecorated cake. Hip pads and wires held her copper-colored gown out at an impossibly wide width. She would have to step sideways through doors to enter or exit. And the gown itself was heavier than a sack of wheat. Every inch was covered in gold beads, jewels, lace, and ribbons.

The hairdresser's touch of whimsy, this one bit of humor, made her feel entirely like herself.

Daniel arrived moments later. His black suit was decorated only by slim gold ribbons at the sleeve and hem. He was dressing more like an American than a French nobleman. She wondered if it was intentional.

"The carriage is ready. We shall leave in...." Daniel stopped talking at the sight of Becca. "I...you." He shook his head.

Becca curtsied, taking his rare speechlessness as a compliment, but she grew serious in moments. "Can we convince him, do you think?"

Daniel's mouth tightened. "I don't know if we can scare Dr. Franklin sufficiently to keep him safe. I have never met a man with more confidence in his own judgment."

Chapter Thirty-Two

The sky lightened to a translucent blue, the last gasp of twilight before darkness fell. Benjamin Franklin stared out the carriage window. He hadn't spoken a word since they'd set out for Versailles. Becca slipped back on the leather seat as the horses pulled up the slight incline toward Versailles's main entrance. There had been real affection between the two men. Becca hoped it wasn't too late to repair their friendship.

"Becca and I will be your shadow for the entire evening. You can't be alone at Versailles, not if you want to be safe," Daniel said.

"I am not a child who requires a nanny." Franklin tapped his cane against the carriage floor with a hollow thump.

"Then don't act like one." Daniel eyed the cane, as if wondering whether Franklin would swat him with it next. "'Tis your own fault. You invented the man with the red rose. You will have to put up with the antidote. One of us will be with you at all times."

Franklin turned to Becca and Lady Augusta, studiously ignoring Daniel. "I couldn't wish for more pleasing company. And you will be quite the sensation tonight, Mrs. Parcell."

"I would rather be invisible." Becca stiffened with dread.

"The way you wear that miniature fur hat is brilliant," he purred.

"Of course you think so," Daniel drawled. "You're wearing the full-sized version."

"Well, there is that." Franklin tapped a finger against his customary fur cap. "I wager the queen will take an interest in your fashion. You may start a trend."

His heavy-lidded eyes were half-closed in thought as he studied Becca and Daniel. "Have you two resolved your differences? You are spending an inordinate amount of time together for a brokenhearted couple."

She opened her mouth to answer, glancing at Daniel. He nodded. "Yes," she said. "I am pleased to say that we have reconciled." But as the carriage door swung open, Becca lost her train of thought.

Her gaze swept the red brick, white marble and stone, bluish-black tile, and gold, gold everywhere on the palace. Gold sculptures of women lounged on the gilded edge of the roof. The upper windows, roofline, and balconies were rimmed with gold, too.

There was too much to see and no place to rest her eyes. She assumed that was the point. "Admire me, but do not become comfortable," Versailles seemed to warn. There was no danger of that. She tried but failed to count the windows overhead.

Daniel flicked a smile in Becca's direction. "The palace has more than two thousand rooms, I've heard. Perhaps you'll count them all."

It was a gentle joke, and Becca responded with a small grin. She did love to count.

Becca stepped gingerly down from the carriage to avoid treading on her hem. At the distant end of a courtyard, musicians in matching red coats and black tricorn hats greeted guests with trumpet music that soared and echoed above Versailles.

The whispers began as they stepped through the soaring gold-covered gate, its metal curves seeming as light as filigree. "Dr. Franklin." His name flew through the crowd.

He waved, smiled, and nodded as they passed from a large courtyard to a smaller one paved in a dizzying pattern of black and white marble squares and rectangles.

A woman floated past in a light green silk gown dripping with jewels.

"Purple sapphires and diamonds," Lady Augusta whispered before Becca could ask.

Another three women sailed by, their feet barely touching the ground.

The skirts of their gowns hardly moved. Their spines were rigidly straight.

Becca tried to mimic their motion but couldn't. "How are those women managing to walk?"

"They slide forward on their toes with tiny, tiny steps," Dr. Franklin chortled.

"Why learn a new way to walk?" Becca asked.

"It seems deucedly uncomfortable," Daniel shook his head.

"Versailles has its own customs. Who follows or leads. Who sits where. How ladies of the court are to walk. It is all defined, and woe to the man or woman who violates the rules."

Becca stiffened and whirled to find Gabriel d'Aumont standing behind her.

He bowed, extending a silk-clad leg. His waistcoat and breeches were a watery blue taffeta, bordered with embroidered vines and flowers in green, purple, and pink. Standing next to him, Daniel appeared almost austere in his black suit.

Gabriel's charm failed to move her tonight. He had pressured Michael to spy on Franklin's household for the French government. Pressure was the wrong word. d'Aumont had threatened Michael with arrest if he rejected the offer, then brought in the police to follow through when Michael refused him.

"Word of Dr. Franklin's arrival is spreading." Gabriel grinned. "It always does. I came to speed your arrival." He extended his arm to Lady Augusta, and they wove their way through the crowd of guests jostling each other beneath a gold and blue clock.

"Oh, dear." Lady Augusta raised her white linen handkerchief to her face as they reached the entrance.

The stench wrapped itself round Becca a moment later. It smelled like a barn that needed a good cleaning. Becca flicked open her fan and fluttered it as if that could draw fresh air.

"Try not to show your reaction, ladies," Daniel warned.

d'Aumont burst into laughter. "Welcome to Versailles. An odiferous cesspool of dead cats is what one visitor called it. There is much improvement, in fact. A few more minutes, and you will hardly notice."

Becca found that hard to believe. "What type of place is this?" How could such beauty and filth coexist?

"It's the jolliest, cruelest, most intriguing place in the world. Come. You haven't seen the best yet." Dr. Franklin plunged through the grand doorway.

Inside the soaring white stone space, knots of guests formed, dispersed and moved on, their white-powdered hair leaving a dusting of flour on every surface. It was a party of ghosts. Becca shivered at her fanciful thought.

A group of women circled Franklin within moments. Their impossibly wide skirts created a wall around him, a rainbow of pink taffeta, gold damask, green silk, and more.

"If he draws a crowd like this all evening, he will be safe enough," Daniel said.

The women all leaned in, listening to the famous Dr. Franklin. One, then another swiveled, then another, until Dr. Franklin's entire entourage stared past Becca.

Who were they looking at? Becca twisted but saw only a red-veined marble column behind her.

"Mrs. Parcell." Dr. Franklin waved her over. "I have told my friends about your hairpiece. Do allow me to introduce you."

They weren't staring behind her. They were staring at her. Becca's throat went dry.

"Lift your chin, Rebecca. Smile, but not too broadly. Back straight." Augusta locked arms with Becca and pulled her forward.

"Is that Franklin's new Paris mistress?" A long-nosed man lifted a monocle to his eye and sniffed as she passed.

Becca tread on his in-step and heard a satisfying *oomph* before murmuring, "*excusez-moi.*"

"I told you," Franklin crowed as Becca drew near. He pointed to his own fur cap and to her miniature version. "What humor, and what an honor to have been the inspiration."

The women studied Becca with critical attention, heads slightly tilted, crimson-painted lips pinched in thought.

Becca returned the scrutiny. Their wigs were elaborate pyramids. One of the women wore a vegetable garden in her hair. Pinned to her three-foot pouf were small porcelain radishes, artichokes, and cabbages. Each garden row in her white-powdered hair was marked with light green crystals. A porcelain rabbit peeked out from a green ribbon fence that edged the garden.

Another woman's coiffure featured small clay ducks swimming on a navy gauze sea. Becca tried not to stare at the scene featured on the top of her two-foot-high wig. There, two miniature clay figures made love next to a tiny windmill.

"Quite original." One of the women smiled at Becca. A pink and white bow covered the bodice of her dress. Smaller pink gauze ribbons curled through her hair.

The woman wearing a miniature rabbit smiled, displaying small, sharp teeth. "You have inspired me. At the next ball, I shall feature all the small animals of France."

"A kitten," one suggested. "A possum," said another. They all murmured their approval.

Becca curtsied her thanks.

"The queen must see her." The woman standing to the left of Dr. Franklin said as if giving an order. Her eyes lit on Augusta, and she smiled. "I was hoping to see you here. Welcome to my home, Lady Augusta."

"'Tis an honor, princess." Augusta curtsied deeply. Becca watched her mother-in-law from the corner of her eye and matched the depth of Augusta's dip. In her gown and whitened hair, Becca hadn't recognized the woman who'd invited them here tonight.

"I recall your daughter-in-law from the perfume shop. She looks almost French tonight."

Becca curtseyed again, uncertain whether she'd been complimented or insulted.

The princess took Augusta's arm and whisked her away. "I shall introduce you to a few people."

"And my daughter-in-law?" Becca heard Augusta ask.

"Do not worry, my dear. We will find her later."

"You can't deprive the rest of the guests of your company, Dr. Franklin," Gabriel slipped into the circle of women to retrieve Franklin. "Come. Let's go up. I want to show Mrs. Parcell the Hall of Mirrors." He led them to the wide white staircase at one end of the massive entryway and into another crowd waiting to have their names' announced.

A servant stood at the side of the stairs, calling each name and title in a voice that carried above the din of laughter and gossip. Gabriel whispered into his ear, and the servant called, "Dr. Franklin, Monsieur Daniel Alloway, and Madame Rebecca Parcell."

"Welcome to my home," Gabriel said as they reached the second-floor landing.

"Your home?" Becca staggered to a stop.

"I am but a humble assistant minister."

"But who are you really?" Becca mumbled. Daniel squeezed her hand, as if to warn her not to challenge Gabriel.

"My rooms face the street in the south wing. One day, I may earn the right to an apartment facing the beautiful gardens." Gabriel lifted his face to the ceiling in a mocking gesture.

"Who else lives here?" Daniel asked.

"The royal family, of course. The nobility. Ministers, Courtiers. Anyone who seeks the king's patronage."

"But that means hundreds and hundreds of people live in the palace."

Gabriel's smile was sly. "Thousands, Mrs. Parcell. Three thousand people have apartments here. So many that each door must be numbered. The stables keep more than two thousand horses. On any day, you might find ten thousand people milling about."

"That is the entire population of Philadelphia. How awful." No wonder Gabriel spent as much time as he could at Dr. Franklin's home. How could he find any rest in this beehive of a building?

A guest with jiggling jowls stumbled past, holding half a glass of champagne. He careened into Gabriel, who grimaced.

"It is the greatest honor of my life to live here and serve my king," Gabriel said.

"That clock-maker? At least he's managed to bed the Austrian slut." The jowly nobleman slurred his words.

The king's clock-making hobby. The queen's Austrian family. Becca gasped at the insult.

"More to drink?" Gabriel called with a smile. When the man turned, Gabriel drew his fist back and punched him in the jaw.

The guest's eyes widened, then fluttered shut as he fell to his knees and collapsed. The glass flute of champagne shattered on the light parquet floor.

The crowd quieted, then turned their backs as if to erase the sight.

The violence was so unexpected that Becca froze in shock. There'd been no exchanged angry words, no change in Gabriel's expression, no warning of violence.

"He insulted the king." Gabriel shook out his hand.

Daniel's hand lightly touched her lower back as if for comfort. Or was it for protection? Dr. Franklin's expression hardly changed, but Becca thought she saw wariness in his eyes.

Two servants rushed toward them.

"Clean this up." Gabriel tapped the man's thigh with his shoe. Its emerald buckle gleamed in the candlelight. Then he flashed Becca a smile as if he hadn't just beaten a man into unconsciousness." Come along. There's more to see."

The soft hairs rose on the back of Becca's neck. Gabriel's emotions were as sudden as a summer squall and as dangerous.

"This is my favorite place to bring visitors. I hope you enjoy it, Mrs. Parcell." Gabriel leaned toward her.

She leaned away.

His sharp eyes caught the motion. "I have upset you. I didn't mean to. But this is my house. My country. I will not tolerate disrespect of my king in my house."

His face was stamped with the same intensity she recalled in Alexander Hamilton's. Was she misjudging Gabriel? Becca forced herself to relax.

"This is no conversation for a happy evening." Gabriel's lips rose into a lopsided grin. "Please, forgive me, and enjoy the Hall of Mirrors." He swept his arm forward, then stepped away.

Through the doorway, a cascade of crystal caught the light of endless candles. A violin quartet played, its music soaring above the crowd.

Two couples swung past Becca, the women's skirts brushing her own. One *tssked,* and Becca realized that she was blocking the door.

She swiveled quickly. There. Dr. Franklin was laughing, already huddled with three women in a corner of this room just outside the large gallery. Daniel stood watch, his arms crossed. She stepped through the opening into a long, crowded gallery.

Hundreds of floor-to-ceiling mirrors endlessly reflected candlelight from rows of crystal-draped chandeliers. Sculpted gold figures stood between each mirror, each lifting more candelabras as if they were weightless.

Becca tilted her head until the pins that held her pouf in place tugged at her scalp. Gold ribbons, cupids, and wreaths danced on the ceiling, along with paintings of heroic battles. She felt a breeze and turned. Couples strolled through open windows to reach a long balcony outside.

Patience Wright's unmistakable bray was the only grating note in the room. The artist stood with Edward Bancroft about fifteen feet away.

He leaned toward Patience, bringing his head close to hers. She raised her face to his, smiling with pleasure.

If the look on Patience's face was to be trusted, then the artist truly had cured herself of her anger toward Jude Fenimore. Becca backed away, not certain why she didn't want them seeing her. Patience and Edward Bancroft were a couple. Patience and Gabriel were not. Becca had seen the portrait Patience painted of Gabriel and assumed the artist and Frenchman were keeping company. She'd been wrong.

Did this make it any more or less likely that any of them had killed Jude Fenimore? She needed to think. Becca retraced her steps to the anteroom just outside the mirrored gallery.

Daniel still stood in the center of the room, watching Dr. Franklin. The young woman facing him patted Dr. Franklin's cheek and trilled, "You are the sweetest grandfather."

Franklin's confident smile wobbled for just a moment.

Becca wandered further, hoping to find a moment of solitude near the staircase. Voices echoed from the entryway downstairs. A few couples floated past, some heading into other rooms, others descending.

Two men stood near the upper staircase. Each leaned their elbows against the banister, facing away from Becca. "On my mother's grave, I swear it. Not one more gold Louis," one of the men said. "They are bankrupting us." From the back, the speaker looked like Gabriel d'Aumont, but his voice was more guttural, the accent less cultured.

"They are fighting for the rights of all men. How can you refuse them?" His companion wore a maroon suit that was too large for his slight frame, as if he had borrowed it from a larger man.

Becca stopped, curious to hear how aristocrats spoke of the War for Independence with no Americans to listen in.

"The peasants whisper of revolution each time their taxes go up now. Give us American freedom, they say." The first man hissed. "Their freedom is a disease that will kill us all."

"Ah, Gabriel, go find a pretty girl to entertain you," the slight man teased. "You worry too much."

"And you should worry more, Étienne." Gabriel d'Aumont poked his friend in the shoulder.

Becca's spine stiffened. Did Dr. Franklin know his good friend Gabriel's true feelings? She sensed Daniel behind her before he took her arm and pulled her away.

"Did you hear?" she asked.

"I am not surprised," he murmured.

"Why not?"

"When he speaks of our independence, his smile doesn't reach his eyes." Daniel shrugged. "It takes a liar to recognize a liar."

"Doesn't that bother you? Have you and he argued about it?" Becca nodded a greeting as they passed one guest, then another.

Daniel shook his head. "The philosophers speak of independence. But our war is popular here because we are poking a finger in England's eye, not because the nobility seeks to share its power."

CHAPTER THIRTY-TWO

"And France and England are enemies," Becca said. "Otherwise?"

They came to a stop in the corner of the anteroom leading to the Hall of Mirrors. No one was close enough to overhear them.

"Otherwise, France might not have sent us a single dollar." His lips curled into a half-smile. "Gabriel sees the threat American independence poses to his France. You didn't see that in him despite the smiles and gifts of chocolate?"

Chocolate and tea. The wisp of a thought rose and was gone. Becca was irritated that she had missed signs that seemed obvious to him.

"If you lied more often, you would see the signs of fabrication in others more clearly." Daniel's half-smile grew into a grin.

"More often? I have told more untruths since meeting you than I have in the first twenty years of my life, Mr. Alloway." Becca's temper flared. "I have pretended to be angry at you. I have pretended to be your wife. I have...."

Daniel's features hardened.

Becca stopped. "What is wrong?"

"These are the lies I hate the most," Daniel said.

"Which lies? There are so many."

"Telling everyone that we were newlyweds in Philadelphia. Telling everyone in Paris that we are estranged. I want no lies between us. Marry me now. Marry me tomorrow. Just marry me."

"I will. I do." Becca had said the same to him just outside the magistrate's office. She'd wanted no lies between them. She felt his warm breath on her cheeks as he exhaled. The tension of the evening disappeared, and the world shrunk to the two of them. It wasn't the moment to remind Daniel that France made it impossible for them to marry, not when he looked at her as if she was endlessly precious to him.

A loud cough and feminine giggle broke the spell.

Dr. Franklin stood nearby. A young woman with a swanlike neck held his arm. Both of them grinned.

Heat rose to Becca's cheeks.

"Grandpapa." The young woman jutted her chin, calling his attention to an elderly servant who stood nearby.

The servant hopped from one foot to another, a surprisingly young gesture for a man who appeared as old as Franklin.

"The queen requests the honor of your presence, Mrs. Parcell. This good man has come to fetch you to the Hall of Mirrors. I predicted that you would be a sensation at Versailles," Franklin crowed. "And now, an audience with the queen. We shall follow to watch. I look forward to your elevation at court."

Becca's stomach lurched.

"We will find you after your elevation, as Dr. Franklin calls it." There was humor and sympathy in Daniel's gaze. "Do not scowl at the queen."

"I am not...." Becca clamped her lips together. Yes, she was scowling. "'Tis not funny. What will I say to her?"

"Not much, I suspect," Daniel answered. "You are a commoner. You will speak only when spoken to."

Chapter Thirty-Three

"Make way, make way," the servant called.

The crowd formed an aisle of blue taffetas, green satins, yellow silks, and more. "Is she with Dr. Franklin?" "Why does she walk so awkwardly?" "What could the queen want with her?"

Walking through the crowd of whispering courtiers was like jumping into a cold lake. It was a shock at first, but one grew quickly accustomed to the remarks, even the unkind ones. Becca focused on the large round black table that had been carried to the center of the Hall of Mirrors. The servant was leading her there.

"Where are you going?" Patience Wright was suddenly beside her, moving forward in lockstep. Edward Bancroft followed in her wake.

"The queen wants to see me," Becca said.

Patience stopped in surprise, then rushed to catch up. Her expression turned to cunning. "Ask if she would like me to sculpt her. I would do it for free."

"Here is Mrs. Parcell, your Majesty." The servant bowed.

Four women sat there, their attention caught by the cards in their hands. Becca recognized the princess. Lady Augusta stood behind her, equally focused on the cards.

The other three women could have been sisters. Their tall beehive hairdos glimmered in the candlelight with matching jewels and dyed feathers. Their collar bones were draped in heavy jeweled necklaces. One wore diamonds and emeralds, the next, rubies, and the third, sapphires. Their faces were masked by white makeup, bright round circles of rouge, and carmine-red lips.

"A warning, Mrs. Parcell." Dr. Franklin materialized beside her, his jovial façade gone. "The rules of propriety here are ancient and complex." He barely moved his mouth as he spoke. "'Tis easy to offend. Do not stare at any of them, and only speak when spoken to. Keep your answers short."

"You are scaring me, Dr. Franklin," Becca whispered.

"I mean to."

Three of the women at the table glanced up, then turned back to the cards. The fourth raised her head for a closer examination.

Becca's heart hammered. *Bend your knees. Keep your back straight.* Augusta had taught her how to curtsy at court. She rose to find Marie-Antoinette's large, bluish-gray eyes still examining her. Becca averted her gaze. *Do not stare.*

Becca tried to stare without being caught at it. Kings and queens were chosen by God, weren't they? That is what King George III of England claimed. If that were true, Marie-Antoinette was touched by divinity. What did that look like?

It—she—looked like a pretty woman in her twenties with bright, curious eyes, a heavy lower lip, and an exuberant love of fashion.

Becca wondered how the petite queen managed to walk in her heavy court gown. The skirt was as wide as a small rowboat, and its pale green stripes were shot through with silver threads. The collar of her bodice was weighed down by diamonds and emeralds. Her hair was worn in a slighter softer, lower pouf than most of the other women here, and Becca wondered if female guests would all be copying the queen's new style within the week.

It was a good thing Marie-Antoinette was a queen and not a farmer. She appeared too fragile to chop wood for a harsh winter. Becca rubbed her thumb along the palm of her right hand. Her calluses were fading. She had earned them last fall swinging a scythe to bring in the wheat and chopping mountains of wood for fires that winter.

"Your daughter-in-law, Lady Augusta?" Marie-Antoinette returned Becca's scrutiny.

"Yes. Although her husband, my son, is deceased."

"My condolences, Lady Augusta. And she is related to the English royal family by marriage to your son?"

Becca's shoulder muscles unbunched. It was surprisingly restful to be discussed as if she were a potted plant.

Augusta nodded.

Royal? She was about as royal as a dandelion on the side of a road.

"She is like us, then," one of the other women said, and they all laid their cards down to study Becca.

"You may introduce us," the queen said.

"You are too gracious, your majesty," Augusta murmured.

Becca repeated her formal curtsy to each of the four women.

"Mrs. Rebecca is but a small twig on the royal family tree for now," Augusta said.

"What do you mean by 'for now'?" Marie-Antoinette asked.

Becca almost answered, but Augusta shot her a warning look. "Mrs. Parcell will no longer be linked by marriage to the English royal family if she marries her betrothed, Mr. Alloway."

Becca turned a gasp into a cough, and Augusta's eyes widened. So much for the fiction that Becca was no longer Daniel's fiancé.

"Ah, the famous Mr. Alloway," Marie-Antoinette said.

"Mr. Alloway is famous?" Becca looked directly at the queen.

A disapproving hiss rose from the guests. Becca clamped her lips together. One did not speak to the sovereign unless directed.

"Some of the ladies of the court are quite taken with him. And you have captured his heart, you say?" The queen sounded disbelieving.

Becca bristled. "I have, your Majesty. Indeed I have."

"Yet you have been in France a while, I understand, and you have not yet married him." Marie-Antoinette gnawed on her bottom lip. No one spoke. "Ahh. I understand. Mrs. Parcell does not want to lose her connection by marriage to England's royal family."

The queen leaned forward and whispered loudly, "Under such a circumstance, it is preferable to be a mistress."

A hush fell over everyone within a ten-foot radius of the queen. "I told you. She is his Paris mistress," a guest said. They'd all heard the queen's hushed message to Becca. Her heartbeat pounded in her throat.

"Do they care about titles in America, Mrs. Parcell?" one of the princesses at the table asked. Her forehead creased.

The four women waited for Becca's answer.

"I cannot say that I give the question of titles much thought," she stuttered, forcing her attention back to the women at the card table.

Their eyebrows rose in shock.

"Then it is true," the princess said. "There are no titles in America."

"Without titles, how can you tell if someone is the right sort?" One of the women narrowed her eyes as if Becca were dangerous.

America was not meant to be a land of the 'right sort,' Becca did not say. It was meant to welcome everyone.

"Monsieur d'Aumont was right," another added.

"Right about what?" Becca asked cautiously. Where was Gabriel? She hadn't seen him in the crowd.

"He says that your country is *pêle-mêle*," one of the women said. At the look of confusion on Becca's face, she added, "higgledy-piggledy, you say in English. Your country is all disorder and confusion."

Becca agreed. But she didn't care to have a foreigner express the thought.

"Melodié, you are being rude," Marie-Antoinette said. "We will not speak of politics." The subject was closed.

Melodié ducked her head at the rebuke, which caused the purple feathers in her hair to shiver. "Then I shall talk about tea. You must thank Dr. Franklin for the special tea he gives to Monsieur d'Aumont. It is rare, but we have all enjoyed it, yes?"

"Monsieur d'Aumont and tea? You are certain?" Becca asked with surprise. Gabriel had presented hot chocolate—not tea—to Daniel with a flourish worthy of an actor. She had never heard the Frenchman mention tea.

And Dr. Franklin wasn't one to hide his light under a bushel. If he'd presented a gift to the court of King Louis XVI, he would have bragged of it. There had been no bragging.

"Yes, Monsieur d'Aumont and relaxation tea. I said so, didn't I?" Melodié snapped.

"*Pardon*, madam." Becca bowed her head, suitably chastised. She might be related by marriage to royalty, but it seemed she was still a commoner in Melodié's eyes. "I will be happy to thank Dr. Franklin on your behalf."

What was it about tea? Something Melodié said struck a chord. "I wish I knew more about tea," Becca prodded. "Was it very special, this tea?"

"Yes, it is the most relaxing of teas," Melodié said.

The most relaxing of teas. Relaxation tea. Becca was missing something

"And Monsieur d'Aumont shared the tea with you?" one of the other women asked.

Melodié preened, stroking the side of her saffron-colored bodice from bosom to waist.

"Ahh, you went to his apartment." The queen giggled. "Does your husband know?"

"He wouldn't care." Melodié's slow smile suggested she had enjoyed other affairs of the heart. "There was a lovely sweet and smoky scent. It was the tea, and I asked for a cup. Monsieur d'Aumont is a gentleman, and he agreed to my request. That was all." Her forehead might have furrowed. The thick white cosmetics Melodié wore made it difficult to tell. "I hardly recall the rest of that evening." She tossed her head as if flinging away some concern she chose not to share.

The tea had put Melodié to sleep, Becca guessed. She didn't remember the rest of the evening.

"Oh, you asked for some tea, and that was all," one of the women drawled in a sing-song voice. The others laughed. Melodié turned away from them; her lips pressed tightly together.

Becca almost felt sorry for her.

Hannah gave Jude a tea for his stomach on their crossing to France. She called it relaxation tea, too. That was the memory that had eluded her. It helped quell his pain and made him sleep. And Becca had mixed relaxation tea powder into hot water for Daniel's head injury to soothe the pain.

Why did Gabriel need relaxation tea? Did he have an old injury or a new malady? Was he having trouble sleeping? Sweet and smoky. The tea was sweet and smoky.

The buzzing of hundreds of voices faded as other memories rose. Faded. On the roof, she's seen faded brown stains on Jude Fenimore's clothing. Blood stains, Becca had thought, dulled by the rain. Blood stains or tea stains? Relaxation tea could have put Jude to sleep. Would enough have killed him? Becca wished her mother was here. She would know more about the herb that made the tea.

Becca launched into speech. "You went to Monsieur d'Aumont's apartment?" she asked Melodié. What had Gabriel told her about his apartment?

"The one in the South Wing? Apartment eighty-seven?" Gabriel had not mentioned his apartment number. She'd made up the number. She needed to see the tea.

Lady Augusta's mouth opened, then snapped shut. One of the women at the table gasped. They all turned to the queen.

A trickle of perspiration crept down the base of Becca's spine. What she'd said was brazen. Announcing that she knew Gabriel's apartment number was akin to saying that they were having an affair or that she was seeking him out. Even worse, she'd broken Versailles rules of civility. She'd spoken out of turn. Becca could just imagine the gossip. The Paris mistress, indeed.

"It seems we do not keep Monsieur d'Aumont busy enough with work." The queen flicked open an ivory fan and raised it to her face. Her laugh was surprisingly earthy.

The three women at the table laughed dutifully. One said to Becca with a mischievous grin, "Not eighty-seven. Monsieur d'Aumont resides in apartment ninety-two. Halfway down the hall. The door is chipped near the knob."

"How do you know that, you cow," Melodié demanded, her voice cracking.

"That is enough," the queen said. Her amusement quickly turned to boredom. "I hear that you have transformed Dr. Franklin's cap into a decoration quite feminine. I cannot imagine such a thing. Come closer."

Becca felt the eyes of the entire room on her as she walked to the queen.

Marie-Antoinette stood, peering up at Becca's hair. "Make yourself shorter." The queen was a good four to five inches shorter than Becca, she estimated. And Becca had been right about the gown. She had never seen a skirt as wide. The material alone must have made Marie-Antoinette's gown uncomfortably heavy.

The queen called to Augusta. "Are all American women so tall?"

"No, your Majesty. We come in all sizes," Lady Augusta said. In English, she added to Becca, "Just stoop, dear."

Becca froze herself into a demi-curtsy.

Marie-Antoinette examined the miniature hat and pheasant feathers, tilting her head one way, then the other. "If you don't care about your own ties to the English royals, why don't you marry Mr. Alloway?" she whispered. "You should."

"France's laws make marriage almost impossible for foreigners. I mean no disrespect, your Majesty. It is difficult here."

Hmmpf. Their eyes met for one moment before Marie-Antoinette's gaze dropped.

Becca winced at her latest verbal misstep. France was still making life difficult for the queen, a foreigner born in a country long considered an enemy of France. The man Gabriel had punched tonight called Marie-Antoinette "that Austrian slut."

"Go home, Mrs. Parcell." The queen's lips barely moved. "Home is best." Raising her childlike voice, she turned to the crowd, "Madame Parcell's *coiffure* is quite witty. An excellent homage to America and the natural world. I approve."

Becca deepened her curtsy and rose. She'd almost forgotten her promise. "A wonderful sculptor is asking to create your image in wax. Her name is Patience Wright, and she says that it would be her honor."

The queen seemed to grow more distant without moving. Becca wondered whether she'd broken another Versailles rule of civility by offering Patience's services. Without another word to Becca, the queen took her seat, picked up her cards, and set one face-up on the table.

"You have all the luck," her tablemates trilled.

Becca hovered, uncertain what to do now until Patience Wright pulled her away.

"You have been dismissed," Patience said. "It happens quickly. I don't think we are quite real to the French court. Did you ask for me?"

"I asked, but the queen did not respond. I am sorry."

Patience's face brightened. "Perhaps she is thinking it over. I cannot thank you enough."

Chapter Thirty-Four

Music soared at the far end of the long gallery, and the crowd surged toward the violin quartet. Becca was trapped, pulled along by strangers as if she were caught in the current of a flooding stream. She elbowed her way to the side of the room, excusing herself as she careened into one guest after another. She reached the open windows and inhaled the cool night air, her rib cage pressing hard against the stays beneath her gown.

Becca swiveled, searching the crowd for Daniel. One of them could stay with Dr. Franklin. The other could search for Gabriel's relaxation tea. It should have been simple to find a man in a black suit in a room full of men dressed like peacocks. But she didn't see him. Exasperation turned to worry.

The crowd was settling, guests joining the dance or watching from a distance. Men and women formed two lines, and they met in the center with arms half raised, fingers elegantly bent, and steps more complex than Becca had ever seen. The minuet was a child's game of hopscotch in comparison.

The quartet began a new song, a faster one, and the dancers increased their pace to match the rhythm. Patience Wright and Edward Bancroft flickered in and out of view behind the dancers. Bancroft slapped Dr. Franklin on the back. They strolled toward the queen and a door behind her.

Becca's perspective changed in an instant. Was the relationship between Patience Wright and Edward Bancroft merely romantic? What if they were joined by hatred as well as attraction?

Patience had hated Jude enough to kill him. Bancroft must detest Dr. Franklin. What else could motivate someone to spy against an old friend?

What if Patience murdered Jude, with Bancroft placing his body on the lightning rod for the sheer pleasure of humiliating the good doctor?

It was all possible, possible enough that Becca lifted the hem of her gown and ran through the dancers to reach them. The musicians stood to see who had broken the beautiful symmetry of the dance at Versailles. A violin screamed in protest.

She came to a sudden stop, feet from Dr. Franklin, still too out of breath to speak.

"I do not require a nanny, Mrs. Parcell. I thought I was clear." Franklin turned his back to her.

Marie-Antoinette raised a graceful hand to her collarbone either in surprise at Franklin's unusual lack of manners or at Becca's disheveled appearance.

But Patience Wright looked positively beatific. "I am in your debt, Mrs. Parcell, for recommending me to the queen."

"Her Majesty is graciousness herself." Franklin bowed to Marie-Antoinette, who smiled shyly.

The queen raised her fan and whispered to a grim middle-aged woman standing behind her, who spoke to Patience. "You shall come next Thursday for a first sitting with the queen."

It seemed the queen did not speak directly to commoners, at least not at Versailles.

Marie-Antoinette raised her fan again to speak to the grim woman, who nodded. "You will ask for Nicolette when you arrive."

Patience didn't appear offended by the queen's indirect directions. She dipped a deep awkward curtsy and grabbed Bancroft's arm to rise. The two of them backed away.

Franklin smiled as if he and Becca were having a friendly conversation. They were not. "I am old, Mrs. Parcell," He spoke in English. "That does not make me an imbecile, nor does it deprive me of the good judgment I have employed since I was younger than you."

Becca winced and widened her stance. She had earned this reprimand.

"I intend to remain safely here in the bosom of the French court." He bowed again to the queen. "With France's most exquisite queen."

Marie-Antoinette glowed. She was not immune to Franklin's charm, even when he spoke in a language she didn't understand.

His smile was frozen in place. "Because that is the safest course in my judgment. Not your judgment. Not Mr. Alloway's. Now, go away, Mrs. Parcell. Enjoy the ball. Enjoy Versailles, and leave me alone. I shall be fine."

"I cannot decide whether to be relieved or appalled at myself," Becca said

Franklin's expression softened. "Be relieved, Mrs. Parcell. Enjoy the ball."

Becca was being dismissed again. She curtsied and backed away. More couples joined the dance. Becca scanned the room for Daniel.

Patience and Edward Bancroft stood near one of the doors leading out of the Hall of Mirrors. There was no point in asking them outright whether they'd killed Jude. But there was another matter she could settle.

She wove through the crowd to reach them just as Edward Bancroft turned away to speak to a gentleman in matching purple breeches and jacket. Becca leaned toward Patience. She forced amusement into her voice. "You and Mr. Bancroft have developed a tenderness for each other."

"Now that we are friends, Mrs. Parcell, I can say that I am happy. But we will continue to be discrete."

Becca nodded. "And you and Mr. Bancroft were together the night of Dr. Franklin's carriage accident?" Patience and Edward had refused to explain why they had not returned with Dr. Franklin to the mansion. How would the artist interpret her open-ended question? Would she answer at all?

Patience's forehead furrowed. "How shall I put this? Mr. Bancroft and I were being discrete that night. Well into the night."

Becca felt her eyebrows rise. "At the neighbor's house?"

Patience shrugged. "There are as many bedrooms there as at Dr. Franklin's house." Her lips rose in a smug smile. "Have I embarrassed you? I did not intend to."

Becca did not want any more details, though it appeared Patience would be happy to share. She changed the subject. "Have you seen Mr. Alloway?" she asked. Dr. Franklin was safe for now, and she was still curious about Gabriel d'Aumont's tea.

Patience shook his head.

Near the violin quartet, Becca caught a glimpse of Gabriel flirting with a woman who wore a glistening silver gown. Gabriel had secrets. That was clear. His violence tonight was a shock. So was his hatred for American-style independence. But did his secrets have anything to do with Dr. Franklin or Jude Fenimore's death?

If she was going to examine Monsieur d'Aumont's apartment, it would be safest to wait for Daniel. *Go. You won't have another chance.*

Go. "If you see Mr. Alloway, will you let him know that I am visiting Monsieur d'Aumont's apartment?" Becca asked Patience.

The artist's eyes sparkled. "You want me to tell your former lover that you are taking a new one?" Patience honked a laugh.

"I wish to make Mr. Alloway jealous." Becca sent Melodié a silent thank you for providing the excuse she needed, a complicated affair of the heart. "I hope the thought of me with another man tears him apart." Becca pulled back her shoulders and mimicked Patience's own bitter, cynical tone.

"You have more spirit than I gave you credit for. Perhaps I will sculpt you, Mrs. Parcell," Patience said.

"It would be an honor." That was another lie. Becca wondered how many she would tell before the evening was over. She dipped a small curtsy before hurrying from the room.

There were fewer guests now in the upper hallway. Their voices ricocheted against the stone walls and banister. Becca came to a stop, her gown bobbing forward and back. She had no idea where to find a staircase that would lead upstairs to Gabriel's apartment. She raised her hand as one servant rushed by. He shrugged and hurried past. So did the second.

Becca pressed her fingernails into her palms. Finding her way around Versailles clearly called for a different approach.

A third servant in red and blue livery shot up the stairs from below.

Becca blocked his way. "You are to take me to Monsieur d'Aumont's apartment. Now."

He stepped left, ignoring her. Becca stepped right. "Apartment ninety-two." She smiled as if he'd already agreed to accompany her.

The man shook his head. The candlelight highlighted the smallpox scars on his high forehead.

"You have never heard me scream," she said in an equally pleasant voice, her smile still intact. "It is a blood-curdling sound, and if I also faint, you will have many questions to answer, and you will be even later getting where you are going." All of that was true. "You will find it much quicker and more peaceful to help me."

"You are a witch." The whites of his eyes shone in the candlelight.

"An American witch. The worse kind." Was this her third lie tonight? She had lost count.

His long nose twitched with doubt. "Follow," he finally said.

Painted cherubs lounging on ceilings and walls followed their progress. White moths beat their wings against darkened windows. Their footsteps echoed in the empty hallways. Left, then another left. Gray stone. Red brocade wallpaper. Back to gray stone. She memorized the turns they took.

The servant pulled a lit candle from a gold-plated candelabra and stopped at a nearby door. The flame flickered as he opened it. He held the candle out to her, his face as closed and unfriendly as ever.

"Aren't you coming?" Becca asked.

He shook his head, pushing the candle forward again.

She exhaled with exasperation and grabbed the taper, careful not to touch his hand. "I can find my way from here. Are all the apartments numbered?"

He nodded. "Make a right, a left, another left, and a right. His nose twitched again. "And don't get lost."

"Thank you. I am sorry that I…." But he was gone before she could apologize for harassing him into helping her get this far.

Chapter Thirty-Five

She stepped into the dark staircase. The candle flame fluttered in the breeze that swooped down the stairwell from roof to basement. Her heels clacked on the wooden treads. She climbed one story, then two. Sound rose from the party below, distorting the music and laughter to a low, discordant moan. At the top of the staircase, she took a deep breath, splayed her hand on the rough wooden attic door, and pushed.

There were no cherubs painted on the walls. No scenes of battle glory etched on the ceiling. No gold-plated candelabras. There was just the scent of a thousand people squeezed in too tight a space and door after door in a hallway lit by her candle alone. Her dress brushed the sides of the narrow hallway as she walked silently on the balls of her feet.

A right, a left, another left, and a right. She repeated the servant's directions. Faded numbers without rhyme or reason were painted on black doors. Finally, she lifted the candle to find a faint ninety-two painted into a black door with chipped paint.

Across the way, a couple argued behind another door. No other footsteps or sound broke the silence.

She pushed her way into Gabriel d'Aumont's apartment. Becca didn't care how much prestige came with living in Versailles. She couldn't imagine living in this jail cell of a room.

There were no windows. She was swaddled in darkness.

The air still held the day's heat and something else, a smoky, sweet scent. There had only been a touch of that scent in the powder Becca had mixed into Daniel's drink. The room didn't smell like any tea she had ever sipped, but still.…

Where was Daniel? She pushed the thought away. There would be time to look for him later.

She raised her candle. The room was as simple as a monk's. There was a chair instead of a night table next to a cot. Becca smoothed her hand along the rough wool blanket to feel for any hidden items. Nothing.

A desk and second chair lined the wall to the left. A large water bowl decorated with blue flowers rested on the floor. One neat pile of papers and a silver letter opener with an onyx handle were the only objects on the desk.

Five sets of colorful clothes—jackets, vests, shirts, and breeches—hung on hooks along the far wall. She jammed her hands into the pockets of his breeches and came away with nothing. Becca tried not to think about what she was doing. It was a personal invasion.

Where was the tea? Had Gabriel given it all away? Her fingers crawled along the bottom of the chair. Nothing. She was wasting time. She crouched, stretching her arms to feel the floor under the bed, then the nubby ropes that held up the mattress. She shook out her hand to fling away the dust.

She had sent herself on a fruitless endeavor. The tea meant nothing. She was merely creating a diversion to trick herself into leaving a party she'd dreaded.

Still crouching, Becca slid her hand along the bottom of the desktop and caught a splinter of wood beneath her index finger. Her hand flew up, knocking the wood and something else that released a sweet and smoky scent. Something soft. Something fixed to the bottom of the desk.

Her fingertips gently squeezed the cloth bag pinned there until she felt an opening near the top. She hooked one finger into the bag, pulling out a round, dried pod. It went into the pocket tied round her waist. So did a handful of loose herbs.

Was this the tea Melodié mentioned? She would show it to Hannah. Her mother would know what it was.

Best to get back to the Hall of Mirrors as quickly as possible. She lifted the candle above her head. Had she left anything behind to suggest her presence? Not that she could see.

233

Footsteps echoed down the narrow hallway in the distance.

Becca swiped the letter opener from the desk. The hard onyx handle was comforting in her hand. The folds of her gown hid the knife. *This damned dress.* She had to turn sideways just to fit through the doorway.

A dim light down the hall bounced its way toward her.

There was nowhere to hide, but she couldn't retreat back to Gabriel's apartment. She'd be trapped within the room's walls if someone came looking for her. She tightened her spine, lifted her chin, and headed toward whoever held the candle.

"It's a good thing you told Mrs. Wright where you would be. I have been searching for you." Gabriel's face puckered with disapproval. "Best to come with me now." He reversed course, retracing his footsteps. He didn't look back to see whether she followed.

She rushed to catch up. "What has happened?"

"You were going to watch Dr. Franklin, and instead, you ran off on some frivolous mission," Gabriel called behind him. "I didn't think you were a frivolous woman, Mrs. Parcell. A tryst," he scoffed. "With me. To make Mr. Alloway jealous. You tell a story at Versailles, and it spreads within moments. What were you thinking?"

A guilty man would not turn his back on her. He wouldn't chastise her for failing her friends.

"I am embarrassed," she said. That much was true. "I have made a terrible mistake." That was true, too. What had she been thinking entering Gabriel's apartment and stealing his possessions? "Please. Are they all right?" Her breath came in short huffs.

Daniel had disappeared, and she had walked away without a thought for his well-being. If he was hurt, she'd never forgive herself.

Three strides brought Gabriel to the stairway. Becca followed. He swung the door open.

"Mr. Alloway disappears, and do you wonder for one second whether he needs you? Did you stop and think?"

"What has happened?" She grabbed Gabriel's arm with her free hand and yanked him around.

"Mrs. Wright is unbalanced. You know that. You have seen her." His voice echoed in the stairwell. He shook off her hand and entered the stairwell. Becca followed. Light from their candles danced on the walls. "She is telling everyone that you are her best friend, since you helped her secure a commission from the queen.

"And now that the two of you are such friends...." Gabriel's voice crackled with sarcasm. "...she hates Mr. Alloway with as much passion as she hated Jude Fenimore."

"Take me to him," was all she said. Gabriel's explanation rang true. Mrs. Wright was a woman of strong, sudden passions. What had she done to Daniel?

He slowed at the next landing and opened the door. Lights blazed from chandeliers. "Go back to the party, Mrs. Parcell. I will come get you later and let you know."

"Know what?"

"This is no sight for a woman."

"Damn you, Monsieur d'Aumont. Bring me to him."

Gabriel appeared uncertain, almost meek. "If you insist."

They blew out their candles, handed them to a passing servant, then hurried down the grand staircase.

Becca's thoughts slowed, and her senses quickened. She would remember the rough feel of the stairway banister under the hand, the sound of Gabriel's even breath, the dip in the center of each stone step carved by a hundred years of footsteps. Because disasters are all sound and sight and feel. A blur. A pain. A scream. Only afterwards, did thought return. For now, she put one foot in front of the other, took one breath and the next, and followed Gabriel d'Aumont.

"Dr. Franklin, he is all right?" Becca called.

"Yes, he and your mother-in-law are in the Hall of Mirrors surrounded by his friends. Quickly." He led her out into the night through the black-and-white marble courtyard. They turned left and entered a wing of the palace.

Becca couldn't have felt more disoriented if Gabriel had blindfolded her.

Down another long hallway they ran, past galleries, and too many rooms to count.

Running was mathematics in motion. 1–2–3. 1–2–3, she counted to the rhythm of her stride, taking her first deep breaths since Gabriel confronted her in the residence hall. 1–2–3. Gabriel had rattled her, tugged at her guilt for leaving Daniel behind. *What if Daniel isn't here? What if Gabriel is lying?*

"How much longer?" She fell behind. Their footsteps were the only sounds Becca heard.

"We are almost there," Gabriel called. "Brace yourself. I don't know what we will find."

She picked up her pace again. *What if Gabriel is telling the truth, and I retreat now?* "Where is Patience Wright?"

"Patience? She is gone." Gabriel brushed away Becca's concern.

They burst through the final door into a room larger than any Becca had ever seen, overlooking a stage and seats two stories below.

Chapter Thirty-Six

"Look what France is capable of building, Mrs. Parcell. The grandest opera house in all of Europe."

They stood on a balcony overlooking a canyon of dark, empty space that made Becca feel as if she were floating in air. A few paltry candles on wall sconces near the door cast the only light. In front of Becca, a carved gold railing blocked guests from plummeting to the ground below. The curved ceiling was impossibly high, carved and decorated in gold, and capped with a painting of cherubs, clouds, and ancient gods. Gold columns supported veined marble along the walls. The massive crystal chandeliers hung round the ceiling seemed almost dainty.

What did she care about an opera house? "Where is Daniel?"

"Here, Mrs. Parcell. I placed him in a fine seat." Gabriel's voice was soothing. He stepped back from the balcony railing.

Daniel sat slumped forward in the first of two rows of balcony chairs. His chin rested on his chest. His eyes were closed. His arms flopped lifelessly at his side.

She squeezed between the balcony railing and the first row of seats. Her heart hammered in her chest, and she sank into the chair next to Daniel.

Gabriel stood behind them.

Her hand went to Daniel's chest. His breathing was slow, maybe slower than normal, his heartbeat quicker. Gabriel had told her the truth. "I can't thank you enough for bringing me here." Daniel was alive, and she almost cried with relief. She thought his eyelids fluttered.

"I'll stay with him if you want to go for more help. Two male servants with a sheet, perhaps. They would be able to move him easily." Now that she knew Daniel was safe, she was chattering on. "What on earth was Mrs. Wright thinking? What did she do to Mr. Alloway? Are you certain...."

From behind, Gabriel grabbed a hank of hair and jerked her back. Her head banged against the seat. Becca went limp with shock, air pressed from her lungs. Then she bucked, kicked, and threw her arms back, scrambling for purchase.

The violent assault was as sudden as Gabriel's attack on the partygoer earlier this evening and even less understandable.

"You bitch." Gabriel clapped a handkerchief over her nose and mouth, his hand pressing against her face. Through the linen, he pinched her nose, forcing her mouth to open in order to breathe. She screamed.

A small, soft ball dropped from the handkerchief into the corner of her mouth. She pushed it away with her tongue, then locked her lips together.

"This will be simpler if you remain calm, Mrs. Parcell."

She did not remain calm. Her nails gouged his cheeks. She tore at his neck and struggled to face him. His hands trapped her head. Her petticoats trapped her legs as effectively as rope.

The knife. What was the good of having it? She couldn't pick it up without turning it around first to grab the letter opener by its handle and not the blade.

The handkerchief was gone. Gabriel smashed her head against the hard back of the seat twice more. Her vision narrowed. Her ears filled with the roar of the ocean, and her hands fell to her sides.

Gabriel's hand pressed on her lips, her cheekbones, her jaw. He rolled the object toward her mouth again. She locked her lips and jerked her face in Daniel's direction. Gabriel's hand followed her motion.

Daniel stared at her, eyes open. Shook his head. Closed his eyes, then opened them again. A surge of energy—or was it hope—pulsed through her at this sign of life.

And she understood his message. Becca went limp, as if she'd given up. She almost had. She forced herself not to gag when the bitter pill touched her tongue. She pushed it to the side of her mouth, catching it between her cheek and upper teeth. She would have bitten Gabriel's hand, but that would have forced the pill down her throat.

As he stepped away from her, Becca tipped her head forward, as if she'd fainted. She opened her mouth just enough to drop the tablet into her lap. She shifted her hand to cover the pill, then let it fall underneath her seat.

Daniel closed his eyes again.

Becca did, too.

"You can hear me, can't you, Mrs. Parcell?"

Daniel's chin dipped in a barely noticeable nod.

"Yes." Becca slowed her voice, slurring her words.

"You'll sleep soon, just like Mr. Alloway."

Becca hoped not. "Sleepy," she said. She was a bit sleepy, and her face and neck felt hot. "Why all of it?"

"You know why, don't you?" Gabriel asked. "You and my friend Mr. Alloway have been asking questions, following those with whom I've spoken."

"Kill Franklin," Becca murmured.

"Very good, Mrs. Parcell." Gabriel sauntered forward, coming to a stop between Becca and Daniel as if he craved an audience. He leaned back against the railing. "The charming, brilliant, sly Dr. Franklin will destroy my country."

Gabriel had said the same thing outside the Hall of Mirrors tonight. American freedom was a disease that would kill them all. Even if that were true, how could killing Dr. Franklin change any of that?

"The king will not hear a word against him. The ministers do not listen me. So I must act to save us all." Gabriel lifted his chin as if leading an army.

"I don't know what you mean." She yawned. Some of the pill must have melted in her mouth.

"The king says 'no' to all of the other diplomats your country sends to Versailles. He does not care for any of them. But Dr. Franklin makes America sound like the land of milk and honey. Each time the brilliant, charming Benjamin Franklin asks France for money, the king opens his purse. Each time. Too many times."

Gabriel's voice rose. "He is bankrupting this nation—my nation—and leading us into revolution. Michael the baker calls for rebellion. Others do, too. There is still time to stop it. I can stop it."

He paused. "All it will take is the death of one man. A small sacrifice. The loans to America will stop. The taxes will not rise. The workers will stop crying to turn France into America."

Gabriel was confessing his crimes, and that was not a good sign. Becca felt the reassuring weight of the letter opener in her pocket along the side of her thigh. *Not yet. Soon.*

"You killed Jude first." Her tongue felt too large for her mouth. It was hard to speak. She jammed her fingernails into the palms of her hands to stay awake.

"That was your fault." Gabriel shrugged.

"How? How was it my fault?" It was not her fault he'd killed Jude. It was not her fault that she and Daniel would die by Gabriel's hands. She shook with anger and welcomed the discomfort. It would keep her awake. She let her eyes flutter shut, then half opened them.

"Dr. Franklin shows me the letter about the man with the red rose," Gabriel said. "Already, I do not think the letter is real. Perhaps it is one of Dr. Franklin's little tricks.

"This is when I know what I will do. I will embarrass Dr. Franklin with this letter. I will find someone to play the man with the red rose. I will make the letter and your trip to Notre Dame public, and I will whisper questions about the whole affair at Versailles. People will wonder whether Dr. Franklin accepted the bribe. They will wonder whether he is too old to negotiate a peace. There will be gossip. He will lose credibility here with the king and the court.

"After, I will pay someone to suffocate Dr. Franklin in bed. I do not want any possibility of being blamed. I have Mr. Fenimore's card. I invite him to dine. He is in pain. He is dying, and he needs money. He is exactly who I need." Gabriel twisted, looking out at the dark opera house.

Goosebumps rose on Becca's arms. "You gave Jude money and the poppy pods for pain." She forced herself to slur her words. Becca thought of her mother's poppy remedies and of the poppy pods missing from Michael's kitchen. Gabriel stole them. He must have. And she, in turn, had taken them from Gabriel's apartment.

She glanced at Daniel, who nodded. Gabriel had used poppy to sedate them tonight.

"Fenimore agreed to my offer. He will go to Notre Dame, he says. I make him a map of Dr. Franklin's house and of the staircase to his bedroom. He agrees to that task, too."

That task. Jude agreed to kill Dr. Franklin. He probably didn't think he'd live long enough to go to trial. And he'd judged murder a lesser crime than leaving Renée and the baby in poverty. Her body grew heavy as if it carried Jude's despair.

"But when he sees you at Notre Dame, Mrs. Parcell, he changes his mind." Gabriel grimaced. "He runs from the police. He threatens me late one night. I had no choice, then. You see. This is how it is all your fault."

"You killed him," Becca whispered.

"And tied him to the lightning rod." Gabriel's smile was gentle. "It is your fault really, as I said. His tolerance for poppy was quite high. It took only a little more to kill him. He did not suffer. I did not know there would be a lightning storm that night. But the clouds erase the stars, and I hear thunder coming closer." He shrugged. "That was a nice touch."

"You hurt Daniel and Renée," Becca whispered.

"Unfortunate but unavoidable. And the carriage accident almost killed Dr. Franklin. He survived, unfortunately." Gabriel shrugged. "I have not treated your Mr. Alloway well, either, I am afraid. Also unfortunate. He is very amusing."

"You were at the Tuileries Garden?" Becca hated this man.

"Yes," Gabriel laughed. "I arrived at the Hôtel de Valentinois to play chess with Dr. Franklin. I hear Daniel has just left for Paris, and I think I might rid myself of him. I send Dr. Franklin my regrets and follow your Mr. Alloway."

Becca knew the rest of that story. "Mr. Fenimore's lover?"

"Ah, well. I am a gentleman. I felt badly about pushing her."

"And tonight?" Becca made sure to slur her words again. "How?"

"Champagne," Gabriel said. "Mr. Alloway suspects I am behind these events. He should be following Dr. Franklin, but he is following me." Gabriel's eyebrows rose in mock surprise. "I gather a few friends to show Mr. Alloway the grand opera house. But first, a servant brings a tray of champagne so we can all toast American independence.

"How can Mr. Alloway refuse the toast? I pay the servant for a small favor. He is to hand out each drink and save one for the American. This is the one to which I add poppy. By the time Daniel arrives here, he is sleepy. I tell my friends I will take care of him. Simple, no?"

Evil could hide anywhere, even in glittering palaces. Even behind bright smiles. She resisted the urge to turn from Gabriel. It was important to look evil in the face.

"You and Mr. Alloway have complicated my plans. I wish it weren't so." Gabriel leaned back on the railing, crossing his arms. "I do not know when I will have another chance to save my country from your Dr. Franklin." He turned from Daniel to Becca and back with a bright smile. "I think you will be more trouble, Mrs. Parcell. I shall start with you."

He shifted, bending in a single motion, his left hand behind Becca's back, his right, under her thighs, and lifted her from the chair.

Daniel launched from his seat. He tackled Gabriel from the side, shoving him off balance.

Becca scrambled up, pushing away from the Frenchman. She lifted the gown of her skirt, climbing over the seats and away from the railing. Her breath rasped in the back of her throat.

Gabriel lunged for Daniel, who tripped back. He grabbed the railing with his one good hand to catch his fall.

Becca jammed her hand into her pocket. She didn't feel the pain when the blade sliced her palm.

Gabriel and Daniel wrestled, with Daniel bent half back over the railing, his hands pushing Gabriel away. He kneed the Frenchman between his legs.

Gabriel collapsed between the front row of seats and the railing, then launched himself again at Daniel. His hands circled Daniel's neck.

Daniel's movements were awkward, too slow, Becca thought. Wet with blood, her fingers clamped round the onyx handle in her pocket. She swung her arm up. The blade ripped through her skirt as she jumped toward the men.

* * *

Afterwards, when Gabriel lay dead two stories below before the stage of the Opera House he loved, Daniel peeled her bloody fingers from the knife.

Becca studied her fingers as if they belonged to someone else. They were a woman's hands, strong, scarred, calloused, and competent. And now they were hands that had killed. "It doesn't feel real what I did," she said.

"That may take a while," Daniel said.

Becca nodded. Because, in the moment, disasters were all sound and sight and feel. A blur. A pain. A scream. But afterwards? She started to shiver.

Chapter Thirty-Seven

Becca swirled the sage she'd plucked this morning in a bucket of cool water. She shook off the moisture, then handed the herbs to her mother to be tied into small bundles and hung to air-dry behind the kitchen.

The two women worked together quietly, and Becca was grateful for the silence. She took a deep breath, inhaling the earthy aroma of the morning's harvest. She didn't want to answer more questions about the Opera House, Gabriel d'Aumont, or the ball at Versailles two nights ago.

And she didn't want to think about those final few moments. After Gabriel plummeted to his death, Becca had collapsed, and Daniel had caught her. Last night, she dreamed that Gabriel d'Aumont and William Cunningham, the man who'd hunted them in New York City, both stood in the basement of the Morristown Storehouse. They smiled as they climbed toward her. Daniel held her when she woke sobbing.

Hannah peeked at Becca, then turned away. "'Tis a good thing Monsieur d'Aumont didn't know more about poppy." She tied bundles of rosemary and thyme to join the sage.

Becca tilted her head.

"They found the concoction he tried to force down your throat," Hannah said. "He mixed sweet figs with the chopped dried poppy straws to make it more palatable. It is a bitter plant on its own."

Becca swished more sage in the water.

When she didn't object, Hannah continued. "Monsieur d'Aumont did not make his pill strong enough. He used too much fig and not enough poppy."

"And that is why Daniel awoke too soon?" Becca concentrated on the sage.

"And why you did not sleep in time," Hannah said.

"That is enough," Becca said.

"You did not have a choice, Becca."

"Enough," Becca looked up, and Hannah nodded.

Becca's stomach grumbled, and she looked expectantly to the kitchen door. For the last two days, she'd spent the early morning hours with her mother and the herbs. Cook sent breakfast out for them at about seven a.m. The breads and brioches had been lackluster since Michael's departure, but Becca was grateful for the outdoor meal.

A petite kitchen maid backed out of the nearby door with a tray holding a pitcher of ale, eggs, ham, jam, and the slightly sweet, rich brioche. She lowered it onto a wooden box near the two women, bobbed a curtsy, and retreated to the house.

Hannah wiped her hands on one of the two towels on the tray, then took a bite of brioche. She swallowed and examined the sweet bread, taking another bite. Her eyes filled with tears.

Becca rushed to her as the kitchen door clicked open again.

Hannah sobbed a laugh, and Becca whirled toward the house.

Michael stood at the top of the steps. He crossed his arms, pushing out his lower lip. "Do you have a complaint about my bread? Is that why no one here is eating?" He grinned and took the five steps from kitchen to lawn in seconds, scooping Hannah up and whirling her round.

"When did you arrive?" "Why are you here?" "Are you safe?" "Can you stay?" Becca and Hannah peppered him with questions.

Michael lifted his hands, palm out. "I will tell you what I know, but you will have to ask Dr. Franklin. Mr. Alloway gets word to me yesterday that I may return here. I ask him to keep it a surprise, even from you, Mrs. Rebecca."

"You are safe now?" Hannah asked.

"Mr. Alloway says that Dr. Franklin swears I am safe, at least for now. He says that something important has changed."

Monsieur d'Aumont was gone. That was what had changed, Becca thought.

245

He must have been hounding the police to find Michael.

He turned to Hannah. "I told you we would never be separated again, and I am here. But I am safe here in Dr. Franklin's home only for now and only if I agree to leave France forever." Two vertical lines carved themselves between Michael's eyebrows. "This is a harsh punishment."

"Come back to Morristown with us," Hannah said. "You love America and independence. Come see if we live up to your dreams. Fight for American independence, if you like."

Michael's dark brown eyes lit with interest.

"Michael can live with us, can't he? For a while?" Hannah asked Becca.

"Of course, he can." A sudden wave of homesickness crashed over Becca. Who knew how long she and Augusta would remain in France.

"No." Michael pushed his lower lip out again and crossed his arms. "I cannot live with you in a house in America when we are not married. Do you think I would show you such disrespect? Do you think I would expose you to gossip? No. I cannot."

Michael's gaze rose beyond Hannah. He took two heavy breaths as if his thoughts required courage.

There was something in the way he stood, the way his chest rose and fell. Becca's jaw dropped.

"My childhood friend, my Hannah, my love, will you do me the honor of...."

Hannah leaped into his arms before he could complete his proposal.

Becca was not capable of happiness this soon after the evening at Versailles. But she watched Hannah and Michael long enough to borrow some of their joy. She left them there and grabbed one of Michael's brioche, which she ate while drifting through the gardens.

An hour or so later, she returned to the sitting room.

"Something for you, madam. A package from America." One of the servants held out a tray on which rested a small wicker basket tied with rope and a knife. Becca's name and Dr. Franklin's address were written on a tag, which was also tied to the basket.

"Thank you." Becca examined the package before opening it. Who would

246

be sending her anything here? She cut the ropes and opened the basket top to find a round jar of cosmetic powder. She clasped the jar between both hands, then opened the note that accompanied it. She knew exactly who'd sent the gift.

Dearest Mrs. Parcell, I wish that this Letter finds you well. I enclose for your Delight a Supply of that American Face Powder you and I have enjoyed so thoroughly. I write, as well, to Remind you of the Invitation I have extended for you and Mr. Alloway to visit us here in Virginia. That Invitation is Evergreen, and our hospitality is always available to the two of you. I am well, although we are continually Broken in upon by the Sons of Tumult and War. With Kindest Sentiments, Martha Washington.

Becca smiled, then laughed. Holding the powder, she strode from the room in search of Daniel.

They placed an old newspaper under the round jar, then fished out the small strips of paper she and Daniel expected to find there. Despite their care, white powder pockmarked the mahogany table around the French paper.

They sat next to each other on the sitting room couch. With no one else in the room, Becca allowed her upper arm to rest against his.

He grinned. "The old trick still works."

In Philadelphia last year, they sent their messages to General Washington, buried in face powder that they addressed to his wife, Martha. Spies who regularly stole politicians' correspondence never bothered to search cosmetics exchanged by women.

The message was simple. General Washington requested their assistance again. Daniel's employer had graciously granted him a leave of absence to assist the general with a small matter of concern. How soon could they leave Paris?

"There's a ship leaving from Le Havre and another from Bordeaux in a month," Daniel took her hand. "I'll purchase passages home for us all."

Chapter Thirty-Eight

The early morning sun cast a soft glow on the dining room walls. Despite the hour, all of Dr. Franklin's guests were gathered in the dining room. The servants set out breakfast hours earlier than usual. Silver clinked against porcelain.

Daniel took another sip of coffee, distracted by the racket of hammers striking wood outside the great front hall. He imagined the servants nailing shut the boxes of curtains, gowns, petticoats, sheets, and embroidered napkins—Becca's unused trousseau—that waited there. The boxes and trunks would be hoisted onto an open cart and carried separately to Bordeaux for the voyage home.

At the head of the table, Dr. Franklin cleared his throat. His customary bowl of oatmeal was untouched. "The weather here is glorious in early fall. Why not stay another month or two?"

"The risk of storms on the Atlantic rises then." Daniel smiled. It was easier to be amused by Franklin's attempts at manipulating them on the day they were leaving. "If we wait, we'll have to stay with you until the following spring."

"I will miss you," Franklin sighed. "You will write and let me know how you fare?"

Daniel nodded.

"We shall miss you, too." Becca patted the letter Franklin had given her. It was addressed to his daughter. "I promise to deliver your correspondence to Sally as soon as we arrive home."

"I cannot thank you enough." Michael Corbin sat next to Hannah. He leaned forward to address Dr. Franklin. "I will fight to the death for my new country."

"Hopefully, not to your death, Mr. Corbin. That would be a waste of all my effort and all of your talents." Franklin toasted the baker with his morning tea. "The king was happy to sign the letter granting you freedom so long as you leave the country quickly."

Daniel's eyes slid to the folded parchment lying near Michael's plate. It bore the king's signature and red wax seal. They would all travel home to Morristown together.

"I will repay you the cost of the ticket as soon as I am able, I swear." Michael's hand formed a fist. "And I will return to fight for France one day. I swear this, too."

Hannah covered his fist with her hand. "I will return then, too."

"What other gifts did you extract from the king?" Daniel asked their host.

Franklin's chest puffed as if he were giving a speech. "Given that Monsieur d'Aumont's crimes in the name of the monarchy were monstrous, and, in a spirit of amity between America and France...."

"Yes, you agreed to keep this entire affair quiet in exchange for what? Please, sir, we need to make a start toward Bordeaux," Daniel said.

Franklin scowled at Daniel, then winked. "I shall be brief. I made the most of the king's desire to erase this entire matter. Mr. Corbin is free to go, of course. And the king has arranged another quite large private loan to our army."

Franklin's gaze flicked to Mr. Bancroft, who was tapping the shell of a soft-boiled egg across the table. He appeared to pay little attention.

There was no loan, Daniel guessed. France's support for America had bled the country dry. Its treasury was nearly empty. Did Dr. Franklin want Bancroft to send the misinformation along to England? If Franklin won other concessions from King Louis XVI, he was keeping them to himself.

"Will you be married as soon as you make landfall?" Franklin asked casually.

"We have been asking the same question." Lady Augusta leaned forward. She sat with Patience Wright and Edward Bancroft across the table from

Becca, Daniel, and Hannah.

"Not right away." Daniel exchanged glances with Becca. "We thought we would marry at Mt. Vernon. Lady Washington has invited us for a visit, and we intend to accept."

"The other night's events would have crushed a lesser woman," Franklin said. "You must take time to recuperate. I would rather have you stay, but I understand the desire for home."

"Lady Washington's invitation came at an opportune time. But you are right, sir. My spirit is rattled. Home is best."

Becca didn't easily speak of her own emotions, Daniel knew. The fact that she mentioned them now was a sign that she was deeply troubled by Gabriel's death. Daniel wasn't entirely sure they would accept General Washington's next commission. But Becca needed to go home.

"Will you continue to work for Mr. Barnes in Philadelphia?" Franklin asked Daniel.

Daniel had been toying with a half-formed idea for weeks. "I have a thought."

"Go on, man." Franklin's eyes lit.

"Paper," Daniel said. "I'd like to look into manufacturing good quality paper in America once the war is over."

"There's almost none to be had," Franklin said.

"Exactly. I would start by importing paper from France, perhaps from Italy."

"That would be expensive," Franklin said.

"But it would make my name, and then...." Daniel's gaze skimmed the table. "I apologize. I won't spend my last morning here boring you with talk of paper."

The hammering outside changed tempo. Not hammering. Knocking. Someone was knocking at the massive front door using a metal baton.

Footsteps clattered toward the door. The hammering outside stopped. So did the knocking. A servant ran into the dining room. He licked his lips and swallowed, preparing to speak.

"I suggest you all join me." Franklin pushed himself to standing before the servant could say a word, grabbed the silver-headed cane leaning against the side of his chair, and limped into the great front hall. His expression filled with triumph.

Becca looked quizzically at Daniel, but he shook his head.

Servants filled the hallway, all leaning forward, all whispering and staring out the now-open door.

Framed by the entrance was a white carriage. Its door was decorated with the king's coat of arms, three fleur-de-lis in a dark green oval surrounded by yellow flowers and capped with a gold crown. The driver held a metal baton in his hand. He stood at attention near the coach's four white horses.

Franklin stepped through the doorway, gesturing for the rest of them to follow.

* * *

The coach held a single passenger, an impatient woman already drumming her fingers on the open window. She wore a broad-brimmed straw hat, and wide lace at the neck of her low-cut bodice barely covered her breasts.

"Melodié? I didn't expect you." Becca took a step back, catching a heel on her hem.

Daniel reached for her elbow, and she inched back, letting her back rest against his chest a moment longer than absolutely necessary. It was obvious to him that Becca wasn't happy to see the visitor.

"The king and queen ordered me to deliver these to you. You are to sign both," Melodié said.

Becca took a step forward, then another. She tilted her head to peek at the papers, curiosity overcoming whatever distaste she had for this woman.

Franklin slapped Daniel on his back.

What trick was the old man playing now?

"You will need two witnesses," Melodié continued. "You shall keep one copy and give one back to me." She flung the folded sheets at Becca, then sat back in the carriage, staring forward.

"We offer you the hospitality of our home, madam," Dr. Franklin called.

"Please, join us while my friends sign their marriage license."

Daniel turned to Franklin. "Marriage license?"

Becca fumbled the papers, grabbing one as it fluttered toward the ground.

"Hospitality, you call it? I shall wait here." Melodié grimaced at the massive white mansion, then leaned back into the shadows.

"Marriage license?" Daniel repeated. The words made no sense.

Lady Augusta gripped Hannah's hand. The servants clapped. Even Mr. Bancroft joined in.

"We don't have the right papers. We can barely prove we exist," Becca protested. "And the magistrate said we can never marry in France."

"The king and queen obviously have other ideas." Melodié leaned out the carriage window to ensure she had the last word.

Franklin beamed.

"You negotiated our marriage with the king?" Life could change in a moment, and it just had. He and Becca would be married before sunset. Daniel was wary of luck. Good or bad, it was guaranteed to change. But this wasn't about luck. It was about love and commitment, and that need not change with the winds of favor. His spirit soared.

"Me? Negotiate with the king?" Franklin's eyes shone. His eyebrows rose momentarily. That was confirmation enough.

"I can't possibly repay you." Daniel took Becca's hand. She gripped his as if she'd never let go.

"Nor I." Becca curtsied.

"Invite me to visit when this war is over. That will be thanks enough." Franklin extended a foot and bowed, using his cane for balance.

"Michael made you a raspberry wedding cake," Hannah added shyly.

"You all knew?" Daniel studied them.

"Dr. Franklin told us yesterday," Patience said. "It was beastly hard to keep the secret."

"Back to the dining room." Franklin lifted his cane into the air like a general leading a charge.

"I don't see how we can limit the witnesses to two." Lady Augusta followed him. "We must all witness the wedding."

"We shall all sign," Franklin said.

Becca and Daniel lingered, strolling away from the entrance until they were alone on the sloping front lawn.

"My thoughts have been dark for the last two days," Becca said.

Daniel took her hand. "I know." They would both be haunted by the harm Gabriel d'Aumont had caused in the name of his twisted love of country.

"We can wait to have a proper wedding in America, if you like. I don't want you to be sad on our wedding day." But he hated the thought of putting off the marriage Dr. Franklin had arranged for them.

"This is the perfect wedding and the perfect time for it." She flashed Daniel a broad grin, the first he'd seen since the party at Versailles. "Dr. Franklin's kindness reminds me of something I'd forgotten."

"Which is?" Daniel asked.

"That there are always better times ahead, even if we can't imagine them now, and there will be good company to celebrate along the way."

They stopped to catch their last view of the Seine River, then retraced their steps to the mansion.

A Note from the Author

I hope you enjoyed reading Becca's and Daniel's story as much as I loved writing it.

You may wonder why I set their latest adventure in and around Paris during the waning days of the War for Independence. It's all Benjamin Franklin's fault.

I found a reference to a letter attempting to bribe Dr. Franklin into helping the English end the American War for Independence, then tracked down the original in the National Archives.

The letter offered Dr. Franklin a peerage and a lifetime pension if he would "merely" propose peace terms to reunite America with England. If Franklin was intrigued by the proposal, he should visit the Notre Dame Cathedral in Paris on a specific date and look for the man holding a red rose who would wait for him there.

Dr. Franklin told his friends at Versailles about the letter. The Paris police arrived at Notre Dame on one of the appointed days and arrested the man with the red rose. But even in pre-revolutionary Paris, it was no crime to visit a church while holding a flower. The police released their suspect after identifying him as a former captain in King George III's guard.

Historians still aren't certain who penned the letter nor how the man with the red rose was linked to the bribery plot.

Dear reader, how could I *not* set this book in Paris and feature Benjamin Franklin, the attempted bribe, and the man with the red rose? But I write fiction, not history, and you should know that I changed the date of the bribery letter from 1778 to 1781 to make it "fit" the timing of my Revolutionary War mystery series.

I make several references in the story to Dr. Franklin's messy desk and his habit of leaving out important correspondence about the war. That, too, is true. In a declassified dossier on Benjamin Franklin as "spymaster" in France, the CIA panned our Founding Father. The report also said he was vain, obstinate, and allowed his house to be infiltrated by spies for England.

After reading *The Paris Mistress*, you may be curious about other historical figures who make appearances in the story. One of my characters, Edward Bancroft was, in fact, a British spy who lived and worked with Dr. Franklin in France. Most historians believe that Dr. Franklin knew nothing of his friend's perfidy. One or two disagree, claiming that Dr. Franklin fed Bancroft false information to pass along to the English. My story reflects the minority position.

Patience Wright is another historical figure included in my story. She was one of the most famous American artists of her day, and she spent the summer my story takes place with Dr. Franklin as his houseguest. During her earlier years living in London, the artist is said to have passed along British secrets to the Americans by hiding them in her wax sculptures and shipping them to her sister on Long Island. Patience Wright was a strident Patriot.

Queen Marie-Antoinette has fascinated historians and the rest of us for more than two hundred years. The Queen Marie-Antoinette you'll find in *The Paris Mistress* is a young woman caught between the freedom of her unlimited fashion budget and the rigid rules, the captivity, of French court life.

Finally, the more I learned, the more I wondered whether America could have won its independence from England without French financial support, which almost bankrupted France. That, of course, made me ask whether the French Revolution might never have happened without the crushing taxes workers were forced to pay to keep the almost-empty French treasury afloat. That question found its way into my story.

For more about the brilliant, complicated Benjamin Franklin, I recommend Stacy Schiff's biography of Franklin's years in France, *A Great Improvisation: Franklin, France and the Birth of America*. *The Autobiography of Benjamin Franklin* is also worth your time. It offers Dr. Franklin's views on politics, philosophy, religion, and the status of women, among other topics.

A *Scented Palace: The Secret of Marie Antoinette's Perfumer* by Elisabeth de Feydeau provides a great, fascinating look at the business of beauty in 18th-century Paris and a peek into the life of the sometimes frivolous, tragic Queen of France.

For more on Versailles, *Versailles A Private Invitation,* produced by Chateau de Versailles, offers a breathtaking pictorial view of the world-famous palace. Geri Walton's resources at https://www.geriwalton.com were also a tremendous help in "seeing" Versailles and Queen Marie Antoinette as they would have lived before the French Revolution.

Thank you again for spending time with Becca Parcell and Daniel Alloway. Happy reading.

Acknowledgements

I am forever grateful to Level Best Books, led by Verena Rose and Shawn Simmons. Along with Harriette Sackler, they saw something in my writing several years ago and took on this previously unpublished author. Thanks especially to Deborah Well and, another thanks to Shawn Simmons, who shepherded this story from manuscript to polished book.

I am indebted to Vinessa Anthony, Michelle Cameron, Judith Lindbergh, Ariel Ellman, and Christina Axelrod at The Writers Circle Workshops for keeping me accountable and for their wise counsel. Friends and fellow Level Best authors Lori Robbins and C.L. Tolbert took time to talk me off the proverbial ledge more than once, and the brilliant and talented Mariah Fredericks, Karen Odden, Cathi Stoler, C.L. Tolbert, Gabriel Valjan, and Nina Wachsman took time that could have been put to better use to read and blurb my story. I am so grateful to them all.

To my husband Bob, and to Brian and Katie, who have cheered me on, kept me grounded, and buoyed my spirit throughout this writing journey and well beyond. I love you more than I can say.

And, finally, thanks to my brother and sister, Jeff and Ellin, whose thoughts have improved this book immensely and to whom this story is dedicated. I can't imagine my life without your laughter, bad jokes, Mel Brooks memes, and kindness.

About the Author

Mally Becker is the twice Agatha Award-nominated author of *The Turncoat's Widow* and *The Counterfeit Wife*, books one and two in her Revolutionary War mystery series. She teaches mystery writing at The Writers Circle Workshops, interviews authors for the Historical Novel Society's website, co-hosts Guns, Knives & Lipstick, a crime fiction Podcast, and is a member of Sisters in Crime and the Mystery Writers of America. Mally was an attorney and a volunteer advocate for children in foster care until becoming a full-time writer. She and her husband live in New Jersey, not too far from Morristown where her first book is set.

SOCIAL MEDIA HANDLES:
https://www.facebook.com/mally.baumelbecker/
https://www.facebook.com/mallybeckerauthor/
https://www.instagram.com/mallybeckerwrites

AUTHOR WEBSITE:
www.mallybecker.com

Also by Mally Becker

The Turncoat's Widow (Historia, an imprint of Level Best Books 2021)

The Counterfeit Wife (Historia, an imprint of Level Best Books 2022)

Printed in the USA
CPSIA information can be obtained
at www.ICGtesting.com
CBHW020329050124
3181CB00005B/75

9 781685 124304